MANNA FROM HADES

A Cornish Mystery

CAROLA DUNN

MINOTAUR BOOKS

NEW YORK

MANNA FROM HADES. Copyright © 2009 by Carola Dunn. All rights reserved. Printed in the United States of America. For information, address St. Martin's Press, 175 Fifth Avenue, New York, N.Y. 10010.

www.minotaurbooks.com

Library of Congress Cataloging-in-Publication Data

Dunn, Carola.
    Manna from Hades : a Cornish mystery / Carola Dunn. — 1st ed.
       p. cm.
    ISBN-13: 978-0-312-37945-2
    ISBN-10: 0-312-37945-5
    1. Widows—Fiction. 2. Cornwall (England)—Fiction. 3. Murder—Investigation—Fiction. 4. Jewelry theft—Fiction. I. Title.
    PR6054.U537M36 2009
    823'.914—dc22

                                                     2008033963

First Edition: March 2009

10 9 8 7 6 5 4 3 2 1

MANNA FROM HADES

BOOKS BY CAROLA DUNN

Cornish Mysteries
Manna from Hades

The Daisy Dalrymple Mysteries
Death at Wentwater Court

The Winter Garden Mystery

Requiem for a Mezzo

Murder on the Flying Scotsman

Damsel in Distress

Dead in the Water

Styx and Stones

Rattle His Bones

To Davy Jones Below

The Case of the Murdered Muckraker

Mistletoe and Murder

Die Laughing

A Mourning Wedding

Fall of a Philanderer

Gunpowder Plot

The Bloody Tower

Black Ship

In memory of my godmother, Bet (Beatrice Helen Jellinek), to whom I owe many happy holidays in Cornwall—and so much more.

Also, many thanks for all their help and support, above and beyond the call of duty, to my "full-service" agent, Alice Volpe, Northwest Literary Agency, Inc., and to Alan and Slick.

AUTHOR'S NOTE

Port Mabyn is a fictional village in a fictional world lurking somewhere in the 1960s and '70s, between my childhood memories of Cornwall and the present reality. No computers, no cell phones, no GPS, no nose or navel rings; female police detectives were an anomaly; the Beatles were top of the charts, not golden oldies; instead of the Mediterranean or Caribbean for their summer holidays, the English still flocked to the Cornish Riviera, leaving it to the locals in the off-season.

Though in many cases I have used the irresistible names of real places, the reader should not expect necessarily to find them where I've put them. The topography resembles the North Coast of Cornwall in general, but not in particulars. The Constabulary of the Royal Duchy of Cornwall (CaRaDoC) has no existence outside my imagination. For information about the real Cornwall, I refer the reader to countless works of non-fiction, or, better still, I suggest a visit.

Pronunciation note: The town of Launceston is pronounced Lanston or even Lanson. Rough Tor rhymes with doubter.

ACKNOWLEDGMENTS

My thanks to Beth Franzese for advice about Aikido, and to her husband, Carmine, for letting her practise on him the moves I needed.

MANNA FROM HADES

ONE

"We put in several frogs, Mrs Trewynn," said Miss Annabel Willis anxiously. "You did say they were well received?"

"Very well indeed, Miss Annabel. They sold in no time. My thanks to both of you for your hard work and generosity." Eleanor lifted the big cardboard box, whose faint, sweet fragrance bore out the logo on its sides: Co-op Tea. It was more awkward than heavy.

"It's a pleasure to do what little we can to help," the elder Miss Willis assured her from her wheelchair, her knitting needles clicking away tirelessly, producing yet another green and yellow frog. "Annabel, stop fussing and give Mrs Trewynn a hand."

"Yes, of course, Dorothy." Miss Annabel dithered.

"Perhaps you could open the car door for me," Eleanor suggested.

"Certainly." Beaming, Miss Annabel buttoned her cardigan over her flower-print dress and trotted ahead out of the tiny cottage. She was over eighty if she was a day. Eleanor only hoped she herself would be half as spry at the same age, a couple of decades hence.

The aged lady opened the door of the aged pea-green Morris Minor (age being a relative term). Teazle seized the chance to hop out and stretch her short legs.

"Oh, the dear doggie! We always had West Highlands when I was a child," said Miss Annabel wistfully. "Dorothy says we haven't room for a dog. She's right, I'm afraid. She won't hear of my wearing trousers, either. They look so comfortable and practical, but in our time, ladies simply didn't." She eyed Eleanor's royal-blue tracksuit and white trainers with envy.

"Nor in my time. Not even in the 'fifties. The 'sixties seem to be altering so many of our ideas." Depositing the box on the passenger seat, Eleanor closed the door. "Thank you for the cup of tea, Miss Annabel. It was just what I needed. Come on, Teazle, we must be on our way."

With a shove from behind, Teazle scrambled up on top of a bag of old clothes on the back seat. Eleanor waved a final goodbye and drove back past the other half-dozen cottages of the hamlet. The lane, scarcely wider than the car, wandered through greening valley-bottom woods for a quarter mile and ended at a T-junction with another lane not much wider. Eleanor turned left, up a steep, twisting hill between high banks starred with pale clumps of primroses, the bright gold of celandines, and patches of purple violets.

The slope levelled off for a short stretch. On one side was a grass verge, with a car parked on it with two wheels in the lane. A gate in the bank led to a summer cottage, a tiny farm-labourer's dwelling expanded and modernised to provide a country get-away for Londoners. Most of the summer cottages and bungalows with TO LET signs she had passed were still closed up, but the Hendersons appeared to have come down early. They were pleasant people with two teenagers.

She pulled over in front of their car, blocking half the lane, but she wouldn't be more than a moment and she'd hear anyone honking to get by.

Mrs Henderson was delighted to see her. The children were doing foreign exchanges over the Easter hols and she and her husband were going to Italy. They were lending the cottage to friends, so she had come down to prepare the place. She hadn't realised—one never did, did one?—how much clutter had accumulated over the years, much of it perfectly good but unnecessary. If Mrs Trewynn could just take this box of kitchen stuff—nobody needed two egg-beaters and three potato peelers, let alone five cake pans when one never baked on holiday!

The box was somehow squeezed into the boot on top of two boxes of books.

"And I'll bring more in to the shop when I've sorted it all out," Mrs Henderson promised.

Groaning a bit, Eleanor's little Morris tackled the hill again.

"Yes, we'll go for a walk when we reach the top," she said in response to an interrogative bark. Teazle raised her black nose from her little white paws and sat up. "If we reach the top," Eleanor amended, leaning forward over the steering wheel to aid the ascent.

One last, steep upward bend and the Morris bounded forward, demanding a change into third gear. The lane straightened, the banks gave way to drystone walls. A moment later Eleanor pulled across the road and parked in a lay-by beside a stile marked by a green PUBLIC FOOTPATH sign.

"Come on." She opened the door.

Teazle scrambled over the handbrake, paused a moment to nose interestedly at the tea box on the passenger seat, then launched herself across Eleanor's lap and out. Before following the terrier, Eleanor remembered to take the keys from the ignition.

Dear Megan was so insistent about the need to lock one's car, wherever one left it, even if it contained nothing of value. Megan said crooks often stole cars just to use to commit other crimes, and being a policewoman, she must know. Though why should anyone choose a car that had barely scraped through the MOT test a month ago? Eleanor had had to pay for several repairs before the examiner would give her that indispensable certificate of safety.

As she closed the door and inserted the key in the stiff lock, she heard a vehicle drawing near. Quickly she turned to look for the dog.

"Teazle?" From the other side of the stile, two bright brown eyes peered at her through a tangled white fringe. "Stay!"

The car that approached was one of the few that she recognised, black and white with a blue light on the roof and POLICE blazoned across the door. Panda cars people called them these days. She waved a greeting to the driver.

Constable Leacock slowed down. "Everything all right, Mrs Trewynn?"

"Oh yes, thank you, Bob, we're just going for a walk on the cliffs."

"Beautiful day for it." He waved and drove on down the hill.

A nice boy, she thought as she went to join Teazle. She was climbing the stile when she heard another car engine, groaning up the hill. Probably someone from one of the farms. The beginning of April was early for tourists or ramblers, especially with Easter late this year, and few others used this lane from nowhere to nowhere.

She glanced back. The grey car that came into sight was not familiar, but then, she never noticed people's cars. Sunlight gleaming off the windscreen concealed those within, but it might be an acquaintance who would be hurt if she failed to acknowledge them. She waved.

"*Wuff!*" said Teazle in a *come-on-let's-get-going* tone. Eleanor stepped down from the stile and they set off across the field. Sheep raised their heads to watch suspiciously. Teazle stuck close to her mistress's heels.

Behind them, the sound of the car's engine suddenly died. Eleanor hoped that did not portend someone following her along the path. She wanted to practise her Aikido, and spectators always distracted her. Strangers tended to be alarmed when they saw a small woman with snow-white curls twisting and twirling and making strange gestures.

Peter had insisted that she learn to defend herself if she chose to accompany him to the more perilous parts of the earth. Aikido, a then recent development of the martial arts, appealed to both of them with its philosophy of deflecting aggression without harming the aggressor. Now she was safe home in England, she'd never need to use it, but the exercise improved her health and the mental discipline brought tranquility.

Nothing could be more tranquil than the present scene. In the quiet, a meadowlark trilled, invisible in the pale blue vault overhead.

Then a car door slammed. A few moments later, the engine started up again and Eleanor breathed a sigh of relief.

On the far side of the field, she climbed another stile while Teazle wriggled underneath. Here they joined the footpath that led around the entire coast of Cornwall and Devon. A grey-green heather-covered slope rose to the cliff's edge, with nothing but sky and wheeling herring gulls visible beyond from Eleanor's viewpoint. A thicket of yellow gorse in full bloom sent forth its sweet, coconutty fragrance.

Teazle dashed ahead, making brief forays into the heather. They came to a level area carpeted with wiry grass, dotted with clumps of pink thrift and patches of wild thyme. A rough, lichened bench overlooked the sea, the slow green rollers shattering in bursts of spray on rocks three hundred feet below.

Eleanor sat down for a minute to collect her thoughts in preparation for the necessary concentrated effort of body, mind, and spirit. She breathed deeply of the scented air. Teazle gave her a sceptical, resigned look and went off about her own business—chiefly rabbits up here. Dismissing irrelevant concerns, acutely aware of her surroundings and of her precise position in the centre of things, Eleanor rose to begin her practice.

When she and the dog returned to the Morris, an hour later, the sun was low in the west and the first scattered drops of an April shower were falling. She felt in her pocket for the car keys.

"Don't say they fell out while I was . . . Oh, there they are."

In the car door. And she had left the passenger-side window wide open. What Megan would say if she ever found out! How fortunate that Teazle told no tales.

She gave the little dog a boost onto the high-piled backseat and they headed for home.

The shower was ending and sunset blazed through the clouds when they reached the hill down into Port Mabyn. At the top, before the slope steepened, a rash of pastel holiday bungalows spread across what had been meadows. There was a mini-supermarket, closed now, and a gravelled public car park. From here there was a good view over the old part of town: Grey stone and whitewashed cottages, slate-roofed, clustered about the stream and up the steep slopes on either side. Most were accessible only via a labyrinth of footpaths and steps. A narrow stone bridge crossed the stream just before it widened into a crooked inlet of the sea, between rocky, precipitous headlands. Within the sheltering arm of a stone-built jetty, three fishing boats at anchor bobbed on the dark water.

Eleanor drove on down, past the post office–newsagent–sweet shop, past the Trelawney Arms, Bob Leacock's police station, B&Bs, antique and curio shops, Chin's Chinese and the fish-and-chip shop next door. Daffodils and hyacinths flourished in window-boxes and tubs, obstructing the narrow pavement. A few people were about, but hers was the only car.

Halfway down was the Mabyn Bakery (*Cornish Cream Teas and Hot Pasties*). The smell of baking pasties wafted through the open car window and made her nostrils quiver like Teazle's. Could her waistline and her wallet afford one of the savoury steak-, potato- and onion-filled pasties for supper, she wondered. Probably not. She had a packet of chicken noodle soup in the cupboard.

She drove across to the wrong side of the street and stopped before a shop window. Above, large gilt letters announced LON ★ STAR; and below, smaller, in black script: *The London Save the Starving Council*.

She had pulled the Morris as far out of the roadway as possible, with two wheels on the pavement, two on the double yellow lines. The bonnet nudged a NO PARKING sign, leaving Eleanor barely room enough to open the door.

"Wait," she said firmly to Teazle, then once she was out, "All right, come."

The Westie sprang over the handbrake and down to the pavement and went to sit before a blue-painted door to one side of the shop. Her short tail vibrated with impatient joy. Home!

Eleanor retrieved the keys from the ignition and went to unlock the door. After some fruitless fiddling, she discovered she had forgotten to lock it when she left, a not infrequent occurrence. Really, modern Western life was so complicated, she reflected with a sigh. It made one quite nostalgic for the rondavels of Botswana or the stilt villages of Malaysia.

She let Teazle in and the terrier scampered along the passage to the far end, then up the stairs on the right. Once stepped on, twice shy, she would wait outside the door to the flat, well out of the way of the hordes of tramping feet that would soon be carrying goods to the stockroom at the back. Eleanor turned on the light in the passage, a dim bulb dangling from the ceiling near the top of the stairs. Then she went back to the car to begin unloading, serene in the expectation that those hordes would arrive at any moment to help.

Tipping forward the driving seat, she reached for the bag of clothes Teazle had been sitting on. Beneath it was a black attaché-case. Eleanor frowned. She didn't remember anyone donating an attaché-case for LonStar. Her memory for practical matters had never been of the best, but she usually knew exactly who had given her what.

Picking it up by the handle—it was surprisingly heavy—she carried it and the bag of clothes through the blue door. Near the far end of the passage, opposite the foot of the stairs, was the door to the stockroom. This she had inconveniently remembered to lock, or, more likely, Mrs Davies had locked it when she left after closing the shop. Eleanor set down her burdens and felt in her pocket for her keys.

Where on earth had she left them now? Ah, dangling from the lock of the street door, of course.

Keys retrieved, she took the clothes and the attaché-case into the stockroom. The bag of clothes she dropped on the floor in the back corner, out of the way of the shelves and racks of already-priced goods awaiting space in the shop. The attaché-case she set on the long trestle table used by volunteers more businesslike than herself to sort and price the donated items.

Through the high window, the setting sun flooded the room with rosy light. As far as Eleanor could tell, the attaché-case was real leather, not one of the modern substitutes. It was in good condition, one corner just a trifle scuffed, but unfortunately on the top edge was an embossed monogram, the kind with super-imposed, intertwined letters which are hard to make out—D, A, and W, she thought. One couldn't expect a customer with the same initials to happen to come into the shop in search of an at-taché-case. The letters weren't conspicuous, though, half-hidden by the handle and not picked out in gilt.

She'd better see whether anything had been left inside it, on purpose or by accident. Laying the case flat on the table top, she pressed back the shiny brass catches, opened it, and gasped. On a bed of black velvet, a tangled heap of jewelry glittered and gleamed, gold, ruby-red, emerald-green, sapphire, amethyst, and the hard sparkle of diamond.

With tentative fingers, Eleanor picked out a bracelet and held it up to the light. Purple stones glowed with an inner fire.

Paste, of course, or the modern equivalent, but paste of excel-lent quality. Even if they were artificial gems, they must be quite valuable. How very generous people were, she thought, a little misty-eyed.

And doing good by stealth, too, not wanting to be thanked, slipping the case into her car when she was not watching, as if it were manna from Heaven.

What the kind donor unfortunately didn't realise was that valuable gifts had to be documented. Jocelyn was going to have forty fits when she discovered that Eleanor had no paperwork, no signatures, to vouch for the provenance of the jewelry.

Nor had she the slightest idea of the identity of the giver.

TWO

The number of the safe's combination was the date she had met Peter in India, between the wars. Even Megan agreed it was as secure a number as any, and it had the immense advantage that Eleanor would never forget it.

The anodised metal door swung open. She scooped the jewelry from the attaché-case with both hands and dumped it in the safe.

Making sure the door closed with a solid click, she re-hung Nick's painting of Clovelly, a Christmas present. No connoisseur of art, she liked the little donkey traipsing down the steep cobbles, the bright splashes of geraniums in window-boxes. It cheered up her small sitting room.

Teazle was already asleep in her bed in the corner, exhausted after all that fruitless rabbiting. Nose and paws twitched.

"Good luck with the dream rabbits," Eleanor wished her, wondering in a vague way whether talking to a sleeping dog was even more eccentric than talking to a wideawake one. Teazle raised her head and blinked. "I'll leave the front door open for you, in case you want to come down and see what's going on."

As she started down the stairs, empty attaché-case in hand, a voice rose from below.

"You there, Mrs Trewynn? This stuff need bringing in?"

"Yes, please, dear."

"Okay. Come on, kids." Donna, teenage daughter of the landlord of the Trelawney Arms, her face plastered with anti-acne makeup and fluorescent eyeshadow, was accompanied by two small, solemn Chins with straight black hair and almond eyes.

Eleanor stood the attaché-case against the wall at the foot of the stairs and went after them out into the dusk.

"I better put the parking lights on for you, Mrs Trewynn," Donna suggested, diving headfirst into the Morris. "Okay, Ivy, Lionel, you can take this box. It's not too heavy. Okay?"

"Okay, Donna." The children awkwardly bore off between them the box of ever-popular stuffed animals knitted by the Misses Willis.

Donna plunged back into the car. "Mostly clothes, this lot, innit, Mrs Trewynn. Get anything good today?"

Eleanor doubtfully eyed her plump rear end, clad in scarlet tights that appeared to be made entirely of elastic, beneath a nearly non-existent skirt. "Mrs Prendergast gave me three boxes," she said.

"That's the lady goes to a fancy London dressmaker, innit? I'd look a right charlie in her stuff. Looks a treat on Mrs Stearns, though. Dad says we got the dressiest vicar's wife in Cornwall."

Eleanor stored up the compliment to relay to Jocelyn, then decided her friend might be less amused and flattered than dismayed that everyone knew she bought her clothes at LonStar. Eleanor herself only wished she was the right size and shape to profit from Mrs Prendergast's aversion to wearing a dress more than once, or a suit for more than a season.

From his gallery next door, Nick came to join her, silent on sandalled feet, accompanied by the usual faint miasma of turpentine. He reached out towards the scarlet tights. Eleanor slapped his hand before thumb and forefinger met.

He grinned down at her, a teasing gleam in eyes as blue as the seas he painted for tourists and suchlike philistines. Tall and lean, he wore his thick, light brown hair long, neatly tied back. Somehow, instead of making him look like a scruffy artist or a hippy, it gave him the air of a dashing Georgian aristocrat. In the dusk, the paint smears on pullover and jeans were invisible.

"Need anything heavy carried in, Eleanor?" he enquired.

Donna emerged from the car, flurried, a box clasped to her bosom. "Ooh, Mr Gresham, you didn't half make me jump." She fluttered improbably long, improbably dark eyelashes.

"The exercise will do you good," he said tolerantly, and she giggled. As she went off with the box, he added sotto voce to Eleanor, "And she'd have jumped a lot higher if you hadn't—"

"Nonsense, Nick, you wouldn't actually have pinched her. There are some books in the boot, if you wouldn't mind."

He tried the boot. "Locked. D'you have the keys on you?"

To her pleased surprise, she found them in her pocket. He unlocked and opened the boot, leaving the keys in the lock. The Chin children reappeared. From the floor, Eleanor retrieved a set of placemats for Ivy to carry and a whistling kettle for Lionel.

"All the latest best-sellers," said Nick, examining the top layer of books by the light from the passage. "Old Cartwright?"

"Yes, and there's another box underneath, of mysteries and thrillers. They sell fast."

"Many of them to me."

"And then you give them back—"

"Sometimes a bit paint-smudged, I'm afraid."

"And someone else buys them. It's good of Major Cartwright

to pass them on to us quickly, before everyone has already read them."

"Poor old chap." With a theatrical groan, he hefted the box and followed Ivy and Lionel. A moment later a yelp of pain floated back to Eleanor's ears. "Sh-ouch!"

She hurried down the passage to find him rubbing his shin while Donna fussed over him and the children politely hid giggles behind their hands.

"What the hell is that monstrosity?" Nick demanded, glaring malevolently at the object in question, which crouched between the stockroom doorway and the long table.

Eleanor bit her lip. "A coffee table, I believe." Four sleek brass dolphins, standing on their tails, supported on notched dorsal fins a circle of thick glass. Their heads and rounded, beaklike noses, grinning mockingly, protruded several inches at each corner.

"I always thought porpoises were charming, inoffensive beasts," said Nick, pulling up his trouser leg to examine the beginnings of a bruise. At least the rounded surface had not broken the skin. "Someone must have been delighted to get rid of the hideous thing. I'm surprised you haven't fallen over it, Eleanor."

"I never walk into things," she said smugly. "Shall I get a cold compress?"

"No, it's all right, I'll survive. Here, Donna, give us a hand to shift the damn thing out of the way before it breaks my other leg."

It was heavier than it looked, but they managed to move it over by a rack of clothes. Without further incident, the car was soon emptied. A stack of boxes, bags, and oddments rose in the corner of the stockroom. Thanking the children, Eleanor gave each of them a LonStar sticker and they ran off. Donna showed a disposition to linger in the passage.

"D'you see *Doctor Who* last night, Mr Gresham?"

"No telly, remember? And if I had I'd be watching the Philharmonia, not the Daleks."

"You coming up the Arms for a pint tonight, then?"

"Not tonight, Donna. Eleanor, shall I park the Incorruptible for you?"

"Yes, please, Nick." She hunted in her pockets for the keys while Donna departed with a pout and what would have been a flounce had she been wearing a skirt of respectable length.

Nick watched her go, shaking his head. "She's driving me to do my drinking at the Wreckers. I'll buy you a sherry there tonight, Eleanor, and then take you to dinner at Chin's. I'm feeling rich."

"Oh, Nick, have you sold one of your artistic pictures?"

"No, just the commonplace but oversize daub of Cambeak, you know the one. An American couple. She said the heather was the exact shade of the couch in their family room."

"Oh dear."

"It'll pay the rent," he said philosophically, moving towards the door. "I left your keys in the car, I think. I'll come by at . . . What's the time?"

Eleanor glanced at her watch. "It's stopped."

"I'll come by as soon as I'm ready. You don't mind walking up to the Wreckers, do you?"

"Not at all. I expect Donna will fancy herself in love with someone else by next month, you know."

"I hope so. The bitter's a penny less at the Arms. See you shortly."

Smiling, she watched him insert himself into the Morris and drive down the hill. She rented a shed for the car from the owner of the small parking lot by the stream, the only level land in old Port Mabyn. Neither the Wreckers Inn, halfway up the opposite hill, nor the Trelawney Arms boasted a parking area.

Eleanor hurried upstairs to the flat, then up again to her tiny dormer-windowed bedroom, to change into a skirt. She was giving the dog her dinner when Nick reappeared in a spotless white shirt and brown corduroys. Teazle spared him a brief but ecstatic greeting before diving at her bowl.

"Let's take her to the Wreckers," he said. "We can drop her off back here before we go to Chin's."

"She's had a long walk today. She'll be perfectly happy at home." Eleanor put on her jacket and bade the dog farewell, receiving in response a reproachful glance.

"Oh, let her come!" Nick took the lead from its hook. Teazle abandoned what little was left in her bowl and dashed to the door. "By the way, here's the keys." He handed them over.

That reminded her to lock the front door of the flat behind her, and she even remembered to remove them from the lock and drop them in her jacket pocket.

By the time she returned home, after a pleasant evening, she had to admit to feeling a little tired. She fetched Teazle down from the flat, where she had left her en route from the Wreckers to Chin's, and let her out of the back door, at the end of the passage.

A steep, narrow asphalt path ran along the back of the shops. Beyond it the rough hillside sank to the south towards the harbour and the inlet, and rose to the west to become the sheltering headland, Crookmoyle Point. From down here Eleanor couldn't see the lighthouse, but by the light shining down from her sitting room window above, she watched the terrier's small white form investigating rocks and bushes. She thought about Nick. What a pity the dear boy had such bad luck selling his serious work.

All the tourists—his chief customers—wanted was pretty pictures to remind them of their holidays. Surely among her vast acquaintance she must number an art dealer or collector to whom she could recommend him.

She'd set her mind to it tomorrow. Tonight all she wanted was a hot water bottle and bed.

"Teazle!"

Short legs at full stretch, the dog raced past her into the passage, then skidded to a halt at the door to the stockroom. She sniffed suspiciously and gave a hopeful bark.

"No. If we really have mice again you can find them tomorrow, but I suspect it's sheer wishful thinking. Come."

They went upstairs.

In the morning, when Teazle came in after a brief airing, she had to be dragged away from the stockroom door and carried upstairs. Perhaps there actually were mice, after all. Jocelyn would not be pleased.

Eleanor breakfasted at the table that separated the small sitting room from the tiny kitchen, cleared up, and then wrote letters at her desk.

Though she had retired from LonStar's overseas staff, she still felt responsible for the projects she had helped initiate. Over the years, she had persuaded scores of villagers, elders, district governors, even ministers, wary of European interference, to allow LonStar to bring aid. Forgetful she might be but she never forgot any of *them*. In schools, clinics, and farming, fishing, and craft cooperatives all over the world, an encouraging word from her might lend new strength to people battling ignorance and hunger. One did not give up just because a riot in Indonesia had slashed a hole in one's life and heart. Peter would have expected her to carry on.

She had run out of stamps and was thinking of popping out to the post office when there was a knock on the flat door.

Jocelyn's pepper-and-salt head appeared around the door. "Eleanor? Oh there you are." The vicar's wife stepped into the sitting room. Her rather angular figure was admirably disguised by a beautifully cut tweed suit, worn with a pale turquoise silk blouse.

"Morning, Joce. Coffee?"

"No time, thanks. It's nearly ten. I'm just going to open the shop."

"Oh, is it your day today? Good. I'll come down in a minute and help you sort the new stuff." Though she was hopeless at pricing, she could bend and lift, unlike some of the stouter, less limber volunteers.

"Anything from Mrs Prendergast? Bless the woman! I'm hoping for a new dress for lunch with the bishop on Saturday. Lois can price anything I want to buy when she comes in this afternoon. Hello, Teazle. Are you coming down with me?"

"She'd better not go into the stockroom until I get there. She seems to have decided there are mice in there and you know what chaos she creates when she's hunting."

"Not again!" said Jocelyn crossly. "I'll have to speak to Mary Todd again about clearing up the crumbs from her elevenses biscuits."

"Must you, Joce? It's so kind of her to give LonStar so much time. I expect Teazle's imagining things."

"We'll see. It'd do Mary good to go without biscuits a couple of times a week. There's no excuse for leaving crumbs about the place." She glanced at her watch, which invariably had the correct time. "I must run."

"I'll be right down."

Eleanor finished her letter and went downstairs. Teazle

demanded to be let out, so Eleanor opened the back door and left it open. Going into the stockroom, she heard Jocelyn moving about in the shop, but the connecting door was still locked.

Eleanor had no key—she only helped in the shop itself in the direst emergencies, since the day she had so upset the cash register that the repairman had to be called. She knocked and called, "Joce?" then headed for the stack of "new" goods.

Muffled footsteps, the click of the lock, the creak of the hinges, were followed by Jocelyn's annoyed voice saying, "I thought Nicholas oiled all . . . Ouch! Who moved that dratted table?"

As they inspected the vicious red mark on Jocelyn's shin, Eleanor guiltily told her about Nick's encounter with the table. "At least there's no ladder in your stocking," she consoled. "I'll get a cold compress."

"Fetch Nicholas, will you? I'll find a place for that thing in the shop if it kills me, before it kills someone else. And if no one has bought it within a week, I'll buy it myself and donate it to Ye Olde Cornysh Piskie Curio Shoppe. Brian and Mavis will love it. They can put china piskies and wishing wells on it."

Nose twitching, Teazle was investigating the table inch by inch, so Eleanor left her. When she returned with Nick, Jocelyn was polishing away dog-nose smears with Brasso and a duster. She had cleared a spot in a back corner of the shop, where no customer was likely to trip over the dolphins. Between the three of them they carried the table through. Nick and Jocelyn compared bruises, then he returned to his gallery.

"You never know when a millionaire art collector will walk in," he said optimistically.

By some obscure connection of ideas, that reminded Eleanor of the jewelry in the safe upstairs. She was about to tell Jocelyn about it, when the bell over the shop door tinkled and a customer came in. The jewelry could wait. She went back into the stockroom.

In the far corner, Teazle was sniffing at some men's shirts spilling out of a carrier bag on its side on top of a box. Her tail was between her legs and she showed none of the frantic excitement mice invariably aroused. Glancing round at Eleanor, she whined.

When Eleanor went over to her, she gave a perfunctory wag of the tail and backed off. Puzzled, Eleanor bent down to right the bag and stuff the clothes back in. Behind the box a pair of boots lay on their sides, one atop the other. The leather, once black but now of no determinate colour, was cracked and the back of the heels, turned towards her, were worn down to the uppers.

"That's odd," she said to Teazle. "I don't remember anyone giving those and I never would have accepted them. No one would buy such disreputable boots."

She set the carrier bag to one side and shifted the box. As it moved, she saw bony, sockless ankles and the frayed, faded hems of a pair of filthy blue jeans. The boots were occupied.

Had some tramp crawled in among the goods? She really must remember to lock doors! In a way, she was glad that he had found shelter from the chilly spring night, but Jocelyn would be furious. Perhaps she could send him on his way before Jocelyn found out.

He must be drunk, or very sound asleep, not to have been wakened by the fuss over the table. She nudged at his thin ankle with a fastidious toe but failed to rouse him.

As she moved boxes and bags away from the prone form, a sick certainty that something was very wrong grew in her. She uncovered the rest of the jeans, a hand in a woollen glove unravelling at the wrist, a khaki anorak ripped under the arm. The man lay motionless.

And then the head, face to the wall: long, lank darkish hair; the angle of a jaw sprouting youthful fuzz; the angle of the neck—

"Joce!" Her call emerged as a strangled squeak. Backing towards the connecting door, she tried again. "Jocelyn!"

"Coming. I've sold . . . Eleanor, you're white as a sheet. What is it?"

"I'm just afraid it's Trevor."

"Trevor?"

"The boy who comes to help when he stays with his uncle."

"Eleanor, dear, calm down. I know Trevor. A scruffy, feckless creature he is, and none too clean either."

"Was." Her voice shook. "Oh, Joce, there's a dead body back there and he looks very like Trevor."

THREE

Detective Sergeant Megan Pencarrow drove through the town centre with the greatest of care. Detective Inspector Scumble of the Constabulary of the Royal Duchy of Cornwall (usually known as CaRaDoC) hated being driven by a woman and was never slow to say so. Wild horses could not have dragged the admission from her, but she found his solid bulk, squeezed into the seat of the unmarked Mini Cooper beside her, just a bit intimidating.

"Close that window," he growled.

She complied, though she had been enjoying the breeze ruffling her short, dark hair. If only Superintendent Bentinck had decided to let County HQ in Bodmin take on the case! But murders were few and far between in North Cornwall and he wanted to give Scumble a chance to take the credit for solving this one.

The inspector's usual partner, DS Eliot, was on sick leave. Scumble had decided it was past time he took a closer look at the work of the only woman detective in his small CID, but he didn't have to like it. Nor did she.

"I suppose it really is a murder," he said as she drove round the new roundabout and took the A30 towards the coast. "Someone's going to catch it if I'm being dragged out to the back of beyond for nothing."

"The victim has a broken neck and the body was concealed, according to Aunt Nell," she responded incautiously.

"Aunt Nell? Who the hell is Aunt Nell?" The rhyme pleased him and he listened with unusual tolerance to her explanation.

"My aunt discovered the body, sir. When the vicar's wife, who was with her, rang Launceston to report it, she asked to speak to me. I gather Mrs Stearns felt it unwise to phone the local officer."

"Oh yes?"

"Not because of any qualms about PC Leacock's competence, sir," Megan hastened to assure him. "It seems his car radio is unreliable and his wife answers the phone at the station. Mrs Stearns felt that half the village would be on their doorstep in no time once Mrs Leacock heard the news."

"No doubt. Murders don't happen every day around here." He rubbed his hands together with unattractive satisfaction. "I take it the doctor and the Scene Of Crime people are on their way?"

"I rang Dr Prthnavi at once, sir. The super ordered out the SOC team from Bodmin and someone's trying to get hold of Leacock. Shall I check?" She reached for the two-way radio.

"No! Kindly keep your hands on the wheel while you're driving, wom—er, Sergeant."

He spoke to headquarters while Megan drove over the northern edge of Bodmin Moor, with the tor of Brown Willy away to the south, and took the A39. As they turned off the main road into the narrow lane leading to Port Mabyn, he signed off and wound down the window. The sun was warm in the high-hedged lane but Megan didn't quite dare open her own window after being instructed to close it.

"So your aunt found the body," he commented.

"Yes, sir. It . . . He was in the LonStar shop, as you know. Aunt Nell and Uncle Peter used to work for LonStar, and when he was killed she retired . . ."

"Killed?" he repeated hopefully. "A murder involving a widow whose husband died in suspicious circumstances—"

She disillusioned him. "A riot in Djakarta. Indonesia. Aunt Nell retired and bought the shop in Port Mabyn, with the flat above. She gave the shop to LonStar and now she works as a volunteer."

Inspector Scumble grunted, acknowledging an unlikely suspect. "She know the dead bloke?"

"I'm not sure, sir. Aunt Nell sounded a bit distraught when I spoke to her."

"What's her name, for Pete's sake?" he demanded irritably. "I can't call the woman Aunt Nell."

"Mrs Trewynn, sir. Eleanor Trewynn."

Rounding a bend, they met a mud-bedaubed lorry. It pulled in close to the hedge and Scumble held his breath as Megan inched past. She was inclined to take umbrage at the insult to her driving ability—until the smell reached her. The lorry's door panel announced Bray Bros. Livestock Transporters, and porcine snouts grunted at them from the slatted sides.

"Too late to close my window," he muttered in what might, in anyone else, have been an apology. "You'd better open yours now, air it out."

She complied, and soon the stink was replaced by the faint seaweedy smell of the ocean.

They passed a caravan park, nearly deserted at this time of year, and then the mini-market and the sprawl of pastel bungalows of the newer part of Port Mabyn. Starting down the steep hill into the old village, Megan glanced at the inspector. His eyes were screwed shut. Being driven really made him nervous, then; she'd assumed his moaning was just part of his general grouchiness.

Just past the pub, she had to give way to a couple of pedestrians crossing the street.

"Are we there?" he asked, eyes still closed.

"Just a little farther, sir."

She parked opposite the shop, offside wheels on the pavement, realizing too late that her massive superior would barely fit between the car and the wall. Which would annoy him more, she wondered, letting him struggle or offering to pull out, thus suggesting that he was overweight? He wasn't, or not much—just tall and brawny.

He swung open the door and she winced as it scraped the whitewashed wall. Hurriedly she got out into the street, resisting the temptation to look back. He was breathing heavily when he joined her, his grey suit slightly more rumpled than usual, but any comment he might have wished to make was forestalled.

"Megan!" Aunt Nell burst from the blue door opposite and, to her acute embarrassment, rushed to hug her. "Oh, Megan, my dear, I'm so glad you've come."

"Aunt Nell, please, I'm on duty," she hissed.

"But you're not in uniform." Aunt Nell stood back and studied her niece's discreet forest-green suit and white shirt. "Are you?"

"No, I'm a detective." Avoiding the interested gaze of the local constable, who had followed her aunt at a more sober pace, she introduced her superior. "This is Detective Inspector Scumble. Sir, Mrs Trewynn."

"How kind of you to come, Inspector, though I'm sorry such a nasty business is the occasion of our meeting. Won't you come in?"

"Thank you, madam, I shall certainly do so as soon as I have had a word with the officer here." Scumble spoke with the heavy patience of one obliged by his position to be polite. "Perhaps you will be good enough to answer a few questions after I have viewed the body."

"Of course, but I have already told dear Bob about finding the poor boy." Stepping back, she patted the constable's sleeve.

To his credit, the young man answered with aplomb, "So you have, Mrs Trewynn, but the inspector'll want to hear it all again, I don't doubt." He saluted. "Constable Leacock reporting, sir."

"I'll go and put the kettle on," said Aunt Nell and returned to the house.

Jocelyn met her at the foot of the stairs. "Eleanor, you really must restrain yourself," she said severely. "I can't believe it's a good idea to embrace Megan publicly while she's working. Try to think of her as a police officer, not as your niece."

Eleanor smiled, unrepentant. The world could never have too many expressions of love, she thought, but she said, "Let's go up and make tea and coffee. I forgot to ask which the inspector prefers."

From the kitchen window she watched the arrival of a police van and another car. The pavement and part of the road in front of the shop were cordoned off, leaving the bare minimum of room for vehicles to pass single file. A curious crowd began to gather, housewives shopping, neighbours coming out onto their doorsteps.

Nick appeared and she heard him talking with the officer guarding the street door below.

"What's happened?"

"Can't say, sir."

"Is Mrs Trewynn all right?"

"Far as I know, sir."

"Let me go and see if she needs any help."

"No one allowed through, sir."

He argued for a minute, then shrugged his shoulders and gave up. Looking up, he saw her at the window, waved, and called, "Okay, Eleanor?"

"Yes, dear. Jocelyn's here."

"Good." He waved again and retreated to his shop. Eleanor rather wished she had asked him over before Bob Leacock had turned up. On the other hand, it was going to be difficult enough fitting Megan's rather large inspector into her sitting room. She hoped he wouldn't want to question her in the stockroom, at least not until the unfortunate youth had been removed. Though she had seen death from violence, death from disease, death from hunger, she had never grown reconciled to the premature ending of life.

A maroon car pulled up behind the police vehicles and a short, slight Indian emerged. A dapper figure in a pearl-grey suit and pale blue tie, he carried a black bag. As he approached the barricade, the policeman saluted and stood aside.

"The deceased's in the back room, sir."

"Thank you, officer." Like Nick, he glanced up and saw Eleanor at her kitchen window.

She leaned forward across the sink. "*Namaste*, Rajendra. You're the police doctor?"

"*Namaste* and good morning, Eleanor. Indeed, I have that honour."

"Do come up for a cup of tea when you're finished."

"Thank you. Should I be so fortunate as to have time, I shall be delighted." He bowed courteously and continued into the passage below.

"Who was that?" Jocelyn asked from the sitting room, which she was tidying ruthlessly. To Eleanor it had looked perfectly all right before she began.

"Rajendra Prthnavi. I suppose he's come to see how that poor boy broke his neck. Oh, Joce, I am glad it wasn't Trevor after all. He looked so very like him."

"That long, matted hair and the tatty jeans are a sort of uniform for a certain type of youth. They wouldn't wear decent clothes if you paid them."

A few minutes later, Dr. Prthnavi knocked at the door. Pouring tea, Eleanor enquired after his family. This took some time as, though born in Birmingham, he had relatives in Bombay with whom she was acquainted. After a quarter of an hour, he announced regretfully that he must go about his rounds.

"Aren't you going to tell us how the unfortunate boy died, Doctor?" Jocelyn asked.

"I ought not, Mrs Stearns, but I am sure I can rely on the discretion of you ladies."

"Of course," she said, slightly offended.

"In any case, there is not a great deal to tell. I expect you saw that his neck was broken? If that had not killed him immediately, he'd probably have died slowly from subarachnoid hemorrhage—bleeding inside the cranium. He was hit on the side of the head with the proverbial blunt instrument, sometime last evening."

Eleanor shuddered. "Oh dear, I was hoping it might somehow turn out to be an accident, but it must have been murder after all, mustn't it?"

FOUR

A heavy tread on the narrow staircase made Eleanor glad her little house was solidly built of Cornish granite. In relative terms, DI Scumble was equally solidly built, but large. As he stepped through the front door of the flat, left open for his expected arrival, his head brushed the lintel and his shoulders brushed the doorposts.

Teazle let fly a volley of barks. Her voice was surprisingly deep for such a tiny dog. Scumble looked a trifle taken aback, and Eleanor had to suppress a quite inappropriate urge to reassure the monster that the mite would not hurt him.

"Hush, Teazle," she said instead. "Do sit down, Mr Scumble. Would you like coffee or tea?"

"Not for me, thank you, ma'am," he said severely, looking round the room for a chair fit to contain his bulk and uphold his weight. The only possibility was one of the old wooden dining chairs, genuine hand-turned beech, a donation from a farmhouse kitchen that had moved "up" to steel and vinyl. Foreseeing the difficulty, Eleanor had tactfully turned one with its back to the table.

As he moved towards it, the floor creaking beneath him,

Megan came into view behind him. She looked rather apprehensive. Remembering Jocelyn's reprimand, Eleanor didn't jump up to embrace her niece. She didn't even venture to offer her a cup of tea after Scumble's adamant rejection of refreshment. A warm but silent smile seemed to be the best choice.

She was rewarded as Megan's apprehension lightened. Squeezing past her boss, the detective sergeant sat down at the table and took out her notebook and ball-point pen.

"Did the poor boy have any identification on him, Inspector?" Eleanor asked. "Do you know who he is?"

"I'm here to ask the questions, madam. You've already told me you didn't know him. I must ask again, for the official record: Were you acquainted with the victim or do you remember ever having seen him before?"

"No, though for a moment I did wonder—"

"But you're quite sure now?" he interrupted.

"Yes."

"Right, tell me about yesterday evening." It was an order, not a request.

From the corner of her eye, Eleanor saw Jocelyn's lips tighten. "I came home just before it began to get dark," she said hastily.

"Where from?"

Eleanor waved her hands. "Oh, all over the place. I was driving, collecting donations, you see. For the shop. And then I walked the dog on the cliffs, not far north of Port Mabyn. There's a footpath sign and a stile but I'm not sure if that particular bit of cliff has a name," she added dubiously. "Oh, but I saw Constable Leacock drive past just after I stopped, and he waved, so he knows where I was and he can tell you, if you need to know. But it was earlier, really still afternoon at that point."

"And then," said Scumble with an air of dogged patience, "you came home."

"Yes, and I parked right outside the shop. I know it's no parking and a double yellow line but it was just for unloading. I had some heavy boxes of books in the boot. Dear Nick came to carry them in for me. Nicholas Gresham, the artist next door. Some of the children helped with the lighter stuff, too."

"Which children?"

"Ummmm . . ." The only face that appeared to her mind's eye was the dead boy's. But the inspector was waiting. ". . . you see, the village children are all very sweet about helping, most of them at least. They understand that it's all for a good cause. Now, who was it who turned up last night?"

"That's what I'm asking you, madam."

"Nick is sure to remember . . . Oh!" The memory of that narrowly averted pinch returned. She mustn't become a dithery old lady just because that was what he obviously considered her to be. "Of course, it was Donna from the Trelawney Arms. And she was organising the two little ones from the Chinese restaurant, Lionel and Ivy."

"So you, Gresham, and these three children all carried stuff in. Where did you put it?"

"In the stockroom, where I found the . . . the body this morning. We put everything at the back there to be sorted. He—the boy—was hidden by some of the clothes I'd brought in." To her dismay, she felt her lips quiver and tears collect in her eyes.

With a defiant glance at Scumble, Jocelyn got up, took Eleanor's empty mug, and went into the kitchen. A moment later she returned with a full mug of steaming tea which she put into Eleanor's hands. "Drink," she said.

A revivifying gulp steadied her, and she went on, "You see, the clothes were spilled and tumbled. I was tidying—"

"We'll get to that shortly. Go on with last night."

"Well, he certainly wasn't there when we unloaded the Incorruptible."

"The *what?*"

"Sorry, the car. It's pea-green, and you know what Carlyle said about Robespierre . . ."

Scumble's scowl suggested he not only didn't, he had never heard of either gentleman.

Eleanor hastened to explain. "He called him 'the sea-green incorruptible.' It's Nick's pun, not mine."

"Could we please get on with the events of yesterday evening?"

"Of course. Where were we?"

The inspector gave her an old-fashioned look and addressed Jocelyn. "If it's not too much trouble, Mrs Stearns, a cup of coffee would not come amiss. Or tea, whichever is easier. Black. And as strong as possible."

"Certainly, Inspector," Jocelyn said graciously. She went back to the kitchen.

"You put all the stuff you had collected in the back room, Mrs Trewynn. At that time there was no body in the room. What happened next?"

"The children went home. Nick told me he'd sold a painting and invited me out to supper to celebrate."

"What time was this?"

"Time? I don't . . . Oh, I remember, Nick asked me the time, and I couldn't tell him because my watch had stopped."

"Didn't you come up here then? You have a clock." He gestured at the pretty flowered-china timepiece on the mantel. Eleanor had agonised over whether she could afford it, at last rationalising that the purchase price would benefit LonStar.

"I didn't look at it. I just had to feed Teazle and change into something respectable before Nick came to pick me up. And comb my hair," she added conscientiously as Jocelyn returned with mugs for Scumble and Megan. Eleanor considered her natural curls could survive most things looking reasonably neat. Jocelyn disagreed.

"The clock's slow anyway," Scumble muttered, checking his wristwatch.

"It runs slow. Anyway, I was ready when Nick came back from parking the Incorr—the car for me. And he had changed, too. We walked up to the Wreckers—that's the other pub," Eleanor explained, as Scumble looked blank.

"Other?"

"Other than the Trelawney Arms, which is where Donna lives. Which is why—But you don't want to know that."

"What don't I want to know?" the inspector asked suspiciously.

"Just that we went to the Wreckers, which is up the other hill and slightly more expensive, because Donna . . . er . . . she's taken a bit of a fancy to Nick, I'm afraid."

"She's a little hussy," said Jocelyn in her forthright way, "and blatantly pursues him."

"You're right," Scumble admitted. "I didn't want to know."

Eleanor beamed at him, seeing Megan, safe behind his back, smother a giggle. "We had a drink at the Wreckers," she said, "then walked back down and up this side to Chin's, the Chinese restaurant, where Ivy and Lionel live. We had a very nice dinner. Much nicer than practically anything I ever ate in China." She was torn between launching into her speech on poverty in China, followed by a plea for a donation, and teasing the detective by starting to list what she and Nick had eaten, followed by an assertion that he didn't want to know that. Megan's agonised expression deterred her. "Then we came home."

Unaware of his narrow escape, Scumble said gloomily, "I suppose you don't know what time any of this took place."

"My dear Inspector!" Jocelyn was shocked. "It's terribly rude for a woman being taken out for the evening to keep her eye on the time. Unless," she added, to be fair, "she has an urgent appointment."

"I didn't," Eleanor put in quickly, before Scumble could explode. "I came up here—"

"You didn't notice anything unusual on the way up? The door was still locked?"

"Oh dear! I'm afraid I'm not sure. In fact, I'm not at all sure I locked it when I left. I know, Megan, Joce, I promised, and I do try, but the trouble is, I've spent so many years in places without doors, let alone locks—"

"Am I to understand," asked Scumble in despair, "that both the street door and the door to this flat may or may not have been locked when you left and when you returned."

"Exactly," said Eleanor.

"And the stockroom?"

"I'm sure I locked that." She gave a guilty glance at Jocelyn. "Fairly sure. I distinctly remember locking something." The car?

"None of the doors shows any sign of being forced. I shall be asking you, Mrs Stearns, who has keys to the shop and storeroom. Now, Mrs Trewynn, did you go out again for any reason?"

"No. Well, yes. Not really. I let Teazle out of the back door, at the end of the passage, by the stockroom door, and I stood at the door watching her. The light was on up here, and she being white, I could see her though it was dark out. She came at once when I called her—she's very good about that—but when she came in she started to snuffle at the stockroom door. I thought perhaps we had mice again. I called her away and we came up and went to bed." She bit her lip. "If I'd investigated, could I have helped—?"

"No. He appears to have died more or less instantly. The dog's behaviour would seem to indicate he was killed while you were out for the evening. You're sure you didn't hear anything out of the ordinary while you stood at the back door, or after you came upstairs?"

"Quite sure. I wouldn't hear anything downstairs after I went to bed, though. My bedroom is upstairs, under the roof, with a dormer window. And Nick had his record-player on. Or perhaps his wireless. He was listening to a piano concerto last night, Shostakovich, I think. He knows I don't mind being able to hear his music."

"I'm delighted to hear it. What about this morning?"

"When I took Teazle down to let her out first thing, she was even more interested in the stockroom door. It was difficult to get her to come away. I was sure there must be mice, and so I told Jocelyn—Mrs Stearns—later. I said not to let her in there without me or she'd create chaos. When I went to start sorting the new stuff, she came with me—"

"Mrs Stearns?"

"Teazle. Mrs Stearns was busy in the shop by then. Teazle came with me. She started sniffing around at the back, and then she began to whine. I called her away and made her lie down by the door. I started tidying a pile of clothes, and that's when I saw him." All too clearly, Eleanor recalled those pathetically bony ankles. She reached for Jocelyn's hand. "I don't think . . . I can't remember if I touched him. I didn't move him. I called Joce—"

"And I rang the police," said Jocelyn decisively. "I was not acquainted with the victim nor did I recognise him. I arrived here at approximately quarter to ten. The vicarage is just two minutes walk. I came in through the street door, which I found locked and unlocked myself. All our more responsible volunteers have keys to that door, so that they can come in to work in the stockroom without going through the shop. I have a list of names and addresses in the shop."

"Excellent."

"I went up the stairs and knocked on Mrs Trewynn's door. When she called out 'Come in,' I entered. I have a key—as a friend, nothing to do with the shop—but the door was not locked at that time."

"That was after I'd taken Teazle down for her morning run," Eleanor explained.

Scumble gave a nod. "Apparently you had locked the street door when you came in last night. Did you lock this door, the door to your flat?"

Eleanor tried to think. She could picture herself putting the key in the lock and turning it, but was that last night? Or the night before? Or when she went out yesterday? "I have no idea," she said a bit crossly, "and the more you ask, the more I can't remember."

Raising his eyes to heaven, Scumble turned back to Jocelyn. "Please continue, Mrs Stearns."

"I exchanged a few words with Eleanor—Mrs Trewynn—and then went down to the shop. I entered through the door from the passage. It was locked. Only I and Mrs Davies have keys to that door. Mrs Trewynn does not."

"Why is that?"

"I don't need one. I never work in the shop because I have only to look at the cash register for it to malfunction."

Scumble looked as if he wasn't in the least surprised.

"I dusted a bit and checked the change Mrs Davies had left in the cash register yesterday at closing time. I should explain that as there's no bank in the village, whichever of us is in charge takes home the greater part of the day's takings. In any case, it's rarely enough to tempt a thief."

"You'd be surprised."

"I put up the blinds and opened the shop at ten precisely," Jocelyn went on. Scumble again looked as if he wasn't in the least surprised. "I served one customer—I can give you her name if necessary—and then I heard Eleanor calling from the stockroom. I had unlocked the connecting door earlier. Again, only I and Mrs Davies have that key. One or the other of us is always here when the shop is open. I went through. Eleanor had found the body. I immediately put up the CLOSED sign, locked the door of the shop, and telephoned the police in Launceston. I wish to make it clear that I rang Launceston not because of any lack of faith in PC Leacock's competence, but Mrs Leacock frequently answers the phone and she is quite incapable of keeping a still tongue in her head."

"Understood."

"Eleanor was in a state of shock. I brought her up here and made tea, which I consider a far more efficacious remedy than brandy."

"I don't have any brandy anyway," said Eleanor, "but I did drink several cups of tea, so if you will please excuse me for a moment . . ." Gathering what little dignity was left to her, she went up the stairs to her bedroom and, more important just now, her bathroom. Teazle, who had been sitting subdued at her feet, naturally followed her.

Behind her she heard Scumble ask whether anything was missing or disarranged in the shop, and Jocelyn telling him all was as it should be, down to the last penny in the cash register. Eleanor reflected on the curious fact that she, who had seen much unnatural death, was so much more shocked than the vicar's wife. Perhaps Jocelyn was shielded by her religion, though in Eleanor's experience, most Christians were as reluctant as those of any other faith—or none—to depart this world for the next.

A few minutes later, Teazle scampered down the stairs ahead of her, as if determined to put the morning's unpleasantness behind her. She gave Megan an ecstatic greeting, embarrassing Megan and making Scumble scowl.

"Mrs Trewynn," he said, "are you aware of anything missing from your flat, or not in its usual place?"

"I don't think so." She looked around. How could she tell after Jocelyn had tidied?

"We'll have to do a thorough search of the premises, the flat and the shop. We'll try to disarrange things as little as possible. We'll need your fingerprints, both of you, for elimination purposes. Constable?"

Megan took their fingerprints, a process Eleanor had been through more than once in some of the places she had travelled, but which exasperated Jocelyn.

"So messy!" she objected.

"Can't be helped, I'm afraid, madam. Now, Mrs Trewynn, is there somewhere you can go while we—?"

"Eleanor will come home with me," said Jocelyn.

"You're the vicar's wife, madam?"

"Yes, the Reverend Timothy Stearns. Our house is the vicarage. Anyone can direct you."

"Good," Scumble grunted. "We'll probably have more questions for both of you."

"You'd better pack up a few things for the night, Eleanor. You won't want to sleep here."

"Oh no—It's very kind of you, Joce, but I'd rather come home, if Mr Scumble says I may."

"Possibly, though I doubt it. In any case, please don't remove anything just yet. If necessary, DS Pencarrow can fetch what you need later."

"There, then, that's settled. I'll just get Teazle's lead. Come on, girl, let's go and see Uncle Timothy."

The little dog bounced to the door and looked back impatiently. Uncle Timothy carried biscuits in his pocket for any stray children he happened to meet. He could often be persuaded to grant well-behaved dogs the status of honorary children.

"You'd better give me your keys, Mrs Trewynn," the inspector said dryly, "so we can lock up when we're done. I'll see they're brought to you at the vicarage."

"Yes, of course. Er . . . I wonder where I put them?"

Scumble's eyes once again turned up to the heavens. "If," he said to the ceiling, "they are anywhere on the premises, we shall find them." He stood up, crowding the room. "Good day, ladies. Please don't discuss the incident with anyone, especially the press."

FIVE

As the door closed behind her aunt, Megan braced herself for a scathing comment from the inspector. All he said was, "You know this artist chappy next door, Sergeant?"

"Not much more than to say hello, sir." Long hair and the smell of turps did not attract her.

"Seen his work? Any good? You reckon he makes a decent living at it?"

"I've never looked around the gallery. It's mostly tourist stuff—picturesque villages, cottages, fishing boats, heather-covered cliffs, I gather. You know the sort of thing, old stone bridges, donkeys at Clovelly." She gestured towards Aunt Nell's painting.

"That one of his?" The floor creaked as Scumble crossed for a closer look. "Hm. I've seen worse."

"It's quite good of its kind. I can't think why he'd go on painting it if he wasn't making some sort of living."

"What do you mean?"

"Just that his other stuff is quite different, sir. Abstract, Aunt Nell—Mrs Trewynn—told me. More . . . well, high-brow, I suppose. "

"Ambitious, eh?"

"I don't think he sells much of it."

"You reckon he'd take Mrs Trewynn out for the evening deliberately to leave the place clear for a confederate to burgle?"

"Surely not, sir! He's not stupid. If I were a burglar, I wouldn't choose a charity shop to rob. I doubt if there's anything here worth more than ten quid or so."

"Let's hope you don't turn burglar," Scumble said with a return to his sour manner. "You'd better not be involved in searching your aunt's place. Go and interview Gresham."

"Yes, sir." Megan escaped with relief.

Halfway down the stairs, she stopped. Ambulance men were carrying a stretcher out of the stockroom, manoeuvring with difficulty around the corner into the narrow passage. The skinny, dirty, pathetic boy was just a lumpy bulge under a strapped-down sheet. Was someone, somewhere, wondering why he hadn't come home? Or had they given up on him months, perhaps years ago?

Megan followed the men along the passage and out into the street, now completely blocked by the ambulance. She heard the collective gasp from the crowd, a mixture of locals and early visitors by the look of them, held back by the police barriers.

No one said, "It's not *So-and-so*, is it?"

Just some feckless runaway from God-knows-where. They might never discover his name.

She turned down the hill to the gallery next door.

The bell on the door jangled as she entered. Nick Gresham was behind the counter at the back, busy making change for a customer. He gave a casual wave to acknowledge her arrival.

She had met him a few times, over polite afternoon tea at Aunt Nell's. They had treated each other with the wariness of dogs wondering whether they were going to have to defend their territory. She had never been in the gallery before, and she looked around with interest.

On the walls and a couple of folding screens hung paintings of Cornish beauty spots, aimed at emmets, as the Cornish call tourists. They were better than most of their kind. Somehow the artist had caught the transparent blue light of Cornwall, sea reflecting sky reflecting sea, never far off even when no sea was visible in the picture. A panel of one screen displayed a number of miniatures of wildflowers. A shelf held sleek porpoises, seagulls, and seals, carved from serpentine mottled and streaked in blues and greens and browns; drawing-pinned to the shelf was a card with the sculptor's name. Not a Cornish piskie, a fake horse-brass, nor a lighthouse table-lamp in sight, she noted.

Half listening as Gresham assured his customer that he knew nothing about what was going on next door, but it was bound to be on the local telly news, Megan wandered behind one of the screens. The painting on the wall opposite her stopped her in her tracks.

It was all dark greys and purples and black, slashed with white, and somehow suffused with brilliant light. It should have been gloomy, even frightening, but it projected a magnificent, powerful energy. She read the title card pinned up beside it: *Storm over Rough Tor.* Yes, there in the lower left corner was a hint of massive solidity—not a clear depiction of the huge, heaped boulders of the tor but enough to anchor the whole in reality. Though she didn't know much about painting, this was obviously of a quite different order from the sunlit seaside scenes behind her. She stepped back to get a better view.

When Aunt Nell first told Megan about her neighbour, she had described Nicholas as making her think of a Georgian aristocrat. Knowing he was an artist, Megan had pictured a foppish dilettante, but the vigour of this picture was a reminder that

Georgians were also swordsmen—duellists—and neck-or-nothing riders.

The jangle of the doorbell as the customer left interrupted her contemplation. She emerged from behind the screen. The proprietor had vanished.

"Hello?" she called.

"I'll be with you in half a tick." Nick Gresham's voice came from somewhere to the rear, beyond the counter. A door stood open, through which he entered a few moments later, wiping his paint-stained hands on a paint-stained rag. There was a dab of blue on one cheek, too. "Sorry. Most people like to look about a bit before I pop out of my . . . Aha, I didn't recognise you for a moment in that garb. It's your policewoman incarnation. Or do you prefer 'lady detective'?"

"Detective Sergeant Pencarrow, sir," said Megan through gritted teeth, taking her notebook from her shoulder-bag.

"Come to give me the third degree, have you?"

"Do I need to?"

"I shouldn't think so. How is Eleanor holding up?"

"Pretty well. She's not exactly your common-or-garden little old lady."

"Far from it."

"Mrs Stearns has swept her off to the vicarage."

"Good. I hope your . . . er . . . large companion doesn't consider her a suspect?"

"He wouldn't discuss it with me if he did. And not only because she's my aunt. He doesn't believe in women in the police, let alone as detectives. In fact, he doesn't even really believe we should be allowed behind the wheel of motor vehicles."

"Do I detect a note of disgruntlement?"

Megan pulled herself together. "I'm supposed to be asking the questions."

"Go ahead. But come on back to the studio. I can't afford to lose the light, and there's been a stream of customers this morning, wanting to know what's up next door." He led the way. "I've sold three pictures!"

Contrary to her expectations, the room Nick called his studio was reasonably tidy. The far wall was mostly windows, with a view of the slope rising to the headland, like Aunt Nell's. Several paintings leant against the low wall below the glass. If she went over close to the windows, Megan thought, and looked down to the left, she'd be able to see the inlet, with the sheer rock wall on the far side and the crooked finger of the quay, and perhaps the inner harbour. Two easels stood facing the windows, one draped with a length of unbleached muslin, frayed along the visible end. The other held a canvas, of which she could see only the back. Beside it was a high wooden stool with a palette and a jar of brushes on it.

One side wall was taken up by wide, deep drawers below open shelves crammed with paints, brushes, a bottle of linseed oil, and a large tin of turps—the smell was quite strong in here—and various paraphernalia Megan couldn't readily identify. The other wall, the one he shared with the LonStar shop's stockroom, was occupied by stairs going up, with a sink and a workbench below, where he apparently framed his own pictures.

"Before you get started, I have to take your fingerprints."

"What the hell for? If you think I—"

"Because you were in the stockroom and there are prints all over the place, and we can't tell which are yours."

"Ah yes, for elimination purposes. You should read detective novels, then you'd have the jargon at your fingertips."

"As a matter of fact, when I left London, war was being waged against jargon."

"Come now, that's hardly fair to the authors of crime fiction! Still, I don't suppose there's much chance of its succeeding."

Megan took his prints. He cleaned his fingers fastidiously, though apparently oblivious of the paint on his face.

She leant against the bench as Nick took his place before the undraped easel, chose a brush, and resumed work on a half-completed painting of a lifeboat putting to sea.

"What time did you first see Aunt Nell—Mrs Trewynn—yesterday?" she asked.

"Quite late." He scratched his ear with the wooden end of the paintbrush. "The sun was setting. I've no idea what time it was, but no doubt the police have access to such information. I heard her car."

"From here?"

He gave her a look as if she was a total cretin. "Hardly. I was sweeping up out there, in the gallery."

"You recognised her car by the sound?"

"I'm not *that* fascinated by cars. I heard a car stop next door and glanced out of the window. Since it was a pea-green Moggie, one of the few cars I can recognise on sight, I deduced that it was the Incorruptible, and further deduced that Eleanor had just come home. As she'd mentioned the day before that she was planning one of her collection runs, I went out when I finished sweeping to see if there was anything heavy I could help with." Falling silent, he dabbed delicately at the canvas.

"And?" Megan asked.

"And?" he echoed absently.

"And was there anything heavy?"

"A couple of boxes."

"Something valuable?" she asked eagerly.

"Paperback books. There may have been a couple of hard-backs. I didn't check."

"Oh, books."

"Don't you read books?"

"Of course I do! When I get time. But no one's going to break into a building to steal books. You'd be surprised how often they're shoplifted, though."

"I wouldn't. Any book I particularly want to borrow from the library is sure to have been pinched. Or misshelved."

She wondered what he like to read. Books about art, probably, or something equally high-brow. "You carried the two boxes to the stockroom?"

"What?" He was concentrating on the painting again.

"The boxes of books." She held onto her patience with both hands, determined not to end up like Inspector Scumble. "You took them to the stockroom."

"Well, of course. That's what I went out there for. And to invite Eleanor out to dinner as I'd had a bit of good luck fleecing a rich American."

Megan frowned. "Fleecing?"

"Don't scowl like that. It doesn't suit you. His wife liked a picture of mine but it wasn't big enough for the bit of wall she wanted it for. So I painted the same scene the size she wanted, on commission, cash up front. He paid through the nose for it. Bigger equals better equals worth a whole lot more money."

"Oh." A disappointing attitude to an artist with aspirations, she assumed. "I suppose you would have noticed if there had been a body in the stockroom when you went in there?"

"Probably," he said infuriatingly. "I didn't root around, but Mrs Stearns keeps everything shipshape and Bristol fashion. I can't state categorically that it wasn't there, but I'd be surprised to hear I'd overlooked it."

"Fair enough. What next?"

"I took the Incorruptible down to Eleanor's shed—you know she rents a shed down by the harbour?—then came home, cleaned myself up a bit, and went to pick her up."

"What about the car keys?"

"Car keys? Well, I must have taken them out of the car, because the key to the shed's padlock is on the same ring."

"Did you have to stop the car, unlock the padlock, and restart the car to drive it in."

"No, actually. Eleanor leaves the padlock unlocked when she's using the car. There's nothing pinchable in the shed."

"So you could have locked the car away without using the key."

"You're right. A deduction worthy of Sherlock Holmes. So I could have locked the keys into the shed, though I'm pretty sure I didn't as I have a vague memory of handing them back to her. Still, I gather Mrs Stearns holds a spare padlock key against just such an inevitable occurrence."

"Aunt Nell's sure to do it sooner or later," Megan agreed, "if she hasn't before now. She has no idea which doors, if any, she locked last night. If you're not absolutely sure you gave her back the keys, and we don't find them in the flat, at least we'll know to look in the garage. What time did you pick her up?"

"No idea. Just a minute, this is a tricky bit."

He picked up a different brush and bent close to the canvas. When he straightened again, it looked no different to Megan, but Nick gave a sigh of satisfaction.

"Sorry, what was the question?"

"You said you don't know what time you picked up Aunt Nell."

"You'd better make sure you write 'Mrs Trewynn' in your report, not 'Aunt Nell.' They might be able to tell you at the Wreckers what time we got there."

"You went straight there?"

"Yes, and they know me pretty well, though I go to the Trelawney Arms more often."

"Why the Wreckers last night then?"

"Oh, er . . . As a matter of fact . . ." His face turned pink. "You see, the . . . er . . . the daughter of the house—the Arms—seems to have taken a bit of a shine to me."

"You don't return her affections?"

"I do not!"

"Pity. You could have celebrated your sale with her last night."

"She's half my age! Too young to go out for a drink, even if Eleanor weren't much better company."

"She's twice your age." Megan felt as if she was betraying her aunt.

"But very good company. Is this relevant? Or are you trying to protect Eleanor from the heartbreak of falling in love with a younger man? No chance of that."

"We can never be sure what might turn out to be relevant," Megan said with as much dignity as she could muster. She would have to leave that bit out of her report. "How long were you at the Wreckers?"

"Long enough for me to quaff a pint and Eleanor to sip a small sherry. Again, you'll have to ask the landlord if you want times. Come to think of it, I did look at the clock, but only to make sure we weren't going to be too late to eat at Chin's. The actual time didn't register."

Megan's sigh was not expressive of satisfaction. So far she hadn't learnt a damn thing Aunt Nell and Mrs Stearns hadn't already told Inspector Scumble. "You left the Wreckers at some yet to be determined time, and . . . ?"

"Walked back down the hill and up to Chin's. Oh, we stopped en route to drop off Teazle."

"You *what?*"

"We stopped to drop off Teazle," he said with exaggerated

patience. "Your aunt's dog? We took her to the pub, but Chin's is a restaurant, so we left her at home."

" 'Left' as in put her inside the street door, or 'left' as in 'took her up to the flat'?"

" 'Left' as in I waited by the street door while Eleanor took the dog up to the flat. She didn't mention it?"

Cultivate inscrutability, Megan reminded herself sternly. He shouldn't have been able to guess from her manner that at last she had garnered a tidbit of new information. She ignored his question and asked another of her own.

"Did you go into the passage?"

"No. The evening was still remarkably pleasant for April. I stood outside and admired the moon. The door was open, though, and I think I'd have heard if anything violent was going on in the stockroom."

"Could anyone in there have heard you?"

"I doubt it. I don't remember saying much, certainly not loudly. I mean, I didn't call out to Eleanor, nor she to me. I don't recall hearing her footsteps in the passage or on the stairs—she walks very lightly. And I oiled the hinges for Mrs Stearns just the other day, the street door and both doors off the passage."

A regular Boy Scout—Inspector Scumble would have said it aloud, sarcastically. Megan was alarmed to find herself thinking it, sarcastically. Scumble's view of the world was contagious. "They'd have heard the door close, though, wouldn't they?" she said quickly.

"Maybe. She didn't slam it, just pulled till the latch clicked."

"And locked it?"

He pondered. "Now that I can't tell you. I have a picture in my mind of her locking it, and another of her not locking it, but which belongs to that particular moment I couldn't say."

"Try putting the moon in your picture."

He raised his eyebrows. "All right." Another moment's thought brought forth: "Good idea. I can see the moonlight glinting on the keys. She locked it that time. Which means I didn't leave the keys in the car," he added, his tone self-congratulatory.

"Had she unlocked it previously, when you stopped after the pub to leave Teazle?"

"I think not, but I wouldn't be prepared to swear to it either way." He grinned. "Isn't it lucky I'm not a policeman?"

"Very." He really was a most irritating man.

"I expect Mr Chin will be able to tell you what time we got to the restaurant," he said soothingly, "and how long we were there. He's good with numbers. If you go Dutch with a group, he can work out in his head what each of four or five people owe. And he keeps his eye on the clock, I daresay. Restaurateurs usually do."

"We have someone asking him."

"Look here, you don't think I had anything to do with this murder, do you? I'm a pacifist."

"Don't tell the inspector. He was hit over the head with a nuclear disarmament sign by an Aldermaston marcher."

"Strewth, you're having me on!"

"It's a fact. It's much too early for us to rule out anyone, but in answer to your earlier question, I doubt DI Scumble suspects Aunt Nell in particular, even if it did happen in her house. In his view, a woman's weapon is poison, not ye olde blunt instrument."

"That's what was used, is it?"

Oh hell, she shouldn't have said that! And he knew it, judging by his knowing smile. Her cheeks felt hot. But she refused to ask him not to tell Scumble. "We won't know for certain what killed him till after the autopsy," she said haughtily.

"Don't worry, I shan't tell on you. If you're finished, I'd like to get back to work."

Megan was sure there must be more probing questions she ought to ask, but her mind was a complete blank. "You can't think of anything at all out of the ordinary, or anyone, that you heard or saw?"

"The only unusual thing was that it wasn't raining. I had a delightful evening with your aunt and I just hope you catch the bugger who's disturbed her peace of mind." With that, he turned back to his painting, immediately engrossed.

Ignored, Megan took herself out through the shop. Nicholas Gresham had no social graces, she fumed. If he was so self-absorbed painting one of his tourist daubs, what would he be like when working on his arty-farty abstracts? Unbearable! His one redeeming quality was his concern for Aunt Nell.

She went to look for Scumble.

SIX

A uniformed constable Megan didn't recognise—from Bodmin, presumably—guarded the street door into the passage beside the LonStar shop. "Move along, please, miss," he said to Megan in the automatic monotone of words oft repeated. "No one allowed in until further notice."

"Detective Sergeant Pencarrow. I'm working with DI Scumble."

"Pull the other one, it's got bells on it."

In silence Megan took her warrant card from the pocket of her suit jacket and held it up six inches from his nose.

His eyes crossed and he moved back half a step, till his back was pressed against the door. "Oops, sorry, miss. No one told me we got lady detectives nowadays. No offence meant." Saluting, he moved aside.

Megan wasn't sure of the truth of either statement, but he wasn't openly grinning, so she let it pass. She'd met the same attitude before in the few months since she moved from London back to Cornwall, in spite of her promotion to sergeant. Perhaps because country manners were still old-fashioned compared to the modern lack of manners in the city, so far no one had been openly rude. Until and unless that happened, she had decided the best way to deal with it was to ignore it.

At least the present oaf had reached behind him as he moved to swing the door open for her. She had feminist friends who would have objected to the assumption that a woman was incapable of opening a door for herself, but Megan was not looking for confrontation. With a nod of acknowledgement, she went in.

The door from the passage to the shop was open. Within, surrounded by racks of second-hand clothes and shelves of second-hand books and china, Scumble stood glowering at a bin of colourful woolly animals. A grass-green, yellow-bellied, goggle-eyed frog grinned back at him.

Megan stopped in the doorway, behind the counter and cash-register. The inspector transferred his scowl to her.

"Dusted! Everything in this place that can be polished has been polished within an inch of its life," he said gloomily.

"Mrs Stearns," Megan assumed. "Did the intruders get into the shop, sir?"

"Probably not." His gaze returned to the frog and its companions. "We haven't found anything they might have been after. I'm wondering whether there could be something hidden in one of these ghastly animals. No doubt Mrs Stearns will disembowel me if we disembowel them."

Megan was stunned by this evidence of a sense of humor, however grim, in her grumpy boss. "Couldn't we just squeeze them?" she asked cautiously. "That would catch anything but a very small piece of paper. Or drugs."

"Drugs are a possibility. The boy ponged of Mary Jane, remember, though the doc didn't find any obvious sign of the hard stuff. We'll have to impound them, at least until we find out where they came from. Anything helpful from Mrs Trewynn's arty boyfriend?"

"Not her boyfriend, sir!" Megan realised too late that he was just trying to get a rise out of her. And succeeding. Lamely she added, "Just a friend. He's half her age."

"What's wrong with him that he can't get a girlfriend his own age? A pansy, is he?"

"Could be, I suppose. I don't think so."

"Drugs?"

"Not noticeably. The smell of turpentine in his studio would cover pot, but I can't see him smoking in there, with customers in and out of the gallery."

"All right, get on with it."

Megan gave her report. She knew she hadn't extracted much useful information from Nick Gresham, but under Scumble's sceptical gaze it shrank to virtually zero. "At least we know Aunt— Mrs Trewynn locked the street door when they went to the restaurant," she finished in desperation.

"Unfortunately," he pointed out, "we still don't know whether she locked the back door. You didn't ask whether he waited long for Mrs Trewynn to come back down?"

"No, sir. Uh, why?"

"Oh, just in case he said she came straight back, and she said she was gone for several minutes, feeding the dog, say."

"Sir, you can't think he was downstairs knocking the victim on the head while she was upstairs feeding the dog!"

"You never know. However, having forgotten to mention bringing the dog home, your aunt is not in the least likely to re-member how long she took about it." He went over to the door to the stockroom and stuck his head in. "Not finished with that bloody list yet?"

"The list's just about done, sir," said Chapman, the scene-of-crime sergeant, "except we're still going through all the blasted pockets."

"Well, don't be all day about it. What have you found in the way of possible weapons?"

He went in. Megan followed him. Laid out on the long, narrow table were a rolling pin; a bundle of brass stair-rods tied with garden twine; an old-fashioned flatiron; an even more old-fashioned copper warming-pan, for which some rich American might pay a pretty penny; and a bent golf club that could conceivably be of use as a garden stake.

"That's it?" Scumble demanded. "Load of rubbish. Any blood or hair?"

"Not that we can see, sir."

"None of 'em looks likely, but we'll let the experts decide. Where's the man who went to the Chinese and the pub?"

"Golloping or gulging," said PC Killick enviously. A true Cornishman, he was given to deliberately incomprehensible pronouncements in the local dialect, though not attempting the renascent Cornish language.

"He better not be," said Chapman, who apparently understood at least those two words, as did Megan. After all, she had grown up in Cornwall.

"Eating or drinking," she translated discreetly to Scumble, who was turning crimson.

It did not noticeably decrease his choler. "He'd better not be!" the inspector seconded the sergeant.

"All the same, sir," said Chapman, "is it okay if we get some pasties in from opposite?"

"I suppose so. Let's have your list of the stuff in here. When the house-to-house people come in, and that includes the grub and booze man, get their reports. If we're not back, bring them to the vicarage. DS Pencarrow and I are going there now."

His sigh was deep enough to have originated in the Antipodes.

Eleanor was invigorated by the walk up the hill with Jocelyn to the vicarage, Teazle trotting at their heels. The sea breeze was refreshing and she didn't mind that it brought with it the beginnings of a sea mist. Crookmoyle Point and Slee Head, to the south of the harbour, were already invisible, and from the lighthouse came the hollow moan of the fog-horn. But the village would probably suffer no worse than a pervading dampness in the air.

The Reverend Timothy Stearns, tall and thin and swathed in yellow oilskins, awaited them on the vicarage's front step. In front of him in the street stood his tan Vespa motor scooter, polished to a gleam. He raised a hand in greeting as he caught sight of them.

"Good morning, Mrs Trewynn," he called out with punctilious courtesy, coming to meet them, then asked anxiously, "Jocelyn, can this be true? Three parishioners have telephoned to say a body has been found at the LonStar shop. Surely they must be mistaken?"

"I'm afraid not," his wife said grimly. "Eleanor found him in the stockroom."

"Who . . . who is it?"

"A stranger, dear."

"Oh dear! Should I . . . I wonder . . . last rites, do you think?"

"It's much too late for that. He was dead when he was found, and for some time before that. Besides, they've already taken him away."

"My dear Mrs Trewynn, what a terrible shock." He held out both hands to Eleanor, dropping his sou'wester. "May I offer . . . That is, do you feel a need for the consolations of religion?"

She took his hands, gave them a gentle squeeze, and released them. "That's very kind of you, Vicar." Though she attended Christmas and Easter services at the little grey stone church because she liked the hymns, Eleanor was not a communicant. In fact, after a Congregationalist upbringing, a Quaker school, and her world-wide travels, she leant towards Buddhism, if anything. "But, truly, I'm over the worst effects of the shock, thank you. I'll be all right."

He nodded gravely. "Jocelyn, do you suppose there's a family in need of support?"

"He hasn't been identified yet, dear. I think you'd do best to get on with your regular rounds. It's your day for St Endellion, isn't it?"

"Yes, I was about to leave when I heard . . . Don't you think I ought to . . . ? But old Mrs Lockhart is expecting me . . ."

"You mustn't disappoint her, Timothy. Off you go, now." Jocelyn picked up the sou'wester. She kissed his cheek, plonked the hat on his head, and tightened the strap under his chin. "Ride carefully, and if it gets very foggy, wait till it clears."

"Yes, my dear. A little medicinal brandy, perhaps, Mrs Trewynn . . . ?"

"I'll take care of Eleanor, dear. Goodbye."

At last the vicar seated himself on his Vespa and started its tiny motor. Teazle backed away, barking her head off. He buzzed away, crouched over the handlebars, like a giant yellow grasshopper as Nick Gresham had once remarked. A benevolent but indecisive grasshopper, he had three parishes in his charge. Without Jocelyn, Eleanor thought, he wouldn't be able to cope even with one.

They went into the vicarage, a cosy, comparatively modern

bungalow that had replaced a huge, hideous, draughty Victorian house. The sitting room was furnished in eclectic style, a few good inherited pieces and some cheap odds and ends from the Stearns' early married days, filled in with once good but slightly shabby charity-shop finds. Two of Nick Gresham's paintings graced the sitting-room walls. One was of Mevagissey; the other of Rough Tor—unless it was Brown Willy, Eleanor was never sure which was which—in sunshine, with a shaggy pony in the foreground. A Welsh dresser displayed a Royal Doulton dinner service, inherited from Jocelyn's parents. The blue-grey broad-loom carpet was courtesy of the Church Commissioners.

Jocelyn had somehow woven these disparate elements into an attractive whole. To Eleanor, who had sat on cushioned divans with turbanned sheiks and on mats on mud floors with loin-clothed Africans, it all seemed very comfortable.

In the depths of one chair, a grey-and-black-striped cat dozed. When Teazle went over to sniff, he opened yellow eyes in an un-blinking stare. Samson and Teazle were old acquaintances, if not friends. Much the same size, they tolerated and generally ig-nored each other.

"Are you sure you wouldn't like a drop of brandy, Eleanor?"

"No, thanks. And no more tea. I'm awash."

"You know where the loo is."

Eleanor retired. One could never be too grateful for modern plumbing.

Returning to the sitting room, she found Jocelyn gazing out of the window. "The mist's getting thicker," she said. "Perhaps I shouldn't have encouraged Timothy to go out."

"His little put-put doesn't do much over thirty, does it? I doubt he'll come to grief, even if he hits a sheep. Anyway, St Endellion is inland. It's probably clear there."

"Yes." She turned away and they both sat down. "I suppose

I've just got the wind up because of that poor boy. Death can come so suddenly and unexpectedly. It's something we need reminding of now and then."

Eleanor didn't want to talk about the murder. Soon enough the police would reappear and it would be unavoidable. "That reminds me, Joce, can't you persuade him to call me Eleanor, so that I can call him Timothy? I've asked him, but he just murmurs vaguely. I do feel awkward calling him 'Vicar,' when I'm not, strictly speaking, one of his flock. We've known each other for nearly two years now. Isn't that long enough?"

"It's not a matter of time. If you live in his parish, he counts you one of his flock, whatever your beliefs or unbeliefs. More to the point, he has to consider his parishioners—the actual members of the church, I mean. If he called you Eleanor, you wouldn't credit the petty jealousies that would arise. Many of the older people would be offended to be called by their Christian names, yet they'd regard it as a sort of favouritism if he used yours, or anyone's over the age of twenty."

"There are places in the world where people only have one name. They seem to manage quite well."

"I daresay, but you're in England now."

Eleanor sighed. "I suppose I've lived out of the country too long. All right, 'Vicar' it is, and evermore shall be so."

"There's no need to feel awkward about it. Think of it as a sort of nickname." Joce smiled. "If you can call your car the Incorruptible, I don't see why you can't call Timothy 'Vicar.'"

"Maybe I'll shorten it to Vic," Eleanor said with a laugh.

"Don't you dare! The ructions—Well, I can't begin to imagine! Now, let's be practical. We don't know when the police will let you back into your flat, whatever the inspector said, so you'd better reckon on staying here tonight. And as long as you like, of course, if you don't feel comfortable there."

"Do you believe in ghosts?"

"Certainly not! Do you?"

"No. So why should I avoid going home as soon as the police let me?"

"My dear Eleanor, I suppose—" She stopped as a piercing shriek came from the kitchen. "Ah, the kettle. That's the water for the peas. You don't mind frozen, do you? I hadn't anything planned for lunch as I was to be at the shop and Timothy's out for the day—Mrs Lockhart always gives him a pasty or a sandwich—so I thought we'd just have an omelette."

"I'm not very hungry."

"You must eat to keep up your strength, my dear. An omelette will be just the thing."

Eleanor abandoned useless protest. Offering to help, she was sent out into the back garden, dripping now, to pick some mint for the peas and parsley for the omelette. Teazle accompanied her hopefully but failed to find a single rabbit hole.

Since Jocelyn cooked as competently as she did everything else, the omelette was delicious. They were sitting over coffee and slices of home-made Bakewell tart when the doorbell rang.

"That will be the police, I imagine." Jocelyn went to open the front door.

Eleanor could hear but not see what followed.

"Mrs Stearns?" enquired a cocky young voice with a touch of West Country in it. "David Skan, *North Cornwall Times*. I understand you were—"

"A reporter! You people are shameless! How dare you come bothering—"

"Joce, let me speak to him." Eleanor came up beside her friend. Obviously Jocelyn had no idea how to handle the press, whereas an important part of Eleanor's job had involved trying to persuade reporters that the efforts of LonStar were worthy of as many column inches as she could squeeze out of them.

She could not ignore the opportunity to do just that, cold-blooded as it might appear to anyone who had never held a child dying of starvation. The boy was dead. Perhaps some good could come from his untimely death.

"Mr Skan, I'm Mrs Eleanor Trewynn. I live above the LonStar shop where this terrible event occurred. I can't tell you any more about it than the police have, or will, but I can tell you this: Horrified as we are by what has happened, we shall not be deterred from our vital mission for a moment longer than absolutely necessary. The plight of the hungry children of the world demands that we put aside our own feelings to continue our work for the London Save the Starving Council." Enough? Too much?

He gave her a considering look, followed by a nod. She could read his thoughts: Yes, he'd buy it. This was a story he could run with. He was young, working for a minor local rag, and ambitious. LonStar was an international charity. Add murder to the mix and it just might be his ticket to the national press.

She spelt her name for him and saw him wondering whether he dared ask her age—he didn't quite. "Elderly," he'd write, or OAP, though her state Old Age Pension was minimal because she had lived so much abroad. She didn't mind, as long as he got the details about LonStar right.

"Trewynn. That's Cornish, right?"

"Yes, my late husband and I were both born in the Duchy, though we met in India, before the war. We both worked for Lon-Star then and continued to do so. Peter was . . . was killed in Indonesia, a couple of years ago." The precise date and time were engraved on her heart, but David Skan didn't need to know that. "I came home and started the LonStar shop here in Port Mabyn."

"So you run the shop, as well as living above it?"

"Mrs Stearns runs it," Eleanor said firmly. Jocelyn had retreated to the kitchen, whence came sounds of vigorous washing up. "I'm merely an assistant. Local people have been very generous with donations and with their time, and many visitors to the area support us with their purchases. We've been able to send worthwhile contributions to LonStar headquarters in London, but we can always do with more help."

He grinned. "Don't worry, Mrs Trewynn, I'll make sure you get your plug, if I have to set the type myself."

"Thank you, Mr Skan."

"And when things are back to normal—" He turned to look downhill and gestured in the direction of the shop. "—maybe I'll get my editor to let me write a feature about your adventures. Ah, here come the cops. Thank you for your time, and please tell Mrs Stearns we're really not all ghouls and bullies. Just wait till the lads from London descend on you."

He went off jauntily down the hill, his thick, Scandinavian-blond hair sticking up like a shock of wheat. Eleanor saw him accost the approaching detectives. Inspector Scumble brushed him off and forged ahead. Megan stopped, presumably on her boss's orders.

Leaving the door open, Eleanor went into the house to warn Jocelyn that the police were about to turn up again.

SEVEN

In a whirlwind of activity, the vicar's wife had washed, dried, and put away every sign of their lunch. "I hope they've already eaten," she said. "Not that I mind feeding your niece, of course, but the inspector looks as if he'd eat us out of house and home."

"I'm sure they won't expect you to give them lunch. That reporter was a nice young man, by the way."

Joce looked conscience-stricken. "I was very rude to him, wasn't I? And he was only doing his job. I'll apologise if he comes my way again, but I can't help hoping he won't."

"Not him, perhaps, but he warned me—we'll probably have London reporters to deal with sooner or later."

Before Joce could express her horror with more than a look, Scumble knocked on the door and called out, "Hello, ladies. Expecting burglars, are you?"

Eleanor went out to the hall. "I saw you coming," she explained as Megan caught up with him, slightly out of breath, "and left the door open for you."

"Glad to hear you had a reason."

Coming up behind Eleanor, Jocelyn enquired, "Have you lunched, Inspector?" Her tone was uninviting.

"Yes, thank you, madam. Your bakery does a good pasty, I must say."

"Don't they?" said Eleanor. "So convenient when I don't feel like cooking and don't want to go out to eat."

"I suppose you have more questions for us. You'd better come in here." Jocelyn led the way into the sitting room.

Scumble handed her a list. "This is everything my chaps have found in the stockroom, barring going through a few pockets they haven't got to yet. I'd like you to check it and see if anything's missing." He turned to Eleanor. "And this is the contents of your flat, Mrs Trewynn. I did it myself, and I don't think you'll find anything out of place when you get back."

"Thank you, Inspector." Eleanor recognised the kindly intent of not letting a horde of policemen paw through her undies drawer, though a horde of English policemen was infinitely preferable to some of the Third World customs officers who had emptied out her suitcases for the world to view. She took the list. "Good heavens, I never dreamt I owned so many *things!*"

He hadn't listed every individual pair of socks or knickers, presumably assuming no thief would want to pinch them. But he'd counted every book in her shelves, every cup and saucer, two salt-and-pepper sets (why did she have two? who could possibly need more than one?), pots and pans, jars of home-made jam (from the village fête; settling down after her peripatetic life, she had intended to cultivate the domestic virtues, but had never found the time), mop and carpet-sweeper. Surely she had nothing worth stealing! Even her few personal ornaments were cheap bangles and bead necklaces given by grateful clients, pretty but not valuable, except that each reminded her of the giver.

All in all, anyone who considered her belongings worth stealing must be in desperate straits and she didn't begrudge them a thing.

"I don't *think* anything's missing," she said doubtfully, handing back the list.

He took it without a word, but his look spoke volumes. Victims of burglary were supposed to assess their possible losses with proper concern.

"You don't own a television?" he asked after a moment.

"No, I prefer the wireless. And books. I never had time for much reading till I retired."

"Hmm."

Jocelyn was doing a far more thorough job of studying her list. She was ticking off items, apparently against a list in her head. When at last she handed the papers back to Scumble, she said, "Not only is nothing missing, a good deal of this stuff doesn't ring a bell. I assume it's the donations Eleanor collected yesterday."

Scumble looked at Eleanor.

"I had a good haul," she said. "Woolly animals and detective stories and—"

"Thank you, madam." He made a move as if to hand her the stockroom list, then changed his mind, clearly deciding there was no point, given the state of her memory. "I'm afraid we'll probably have to come back to you with further questions, but that will be all for the present. I appreciate your cooperation."

DI Scumble was frowning as he and Megan started back down the hill.

Megan felt compelled to defend Aunt Nell. "It's not that my aunt's memory is failing, sir. It's just that she's not very interested in possessions."

"So I gathered," he said dryly. "It's a pity the people we're after aren't equally uninterested."

"You're pretty sure this murder was a quarrel between burglars, sir?"

"I was speaking generally. Most villains are greedy. But yes, I reckon a couple of delinquents walked down that path behind the shops, trying doors. They found that one unlocked and walked in. Like as not, they didn't even realise it was a charity shop."

"What do you think they quarrelled about?"

"Who knows? The victim had been smoking cannabis, so it's good bet the murderer had been too."

"But, sir—"

Scumble held up his hand. "Before you tell me addicts are rarely violent, let me tell you that I've been in this game a lot longer than you, and this generation did not discover marijuana. What it does is reduce the ability to foresee consequences. A couple of students smoking in their flat are not likely to go out and bash an old lady on the head, I'll give you that. But a pair of sneak-thieves on the prowl, that's another matter altogether. Don't tell me your years with the Met have left you with any rubbishy romantic fantasies about honour among thieves."

"No, sir."

"Good. Then let's get moving. We've got a couple of dozen volunteers to be talked into giving their fingerprints for elimination. You get on with that." He shuffled through a fistful of papers. "Here's the list Mrs Stearns gave me. And don't forget to talk to the kids who helped last night, when they get out of school. No need for the younger ones' prints. They're easily distinguished."

Another list! So far, Megan thought, this murder investigation seemed to consist largely of lists.

"I take it you've no great desire to attend the autopsy with me."

She gulped. "If you think I ought to, sir . . ."

"You ought, but there's far too much else that needs doing. You can skip it this time."

Megan breathed again.

That afternoon, an amazing number of people developed a sudden interest in helping in the LonStar shop. Jocelyn took the telephone off the hook, but the vicarage doorbell rang constantly with a stream of would-be volunteers. Though she wrote down all their names, she avoided inviting anyone in by saying in hushed tones, "It's been a terrible shock to poor Mrs Trewynn, you know."

"But I'm quite all right," Eleanor protested. "They'll think I'm utterly prostrated. And a real drip."

"It's only a slight exaggeration. You did have a terrible shock. You don't want them coming in and pestering us for details, do you?"

"No, of course not. Mr Scumble specifically told us not to talk to anyone."

"There you are, then." And Jocelyn went off to explain yet again that poor Eleanor had had a terrible shock.

"Poor Eleanor" gritted her teeth.

In between callers they sat in the kitchen, so as not to be visible from the street through the sitting-room window, and wondered when they'd be able to reopen the shop. Ever efficient, Jocelyn had long since telephoned that day's volunteers to tell them their services would not be required.

"But should I ring tomorrow's people? Or just ring Mrs Davies and let her deal with it, as it's her day? She's bound to make some remark about it all being my fault."

Mrs Davies was a thorn in the flesh of Jocelyn, who was reluctant to admit that the Methodist minister's wife was almost as efficient and undoubtedly equally honest. Eleanor often had to take evasive action so as not to find herself caught between the pair.

"She can't. Yesterday was her day."

"That's right!" Jocelyn brightened and started to stand up.

"No, Joce, you are not to! If you dare to so much as hint at blame, I'll . . . I'll give you the sack!" Though it was an empty threat, at least it showed how strongly she felt. "If it was anyone's fault, it was mine. If I wasn't so wretchedly vague about keys. If I had just remembered to lock the doors—"

"You could remember if you really tried," Jocelyn said severely, but she sat down again instead of going to offend Mrs Davies. "Still, I daresay they'd have broken in if the doors had been locked, and then we'd have had the damage to repair. I must say, it still seems to me inexplicable that they should have taken the trouble to burgle a charity shop full of second-hand odds and ends."

"But if they came in by the back door, they wouldn't necessarily have known what—Oh, I've just remembered. I picked up a donation yesterday that may be quite valuable. I'm not sure. It's some jewelry, paste of course, but it looks to me as if it's quite good. Not that I know anything about the subject. I've no idea what it might be worth."

"Eleanor, really! How *could* you have forgotten?"

"You must admit there's been plenty going on to occupy my mind! Finding that poor boy, and then the police asking questions I couldn't answer, and the reporter—"

"All right, never mind, at least you've remembered it now. Who gave it?"

"I don't know. No one mentioned it. They must have slipped it in with some other donation."

"How very odd. I do wish people would realise that we have to know the provenance of anything of value. You did put it in the safe, I hope?"

"Of course. I'm surprised Mr Scumble didn't ask me about the safe. Do you suppose he didn't find it? Hiding a safe behind a picture isn't exactly a novel idea, is it?"

"Not at all. He can't have been looking for one. After all, that's why we put it in your flat, because no one would dream you had such a thing. Oh bother, there's the dratted doorbell again. I wish I knew how to disconnect it."

"People would only knock," Eleanor pointed out.

"True. Why don't you put on the kettle while I go and get rid of whoever it is."

The day seemed to have gone on forever, but at last it was tea time. Eleanor took the kettle from the stove and was removing the lid when she heard from the hall: "Who . . . ? Oh, it's you, Nicholas. Have you come to offer your services as a volunteer?"

"No." He sounded surprised. "I already do as much as I have time for. Why? I didn't know you were shorthanded. Have people been cancelling because of the murder?"

"Come in." She peered behind him in a hunted way. "Quickly!"

"Hello, Nick." Eleanor had come to the kitchen door, kettle in hand. "You're just in time for tea."

"Good timing. How are you holding up?"

Since Jocelyn had opened the door to him, she assumed she was allowed to say, "Quite well, considering. Have the police been pestering you with questions about last night?"

"How do you expect me to answer that when it was your niece who pestered me?"

"I'm sure Megan was polite," said Jocelyn, taking the kettle from Eleanor on her way into the kitchen. "Unlike That Man."

"I haven't yet had the pleasure of That Man's acquaintance," said Nick with a grin, "but you have me shaking in my shoes, Mrs Stearns."

"Then you'd better sit down. I suppose you're posing as a starving artist?"

"Yes, of course. I were brought up proper, I were. I know it's your Christian duty to feed the hungry, so I'm sure it must be my duty to present the opportunity."

Jocelyn gave him a withering look as she turned on the gas under the kettle, but she reached down a cake tin.

Nick remained unwithered. "That looks promising," he said. "Ah, gingerbread. Excellent! I'm glad you didn't waste it on the rude inspector."

"Mr Scumble wasn't really rude," Eleanor protested. "It's his manner that's at fault, rather than his manners. For the most part. Did Megan ask you about what times we did what last night, Nick? I'm afraid I wasn't much help at all."

"Nor was I," he said cheerfully, "but they can easily check our movements. Don't worry about it. When will you be able to re-open the shop? Give me notice, won't you. I want first shot at those detective stories."

"We don't know yet. We were just talking about it." Eleanor frowned. "And I remembered . . . Nick, you can't imagine Major Cartwright slipping a collection of jewelry into my car when he loaded the boxes of books, can you? After all, he's a widower. He might think that as his wife can no longer wear them—"

"Eleanor!" Jocelyn snapped, setting the teapot on the table

with a bit of a thump. "You really mustn't tell anyone about that."

"Not anyone, dear, just Nick. I won't tell another soul, I promise."

Nick looked as if he would like to protest being classed with "anyone," but could hardly do so with his mouth full of Jocelyn's gingerbread. He swallowed. "Not Major Cartwright," he said. "He's pretty hard up, I think. The books are his one extravagance. If he had jewelry, he'd have been selling it to live on. Someone put real, honest-to-god jewelry in your car?"

"Only paste, of course. It may not be worth much. It's just that I can't think who, of those I collected from yesterday . . . Joce, we must ring them all up and ask . . . But they aren't all on the telephone."

"If it was a mistake," said Jocelyn, "then they will get in touch with us. If it was an intentionally anonymous donation, then finding out who gave it can wait until all this dreadful murder business is cleared up."

Nick looked alarmed. "For heaven's sake, you can't just ring people up and ask if they happened to discard a pile of jewelry by mistake! You'll get half-a-dozen claims."

"Our donors aren't that sort," Eleanor asserted.

"No, he's right. It wouldn't be fair to put the temptation in people's way. If no one calls us, we'll have to work out a way to do it."

"Assuming the stuff wasn't just floating around on the floor of the Incorruptible, couldn't you ask about the container rather than the thing contained? What was it in, Eleanor?"

"A briefcase, rather a nice leather one."

"You couldn't have fitted a briefcase into the safe," said Jocelyn. "What did you do with it? Leave it upstairs?"

"No, I took it down after I emptied it."

"It was not on the inspector's list," Jocelyn stated with absolute certainty. "You'd better tell him right away."

"I can't see the hurry," Eleanor argued. "It was empty, and not particularly valuable in itself."

"You have to tell him about the jewelry anyway," Nick pointed out.

"I'd much rather not. He's going to be angry with me for not mentioning it before, and angry with himself for not finding the safe."

"Tell Megan," Jocelyn suggested.

"That would be much easier. I wonder where she is?"

"As I walked up," said Nick, "I saw her going into the Trelawney Arms. Since it wasn't open yet, I kidded her about special hours for the police, and she told me—rather snarkily, I thought—that she had to interview young Donna. Shall I be terribly noble and go and find her?"

"Would you, Nick? The sooner I confess, the less reason the inspector will have to be upset with me."

"Right, then, I'm on my way. I don't know which scares me more, Donna or Detective Sergeant Pencarrow."

Eleanor laughed. "What nonsense you talk, Nick."

Grinning, Nick was getting to his feet when the vicar breezed in.

"A tea party! Splendid. What, you're not going already, my dear fellow? Sit down, sit down. Have another cup."

"Nicholas has an errand to run, Timothy," said his wife, fetching a cup for him. "He'll be back shortly."

"I certainly hope so. Keep your fingers crossed." Nick departed with a wave.

EIGHT

The vicar was full of his own concerns, the people he had visited, the pleasure of riding through the countryside once the mist
had dissipated, the crack in the wall of St Endellion Church—a
good quarter-inch wider than last week.

"And I heard most disturbing news, my dear," he said to Jocelyn. "Rumour has it that a builder wants to have the church de-
consecrated in order to buy it and turn it into a house!"

"In that case, dear, the crack seems providential. He'll hardly
want to bother if it's crumbling away."

Eleanor listened with one ear, the other cocked to hear Nick's
return. The vicar finished off the gingerbread and drank a third
cup of tea, and still there was no sign of Nick. She hoped he
hadn't got himself involved in a quarrel with Megan. To her sor-
row, those two did not hit it off.

The vicar went off to his den to write a letter to the Church
Commissioners about the crack in St Endellion's wall. Eleanor
helped Jocelyn clear and wash up the tea things. As the last cup
was put away in its proper place, Nick returned.

"Never say I wouldn't risk my life for you, Eleanor!" he exclaimed. "Megan wasn't at the Arms, but Donna cornered me. If we hadn't just had one murder in the village, I swear I'd have done the girl in."

"Don't joke about it," Jocelyn admonished him. "Would you like to stay to dinner? Just shepherd's pie, I'm afraid, but there'll be plenty, and the first asparagus from the garden to go with it. As long as you promise not to talk about murder. I suspect Timothy's forgotten about it, and I'd prefer not have him reminded sooner than need be."

"For asparagus, Mrs Stearns, I'd promise my first-born child if I had one. But I'll come back, if you don't mind, rather than stay. I've got some work to do."

He left again. Jocelyn sent Eleanor out into the spring dusk to cut asparagus while she peeled potatoes.

Endless meals! There were definitely advantages to living alone, Eleanor thought. She tried to concentrate on her task, on Teazle snuffling among the raspberry canes, and on the seagulls wheeling so high in the sky the sunset glow still stained them pink . . . Once she had been very good at putting things out of her mind when she chose. You couldn't get on with your work if you dwelt on the horrors you had seen. But she was out of practice. She kept seeing those pathetic, sockless ankles.

She was glad to go back into the house, to the bright lights and kitchen smells, and Jocelyn's determined chatter about other subjects—any subject but murder.

There were advantages to not living alone, too.

Once more Nick reappeared. The shepherd's pie and asparagus were consumed, followed by rhubarb—also from the garden— and custard. As Jocelyn served Nick with a second helping of pudding, the telephone rang.

"I'll get it, my dear," said the vicar, folding his napkin and unfolding himself. He returned shortly, looking puzzled. "It's for

{ 73 }

you and Mrs Trewynn, Jocelyn. Very odd. Someone called Stumble. He didn't give me his Christian name, only his initials, D.I. And he said he'll be here in five minutes."

DI Scumble arrived, trailed by Megan. Eleanor was concerned to see her niece looking tired, but she managed to refrain from embracing her. She even managed to let Jocelyn do the honours.

"Coffee, Inspector?"

"If it wouldn't be too much trouble, madam."

"We were just about to have some ourselves. I don't believe you've met my husband? Timothy, this is Detective Inspector Scumble. And you know—ah—Detective Sergeant Pencarrow."

"How do you do, Mr—er—Detective Inspector," the vicar said courteously, then turned with obvious relief to his companion and held out both hands. "Megan, my dear, how delightful to see you. I hope you too can stay for coffee?"

"Good evening, Vicar." Megan managed to avoid taking his hands. She glanced at the inspector, who nodded resignedly. "Yes, I'd like coffee, thanks."

"You have a letter to finish, have you not, Timothy?" Jocelyn said with an commanding look.

"What's that, my dear? Oh! Oh yes, the church. Yes, indeed, I'd hoped to catch the first post tomorrow. It's proving rather difficult . . . Not, I'm afraid, a particularly attractive building. You'll excuse me, Mr . . . er . . . Stumble. And Megan." Looking slightly puzzled, he loped obediently away to his den, followed by Teazle.

"And you are . . . ?" Scumble asked Nick suspiciously.

"Mr Gresham," Megan introduced him. "The artist with the gallery next door to the scene."

"What are you doing here?"

"I thought we'd better get together and coordinate our stories," Nick told him blandly. "The police are very hot on discrepancies, are they not?"

"Stuff and nonsense, Nicholas!" Jocelyn admonished him. "He came very properly, Inspector, to enquire after Mrs Trewynn's well-being. I invited him to dinner. Do come into the sitting room, all of you."

The Stearnses' sitting room was big enough for Scumble not to dominate it as he had Eleanor's. He sat in the chair to which Jocelyn waved him, and the rest found seats.

With her customary efficiency, she had already taken in coffee and sufficient cups and saucers for everyone. She lifted the pot to pour, but Scumble stopped her.

"Just a minute, Mrs Stearns. I have something to show you. We'll have coffee while you all think about it." He took several sheets of paper from his inside pocket and unfolded them. "It's quite convenient you being here, Mr Gresham. We shan't have to go looking for you."

"Always a pleasure to assist the police."

Megan glared at him, but Scumble didn't rise to the bait. Stolidly he passed out a sheet of paper each to Jocelyn, Eleanor, and Nick.

Eleanor studied hers, perplexed. It was a Roneoed copy—reeking of alcohol—of a drawing of a peculiarly curved object, vaguely reminiscent of something but she couldn't think what. Jocelyn glanced at hers, then put it down on the table and poured coffee. The picture was the same.

Nick stared at his with a frown. "What is it?" he asked.

"I'm hoping you can tell me. Thank you, Mrs Stearns, a little milk this time, please. No sugar."

Eleanor laid the picture on her knee and gazed at it while she sipped her milky coffee. On closer inspection, a straight line ran out more or less at a right angle—if a curved line could be said to form a right angle—near the end of the object.

"All right, you don't know what it is," Nick persisted. "But you need to know, so it's something to do with the case. The weapon?"

"The pathologist's best guess at the shape of the weapon," Scumble admitted grudgingly. "There's nothing in the stockroom that remotely matches, and we can't find anything in the bushes. Whatever it is, it was probably taken away and disposed of elsewhere, but if any of you has any ideas . . ."

"Could he have been killed elsewhere and his body brought to the stockroom?"

"Conceivable. But why bother, when there are cliffs several hundred feet high within easy reach?"

"Not so easy." Nick was obviously feeling argumentative. "Suppose he was killed somewhere in the village. Lugging him out onto the cliffs would be hard work compared to simply dumping him nearby."

"Which would be less work, but with a much higher risk of being seen by someone out for a stroll, or looking out of a window."

"No one saw anything," Megan put in, "which suggests the victim as well as the murderer was doing his best to keep out of sight."

"Well," said Jocelyn, pushing the paper away from her, "I can't imagine what it might be."

"I'll tell you what it reminds me of," Eleanor said hesitantly, "though it's not very like. My father had a walking stick with a carved duck's head in place of the usual knob or crook."

"We've never had anything like that in the shop," Jocelyn asserted.

"In any case, the curve isn't quite right and this straight line here is in quite the wrong—"

"Not a duck!" Nick interrupted, and started to pull up one leg of his trousers.

The vicar's wife was scandalised. "Nicholas, really!"

"Look! It's the bruise I got walking into that damn table—sorry, Mrs Stearns, that blasted table. Isn't it much the same shape?"

There on his hairy shin was a purpling mark, its shape very similar to the drawing.

"Oh!" Jocelyn's hand went to her own leg, decently clad in 30-denier stockings.

"The *what?*" roared Scumble. "What table?"

"The dolphin table," Eleanor explained. "Both Nick and Joce walked into it."

"Where?"

"In the stockroom. It's a sheet of heavy glass supported by brass dolphins. Four of them, I think."

"There is no glass table in the stockroom."

"We moved it, Inspector," Jocelyn said apologetically. "It was a terrible hazard where it was, obviously, since both Nicholas and I tripped over it."

"Where did you move it to?" Scumble spoke with a terrible patience.

"Into the shop."

"When?"

"This morning."

"This morning. After the murder."

"Before we found the body," Eleanor mentioned hopefully.

"No one could possibly have used it as a weapon," said Nick. "It's frightfully heavy. One person couldn't lift it, let alone swing it at someone's head."

{ 77 }

"Frightfully heavy, is it? How do *you* know?"

"I helped move it. Twice. Last night I walked into it when I was helping to unload the Incorr—Mrs Trewynn's car. Donna and I—that's the lass from the Trelawney Arms—we shoved it out of the way."

"Which is why I fell over it," said Jocelyn. "It wasn't where I expected it to be. We asked Nick to help us carry it into the shop."

"So, Mr Gresham, you were in the stockroom and shop this morning?"

"Yes. I didn't spot the body, though."

"That was before I found it, and Nick didn't go anywhere near it," Eleanor assured the inspector.

The look he gave her suggested he had no faith in her memory whatsoever. "But his fingerprints—all of your fingerprints—will be on the table."

"Oh no, Inspector," said Jocelyn, affronted. "I polished it thoroughly."

"You polished it. The brass as well as the glass, I suppose."

"Certainly. Eleanor's dog was sniffing around it, so it had nose prints as well as fingerprints and dust all over the place."

"The dog was interested in it, was he?"

"She," said Eleanor.

"I beg your pardon, madam," Scumble said with heavy sarcasm, "she. How is it that none of you, *not one* of you, thought to mention either the dog's interest in the table or this exercise in furniture removal to me or my officers?"

Eleanor, Jocelyn, and Nick looked at one another. Nick shrugged.

"It never crossed our minds," said Eleanor. "I forgot about it entirely. When your mind is on murder, you don't think about tables."

"The police do." The inspector let his statement stand for a moment. Then he went on, "I'll have to ask you all to come down to the shop now and show me where the table was before it was 'shoved' aside, and where it was shoved to. We'll be taking it away."

"Thank heaven for small mercies," said Jocelyn, then looked appalled at her own words. "I'll tell Timothy we're going out," she added hurriedly, and made for the den.

Resigned patience emanated from Scumble as he stood waiting for Jocelyn's reappearance and for her and Eleanor to get their jackets.

Nick said to him, "I don't see what the table has to do with anything. Only a circus strong-man could have used it as a weapon."

"You let us worry about that, sir," the inspector advised, almost benignly.

He was suddenly so mellow that Eleanor suspected finding out about the table's peregrination had suggested an answer to a worrisome problem. Pehaps the dolphins' tails had left odd marks on the floor that the police had been unable to account for. As they all started down the hill, she mentioned the possibility to Jocelyn.

"No discussion, please!" Scumble snapped. "I want your unbiased recollections."

"I was just—"

"If you'll kindly refrain from chattering, Mrs Trewynn, then I won't have to trouble myself as to whether you're discussing the table or the weather."

So much for the mellowing she thought she had detected. His words were not particularly harsh—though "chattering" was a trifle unkind—but his tone of voice was decidedly acerbic.

After years of dealing constantly with people to whom English was a second language, or third or fourth, Eleanor was very conscious of the power of tone of voice to turn a successful negotiation into a disaster. She wondered whether the police were taught about such things or had to muddle along in hit-or-miss fashion. She was going to ask Megan, who came back to join her and Jocelyn, but stopped herself just in time not to call down Scumble's wrath upon her head again. They walked on in silence.

A uniformed constable still stood guard on the pavement in front of the shop.

The inspector took Nick into the stockroom first, leaving the women in the hall. He shut the door, so they heard only a mutter of voices and the thud of footsteps.

"I can't see that the table has anything to do with anything," Jocelyn said crossly, though in a low voice. "What *is* he on about, Megan?"

"He hasn't told me," Megan responded.

"You mustn't ask her, Joce. If she knew, she shouldn't tell you." All the same, Eleanor was pretty sure her niece had a good idea of what was in Scumble's mind. She was much too tired to try to work it out for herself. She sat down on the stairs.

"Are you all right, Aunt Nell?"

"Just a bit weary, dear. It's not very late, I know, but it feels as if it's been a very long day. I'm more than ready for bed."

"You shall have a hot water bottle," Jocelyn promised, "and cocoa if you fancy it. Timothy will take Teazle out for her last walkie."

"Mrs Stearns." Nick came out of the stockroom. "The dentist—the inspector, that is—will see you now," he announced.

Jocelyn went in, with much the bearing of one bracing herself to enter the dentist's lair. The door closed behind her.

"Am I permitted to leave now, Detective Sergeant Pencarrow?" Nick asked.

"You're free to go anytime," Megan said uncertainly, "but I expect Mr Scumble would prefer you to stay in case he has any more questions for you."

"Free to go, but your departure will be noted down and may be used in evidence against you. It's all right, I was going to keep Eleanor company anyway. Does your boss actually suspect any of the three of us of complicity in that wretched youth's demise?"

"I don't think so. If he did, seriously, he ought to take me off the case, because I know all of you—"

"You don't know me very well. So it could be just me he suspects."

"Stop teasing, Nick," Eleanor said severely. "It's not something to joke about."

"He'd jump at any excuse to take me off the case, so I'm pretty sure you're none of you under suspicion. Not of the murder, at least, and he'd have a hard time proving you deliberately failed to tell him about moving the table. But don't take my word for it. He hasn't told me—"

"Eleanor, your turn." Jocelyn stalked out of the stockroom. As Eleanor went in, she heard Jocelyn behind her saying, "That man had the nerve to—" The closing door cut off her indignant voice.

"All right, Mrs Trewynn, let's hear your version of the wanderings of this infernal table."

Eleanor turned to point to a space to the left of the door, which from her present perspective opened inward to the right. "It started out there. It was well out of the way of anyone working in here, but directly in the path of anyone carrying stuff in from outside towards the back of the room. Nick had a big box of books in his arms, blocking his view, so it's not surprising he walked into it."

"Mmph. And then?"

"He and Donna half-carried, half-dragged it over there. I should have realised it would be in the way of anyone coming through from the shop. Jocelyn could hardly have avoided it. I went to fetch Nick to help carry it into the shop."

"So you didn't see Mrs Stearns polishing it?"

"She was finishing off the dolphins when I got back. She must have done the glass first. She'd cleared a space for it in the shop, too, but then she's a very efficient person, and Nick had to wash paint off his hands before he could come."

"How long were you gone?"

"Good heavens, I haven't the faintest idea. I hadn't any reason to note the time, and I'm afraid I often forget to wind my watch anyway, since I retired."

"How is it that you remember so clearly where the table was?"

"Two of my friends hurt themselves on it. Of course I remember!"

Scumble sighed. "Thank you. That'll be all for tonight, then."

"There's just one thing I ought to—"

"Can it wait till the morning, Mrs Trewynn? Even the police have to eat and sleep sometimes, you know."

Eleanor considered. The tale of the briefcase and its contents was a complicated story that would take some time to relate. It was already overdue, so surely it could no longer be classified as urgent, and another few hours wouldn't make any difference. Also—the thought flashed across her mind—tomorrow morning she'd be able to blame at least some of the delay on Scumble himself.

Suppose it *was* important? But tired as she was, she simply couldn't face trying to explain tonight to the equally tired and impatient inspector. She'd only make a mess of it. "First thing in the morning," she compromised.

"I'll have someone at the vicarage at eight. If that's not too early?" he asked with a touch of malice.

"I'll be ready. Good night, Inspector. Sleep well."

He ushered her out into the passage. "You're free to leave," he growled. "You'd better escort the ladies up the hill, Sergeant."

"That's all right," said Nick, "I'll see them home. Now that we've all told you where we think the table was, it can't matter if we compare notes."

"True. But make sure you see them right into the house. Don't forget, there's a murderer on the loose, and Mrs Trewynn is the nearest thing we have to a witness."

As they started up the hill, Eleanor shivered. "I wish he hadn't said that."

Scumble beckoned Megan into the stockroom and indicated where the table had started, where it had paused on its journey, and where it ended up, in the corner of the shop.

"We're never going to get that into the car," she said.

"Not a hope. But never mind that for the moment. What do you think happened?"

Megan returned to the stockroom and contemplated the table's intermediate position. The inspector stood in the doorway and contemplated Megan, his expression sardonic.

"You said there were bruises on his arms, sir? And his chin?"

"The one on his chin is several days old. He seems to have collided with someone's fist. The others—looks as if someone gripped his upper arms, hard, very shortly before death."

"And the marks on his head are more or less the shape of those porpoises. The edge of the glass could have caused that straight line, couldn't it?"

"Very likely."

"And there was something there that interested Teazle. It's a pity Mrs Stearns is such a fanatical cleaner."

"Makes it more difficult, but if his head hit the table there'll be traces left in the crack between the beast and the glass. He didn't bleed much, because he died almost at once, but there would have been some blood. The murderer must have done a bit of a clean-up job or Mrs Stearns could hardly have helped noticing more than a few smudges from the dog's nose."

"But would it be possible to break someone's neck by bashing his head against a stationary object?"

"Possible," Scumble said, almost approvingly, "but it would take quite a bit of force."

"So we're looking for someone pretty hefty."

"Or desperate."

"Is that all we know about him?"

"So far."

"That's not much help, is it, sir?"

"No help at all until we know who the victim was. We've got a halfway presentable photo now. You can take it to show to all the neighbours tomorrow, and if there's no bites, we'll go to Missing Persons and the Criminal Records Office. Let's hope we don't have to release it to the press. "

"I was thinking, sir—"

"Don't overdo it," said Scumble with heavy irony, "you don't want to do yourself a mischief."

In the face of this encouragement, Megan held her tongue.

"Come on, how can I tell if it's worth hearing till I hear it?"

"I just wondered, seeing the way the victim was dressed, if they might have broken in looking for clothes, or even for shelter, as much as valuables."

"It's possible."

"But it doesn't actually get us any further."

"No. I still have to put a couple of men on to watch the place in case they come back to search for something we don't know about, or something they've taken it into their drug-hazed minds is here, or—"

"They?"

"We have no reason to believe there were only two of them."

"No. I suppose not."

"I can't see a dozen crowding in here without leaving traces, but there could easily have been three of them, four at a pinch. Now go and radio for a van to fetch away the table. I'm going to poke about in here a bit more."

Megan went out to the car to call the Bodmin nick. Someone strong and desperate, she thought in dismay, and perhaps more than one. What if they decided Aunt Nell might be able to identify them? What if they had been watching and seen her go off with the vicar's wife?

If the DI didn't post a man to keep obbo on the vicarage, Megan intended to propose that he should, no matter how much scorn the suggestion drew down on her head.

NINE

The sun had cleared the hills surrounding Port Mabyn and shone through spotless windows into the vicarage kitchen. Eleanor and the Stearns were just finishing breakfast when the doorbell rang, at eight o'clock on the dot.

"I'll get it," said Eleanor, putting down her coffee mug, blue and white striped Cornish pottery like the rest of the breakfast service. So like dear Joce to have a matching set, though she'd had to collect it piece by piece from the LonStar shop. "It'll be whoever Inspector Scumble sent—I do hope it's Megan."

Megan it was. She followed Eleanor into the kitchen.

The Vicar unfolded. "Good morning, my dear young lady. You want to talk to Jocelyn and Eleanor, I know, so I'll make myself scarce."

"No, please stay a moment, sir. I've got a photo of the victim I'm showing everyone. We still don't know who he was."

"Is it . . . is it very unpleasant?"

"No, no, they cleaned him up. Here."

He took it between thumb and forefinger and peered at it. "No," he said, with obvious relief. "Never seen him in my life.

Here, Jocelyn, what about you?" He handed the photo to his wife and sidled out of the room.

Eleanor looked over Jocelyn's shoulder. The thin face was young, but not too young to be badly in need of a shave. The dark, fuzzy stubble softened but didn't conceal a bruise on the right side of his jawbone, an inch or two up from the point of his chin. The long hair had been combed but still gave an impression of uncleanness.

"No, I've never seen him before," said Jocelyn, handing the photo to Eleanor. "Do sit down, Megan. Coffee?"

However hard Eleanor tried to be charitable, tried to make allowances for the changes wrought by death, she thought the youth looked shifty, even unsavoury. Was it just because he had been found in unsavoury circumstances in the room below her flat? If his eyes were open, his expression full of life, would she feel different about him?

"Do you recognise him, Aunt Nell?"

"No, dear, I'm afraid not. I can't help wondering about his parents. Not knowing what's become of him, I mean."

"Sometimes ignorance is bliss," said Jocelyn. "I expect you'll identify him sooner or later, won't you, Megan? That's when his family will need sympathy."

"We're pretty well bound to find out sooner or later, one way or another. Then we'll start tracking down his associates." Megan put the photo in an envelope and stuck it in her pocket. "It's still a mystery what he was doing in the LonStar premises in the first place. Aunt Nell, the DI said there's something you were going to tell him last night?"

Jocelyn stood up. "Well, I'll just leave you two to it—"

Eleanor caught her arm. "Don't desert me, Joce."

"I never saw them, after all. And it's Megan you're facing, not that man."

"Them?" asked Megan. "What's going on?"

"It's nothing but hearsay as far as I'm concerned," said Jocelyn firmly. "Leave the washing-up. I'll do it later." She hurried out.

"Aunt Nell?"

"I tried to tell him last night."

"But?"

"But I should have told him sooner. He'll never believe I just kept forgetting."

"He'll believe it," Megan said with absolute conviction. "Come on, let's do the washing-up while you tell me. You wash and I'll dry, in case I have to write anything down."

"You will," said Eleanor gloomily. "I don't know what it all means, but I can't believe it has nothing to do with the murder." She started running hot water into the sink, adding a good squirt of Sqezy, the Washing-up Wizard. "That would be just too much coincidence to swallow."

"For pity's sake, Aunt Nell, spit it out!"

"What a very ungenteel expression! All right, all right. I'll 'spit it out.' It wasn't until I got back to the shop that I found it." She handed over a cup to be dried. "When I started unloading the Incorruptible, there it was, and I simply had no idea who had given it to me."

"It? You were talking about 'them.'"

"The container and the thing contained," said Eleanor, with vague memories of English lessons and Nick's earlier remark. "Things, rather. The briefcase I mean, dear, or perhaps attaché-case is the correct term. It's one of those thingummies business-men carry, but not the flat, soft-sided kind, more like a small suitcase, if you see what I mean. But thin, a couple of inches I'd say." She gestured to show the overall dimensions—perhaps two feet by eighteen inches—and soapsuds flew. "Quite heavy for its size."

"I get the picture."

"I took it back to the stockroom and opened it. Megan, it was full of jewelry!"

"Jewelry!" Megan nearly dropped the saucer she was drying. "You're not serious!"

"Absolutely, dear. It must be paste, of course, or whatever artificial gems are made of these days, but still quite valuable, and so very generous of someone. But such a trouble! We aren't allowed to accept that sort of thing without proof of ownership and all sorts of paperwork. Joce always deals with it so I'm not sure exactly what's needed. And it had appeared out of thin air without even a name to go with it."

"So you tucked it away in a corner of the stockroom and forgot about it?" Detective Sergeant Pencarrow asked in incredulous horror.

"Of course not. Do give me credit for a modicum of common sense!" Eleanor said quite crossly. "I took it upstairs and locked it in the safe."

"In your flat? There's a safe in your flat?"

"I had it built in when I bought the place and remodelled it. These old cottages have pretty thick walls, you know. Joce thought it would be a good idea, safer than in the shop. We've both been very careful never to tell a soul about it. I expect that's why I forgot to mention it to the inspector, besides being sure he'd find it, used to searching places as he must be. Only it seems he didn't, or he'd have asked me to open it, wouldn't he?"

"Undoubtedly."

"And I'm afraid he'll be rather annoyed, with me for not telling him, and with himself for not finding it. So, you see, I'm very glad it's you who came this morning and I've been able to tell you, instead of him." She handed over the last plate and started to scrub the frying pan.

Automatically drying the plate, Megan said, "You're going to have to tell him, too. This is going to change everything. It's the first hint we've had of a significant motive for the break-in! He won't be satisfied with hearing it from me, you know. Besides, he's going to have a lot of questions. There's no point me asking them. You'd only have to repeat the answers. I'd better go and ring him right away."

"If you must, dear," said Eleanor with a sigh.

"He just about blew my socks off," Megan reported, "as if it was *my* fault! You're to wait here, Aunt Nell. It's more of an order than a request. While the inspector is on his way from Launceston, I've got to show the photo of the victim to anyone and everyone I can find, so I'll come and fetch you when I see his car at the shop. *Please* don't go anywhere or talk to anyone."

Jocelyn stiffened. "I assume Mr Scumble doesn't propose to put me under house arrest also? I have parish business to be seen to."

"It's not house arrest, Mrs Stearns, just a . . . well, just he's going to be even more upset if Aunt Nell isn't available when he gets here. He didn't actually say anything about you."

"Then I shall go about my lawful occasions, whatever that's supposed to mean. You may take it that I don't intend to discuss the case with anyone."

"Thank you, Mrs Stearns," Megan said meekly.

Jocelyn went off about her lawful occasions and Megan went off to trudge up and down the street, footpaths, and alleyways of Port Mabyn, wielding the victim's photograph. Eleanor found a pile of mending waiting to be done and set about sewing a button on one of the Reverend Stearns' best shirts, hoping her stitches would be neat enough to satisfy her meticulous friend. Probably not, as her mind kept wandering to the best way to present her story to the inspector.

Megan returned looking gloomy. "I've been round half the village and no one admits to ever having seen him. Not that all that many were at home. The inspector's arrived. We'd better not keep him waiting."

Leaving Teazle with the vicar, Eleanor was escorted down the hill to her flat. On the way, several people greeted her and started expressing their sympathy and asking questions. Some were neighbours; others, wielding notebooks and cameras, were obviously reporters. Megan hustled her along, repeating "No comment," and not letting her aunt say anything more than "Good morning."

Scumble was already in the flat. He had taken Nick's picture off the wall, exposing the safe.

"Oldest trick in the world," he grumbled. "I'd have found it in a second if I'd imagined for a moment that you had one. I don't suppose by any chance you remember the combination?"

Sarcasm is the lowest form of wit, Eleanor thought, though for Megan's sake she didn't say it aloud. "Certainly," she replied. "It's—"

"Don't tell me!" He held up both hands to forestall her revelation. "Just open the blood . . . the blasted thing."

Eleanor complied. Scumble flashed his torch into the dim recess. Gold gleamed; gems sparkled and glittered in a myriad colours.

"Ye gods!" the inspector exclaimed. "No wonder someone tried to get in last night!"

"He did?" Eleanor was shocked. "What happened? He didn't get in?"

"I had men watching front and back, hidden. He came down the path at the back. When he stopped at your door, the silly bug—fool posted there tried to jump him and got caught up in a blackthorn bush. "

"Oh dear, I hope he wasn't too badly scratched."

"Not badly enough for my liking," Scumble said grimly. "He swears he didn't swear aloud, but the intruder obviously heard him and ran off."

"Megan, you didn't tell me."

"I should hope not," said Scumble, "after I expressly forbade it. And you're not to say a word either, Mrs Trewynn. I've only told you because you live here and you should be on your guard. If I read about it in the local rag—or anywhere else for that matter—"

"They won't hear it from me," Eleanor assured him.

"That I can believe. You don't talk half enough to suit me. How could you forget about this stuff? There's a fortune in there. If they're real."

"They can't be, surely. Our donors are generous, but . . ." Words failed her.

"Not that generous," Scumble finished for her. "Smells pretty fishy, if you ask me. All right, they'll be safe in there for the moment." He closed the door and spun the lock. "They'll have to be appraised by an expert p.d.q. Is there a jeweller in the village? And I don't mean an artsy-craftsy type turning out pretties for the tourists. A real pro."

"Not in Port Mabyn. I don't know—I expect you'd have to go to Camelford, or Bodmin, or even Launceston."

"Pencarrow, get on the radio to HQ and have them ring up Castle Jewellers in Launceston. See if their Mr Hobbes will come out and give this stuff a look-over. Say someone can give him a lift over here if necessary."

"Yes, sir." Megan went out.

Her footsteps retreated down the stairs. Without her, the room seemed to shrink, and Scumble's alarming bulk to take up more space.

TEN

Abandoned to DI Scumble's tender mercies, Eleanor decided sops to Cerberus was a good idea. "May I offer you a cup of tea or coffee, Inspector?"

"Thank you, I don't mind if I do. Coffee would hit the spot nicely as long as you can talk at the same time."

"It's just instant, not anything complicated."

"That's fine. Tell me how the jewelry came into your possession."

"I went out collecting donations on Tuesday afternoon," said Eleanor, filling the electric kettle. From the kitchen, she could see Megan getting into the police car below. "Not in the village; out in the country, so I took the Incorrupt—my car. When I got back—"

"I don't suppose you've remembered what time that was?" he asked without hope.

"The sun was setting, but that's as close as I can get. Didn't I tell you that already?"

"It'll have to do. Go on."

"I parked just outside the shop, partly on the pavement, I'm afraid, but I was unloading, so it's allowed, isn't it?"

"I'm not in the traffic division," he said dryly.

"What a pity. I really ought to find out if it's legal." Seeing his face begin to purple, she hastened to continue. "Teazle—my dog—jumped down. Milk, no sugar, isn't it?"

"Black, please. Is the dog germane to your story?"

"Yes, in a way." The kettle clicked off and Eleanor poured boiling water into the two cups, stirring to make sure the powder dissolved. "You see, she was in the back seat, sitting on top of the bundle of donated clothes under which I found the jewelry. They were in a polythene bag so she couldn't have damaged them."

"Now let's get this straight: You parked the car, possibly illegally, and the dog jumped down. Did she go out of the window?"

"She'd never do that. Here you are. Won't you have a seat?" Anything to stop him towering over her.

"Thanks." He took the mug, sipped—his mouth must be lined with asbestos—and sat down. "You opened the car door," he said with exaggerated patience. "Which side? Which way were you facing?"

"The wrong way," Eleanor confessed. "Is that illegal too? People seem to do it all the time."

"I am *not*—"

"—concerned with traffic control. I know. Sorry. The driver's-side door. I got out and told Teazle to come. Oh, I put the seat-back down. . . . No, that was afterwards. Teazle jumped from the back onto the driver's seat and down, and I let her into the passage. She's terribly good. She just goes upstairs out of the way while—"

"You unlocked the door into the passage?"

Eleanor racked her brains. "I'm still not sure," she admitted. "I wouldn't want to mislead you."

"Glad to hear it," he muttered.

"I turned back to the car. That's when I put the seat-back down and took out the bag of clothes."

"Hold on. Was your passenger-side window open?"

"Yes, it was a beautiful afternoon."

"Was your back turned to the car for long enough for someone to insert the jewelry under the clothes?"

"I don't know. I suppose so, if they were quick. But there were a few people about. The street wasn't deserted. Someone would surely have noticed."

"Hmm. All right, go on."

"Where was I? Oh yes, I took the clothes and the jewelry back to the stockroom, then, when I saw how valuable it looked, I brought the jewelry up here and put it in the safe. By the time I went down again, Donna and the little Chins were—"

"The *what?*"

"What on earth do you mean, the 'what?'"

"Little chins . . . Oh, the kids!"

"Ivy and Lionel, from the Chinese. Such dear children. They often help me, as does Donna. You always hear about teenagers being difficult, and one must admit she—Well, never mind. Then Nick came to see if there was anything heavy to carry. Nicholas Gresham, from next door."

"The artist whose shin met the table, who carried the boxes of books in."

"That's right."

"Did you tell him, or anyone else, about the jewelry?"

"Good gracious no!" She paused before continuing guiltily, "Not *then*. I was afraid it might turn out to be a mistake, so embarrassing to everyone to have it known and then to have to give it back . . . I did tell Jocelyn—Mrs Stearns. She had to know because it was shop business, but I didn't mention it even to her until yesterday afternoon. Earlier, we had other things on our minds."

"Quite. So you did tell Mr Gresham at some point?"

"At tea-time yesterday. He said we must tell you immediately."

"And quite right he was. So why have I only just been informed?"

"Because of the drawing of the boy's injury, and Nick's and Jocelyn's bruises. We were all thinking about the table, and the jewelry simply got lost in the shuffle. "

Scumble heaved a heavy sigh. "I'll accept that, as a working hypothesis."

"Later, I was about to tell you when you decided to call it a day."

He had the grace to look discomfited, for a fraction of a second. "What happened after all your booty was stowed in the stockroom?"

"I've already told you about that. Nick invited me out to supper as he'd sold a painting, and then he took the car down to my garage. It's just a shed, down in the parking lot by the stream."

"Locked?"

"Padlocked. Usually, when the car is there. But the jewels weren't put in the car in the shed. Earlier, I mean, before I went out in it. I couldn't possibly have helped noticing when I took it out, or at least when Teazle got into the back. Or when I put in the first donation I picked up. Boxes from Mrs Prendergast. The flat kind, you know, dress boxes. I would have seen—"

"I suppose so. We'll have to check the car for fingerprints. The key is on the ring we've got?"

"Yes, the one that's obviously a padlock key."

"Right, let's get back to this collecting trip of yours. Where exactly did you go?"

Eleanor told him whom she had visited that day and what they had given her. She never had any difficulty remembering people, nor the proceeds of their kindness and generosity. The order in which she had called on them was another matter. "Is it important?" she asked.

"I don't know. Can give me their addresses?"

"They're all in my address book, in my desk." She went over to the flap-top desk in the corner, carefully placed where she could look out over the inlet while she wrote letters. "Here. Though the addresses may not help you very much. Most of them are tucked away in odd nooks in the landscape. I can try to give you directions, but you know how it is—after a while one goes by landmarks more than by anything so precise as 'turn left at the next crossroads' and 'bear right where the lane forks.'"

"We'll find them."

"You aren't going to . . . to *accuse* them of anything, are you?" Eleanor was thinking how the arrival of the police would upset Miss Willis and Miss Annabel.

"Donating to a charity is not a crime, Mrs Trewynn. We have to find out whether any of these people put the jewelry in your car, whether accidentally or deliberately."

"Yes, of course. Could you possibly send Meg—Detective Sergeant Pencarrow—to question the Willises? They're elderly, you see, and they won't get so flustered if it's not a uniformed policeman."

"I can't promise. I may not be able to spare her."

Eleanor decided to regard this as a victory of sorts. At least he had acknowledged that Megan was more use to him than a common-or-garden bobby. Megan, who clearly felt unappreciated, would be pleased to hear of the inspector's concession.

Megan returned to the flat just then. Eleanor managed to restrain herself from passing on the good news at once.

"Mr Hobbes is on his way, sir."

Scumble nodded. "You grew up around here, didn't you?"

"At the other end of the county, actually, sir."

He dismissed this with a wave. "Do you know where these places are?" He handed over the list of names and addresses.

Megan read it with dismay. "Not really, sir. Even with a map, the lanes are pretty confusing in places, but I expect I can find them."

"Good. Take Dawson and ask 'em all what they donated to LonStar the day before yesterday. Ask particularly about anything valuable, but don't specify jewelry. You might as well see if anyone can put a time to Mrs Trewynn's call," he added pessimistically, "though I can't see what good it'll do us if they can. You made a note of everyone in Port Mabyn you've shown that photo to?"

"Of course, sir."

"Give your notes to Pardoe. He can finish that up. And take a copy of the picture to show all these people you're going to run to earth in their rural retreats."

"Uh, some of these places probably don't get wireless reception, sir. If they haven't heard about the murder, should I tell them why I'm making enquiries?"

"No! Least said, soonest mended." He turned a ferocious scowl on Eleanor. "Which doesn't apply to witnesses."

"'I tell thee everything I can,'" said Eleanor. "'There's little to relate.'"

Scumble gave her a look of utter incomprehension. Oh dear, she thought, he wasn't brought up on Lewis Carroll. Now he would think her battier than ever. But the image the quotation brought to her mind—an aged, aged man a-sitting on a gate—reminded her of something she *hadn't* related.

"It wasn't a gate," she said, as Megan, who surely was acquainted with the White Knight, made her escape. "It was a stile. I went for a walk on the cliffs."

"That afternoon," the inspector said flatly. "After picking up the goods?"

"Yes. It was a beautiful day. I parked in a lay-by, well off the road."

"I'm delighted to hear it. Did you by any chance lock the car?"

"Well, no. As a matter of fact, I left the keys in the lock, so, you see, I did mean to do it. But I heard a car coming, so I checked to make sure Teazle was well out of the way."

"Did you recognise the car?" he rapped out. "What make, year, colour? I suppose there's no hope of your having noted the licence plate."

"It was a panda car, actually. Or don't you like people calling them that? A police car. Bob Leacock's police car."

"PC Leacock's police car. The local officer."

"That's right. Such a nice young man. He stopped to make sure I hadn't broken down and we passed the time of day. Then he drove on and I climbed up onto the stile. Teazle went underneath. It was a wooden one, not one of those with stone steps built into a wall. That kind I have to lift her over, which is all very well if you have a small dog but how people manage . . . Sorry! Where was I?"

"On top of the stile, I believe. The *wooden* stile."

Sarcasm again. Eleanor was quite indignant. After all, she had apologised for rambling. She was almost tempted to tell him she couldn't remember what had happened next. He'd certainly believe her. But not only would that be childish, the more she thought about it, the more obvious it seemed that the loot must have been put into the Incorruptible while she was walking across the field.

"Another car came by. It's no good asking me the make or year or licence plate, but it was grey. The sun was reflected off the windshield and I couldn't see who was inside, but I waved, just in case it was someone I knew. It drove past. After I had climbed down from the stile and started across the field, I heard the engine cut off. I remember hoping they weren't going to walk the same way and spoil the peace and quiet. A few moments later, I heard a car door slam. Then they drove away."

"In which direction?" Scumble demanded.

"The opposite way to Bob. They must have passed each other as he drove down the hill."

"If he doesn't know the make, model, and year," snarled the inspector, "I'll have him kicked off the force."

ELEVEN

PC Dawson was young, brash, and muscular. Megan wondered whether DI Scumble had chosen him to accompany her because she might need protection. Visiting rural philanthropists sounded harmless but this was, after all, a murder investigation. The fact that she had passed all the police unarmed combat courses with flying colours was not likely to impress the inspector.

Dawson raced the panda Mini along twisting lanes barely wide enough for a single car. The high, banked walls on either side effectively blocked any view of oncoming traffic. It gave Megan a new appreciation for Scumble's dislike of being driven.

She closed her eyes as a bend brought them nose to nose with a tractor. Had it been doing more than three miles an hour, disaster would have been inevitable. As it was, the police car screeched to a halt a scant foot short of its radiator grille. The farm-worker driving it, a red-faced man in a disreputable hat, gave a cheery wave and pointed forcefully at the way they had come.

Dawson reversed, swearing. He shot Megan a half-shamefaced, half-defiant look and muttered, "Sorry," as he backed into a passing niche.

After six years in the police, she still hadn't worked out how to deal with this situation. He'd never have apologised for bad language to a male colleague. On the one hand, he was being polite. On the other, he was treating her differently because she was a woman. She mumbled something indistinguishable even to herself.

The tractor chugged past with another wave and a grin from the farmer. He was pulling a cart loaded with bales of wool. A faint, not unpleasant smell of sheep wafted into the car.

Unchastened by their near miss, Dawson rocketed out of the passing-place and down the winding lane. The high banks ended and tangled woodland closed in. As they neared the still narrower bridge at the foot of the hill, the radio started to squawk. Amid the unintelligible noise, Megan thought she heard their car's call number.

"Was that us?" Dawson asked, easing off the accelerator just in time for the sharp turn onto the old stone bridge over a swift stream edged with mossy boulders.

"I think so." Megan reached for the transmitter. "This is CaRaDoC L7. We're barely receiving your signal. Please wait till we get out of this valley." She let go the transmit button.

The radio resumed its squawking. Megan caught their call number again, and something that might have been Scumble.

"I repeat, we can't hear you properly. We're heading uphill now. Please wait. We should get a clear signal at the top." She repeated variations on this theme until the car emerged from the trees and the lane levelled off between spring-green hedges. Dawson pulled into a lay-by and switched off.

"Okay, this is CaRaDoC L7. Reception should be better here. Please repeat your message."

It wasn't Scumble in person at the other end, just an operator at HQ in Launceston relaying his instructions. PC Leacock was urgently wanted. He wasn't answering his radio. Either it was on the blink again, or he wasn't in his car, or—the operator suggested snidely—he was down at the bottom of some valley where there was no reception. If they came across him, he was to be sent straight to DI Scumble at the LonStar shop in Port Mabyn.

Megan acknowledged the message and signed off.

"I expect he knows too much," Dawson suggested with relish, turning the key in the ignition, "and the murderer's bagged him."

"I expect he's in some cosy farmhouse kitchen being fed on the fat of the land," said Megan sourly.

"Yeah, more likely," he agreed as they zoomed on their way.

She consulted their map. "The next village looks a bit bigger than the last one and it says '*Inn.*' Maybe they'll have pasties."

"Even if not, I wouldn't say no to a pint."

Beer on an empty stomach didn't sound like a good idea to Megan, especially as he was driving. Before she had to decide whether to voice this undoubtedly unpopular view, they drove into Tregareth.

The hamlet consisted of a single street. One of two rows of labourers' cottages had been converted into a quite attractive house. The other had not. They faced each other uneasily across a thoroughfare no wider than necessary to allow two farm carts to pass each other. Gardens, if any, were tucked away behind.

"*El Alamein,*" Dawson read the word painted in black on the whitewashed wall over the blue front door of the house. "Isn't that the old boy we've come to see?"

"Major Cartwright, yes. But let's get something to eat first."

Beyond the cottages stood the pub, long and low, grey stone with a slate roof. On the faded sign a jaunty, green-jacketed pig pranced on its hind legs playing a penny whistle. Below, two smaller signboards swung on short chains. One announced HOT

PASTIES, the other the inevitable CREAM TEAS. A telephone box made a splash of colour at one end of the building.

The rest of the village appeared to consist of a cluster of modern bungalows in the usual pastel hues, a tiny stone chapel, and a larger two-story stone house, half hidden behind a huge, spreading cedar of Lebanon that leant at an angle away from the prevailing winds. No doubt several farms, with associated cottages, lurked in the surrounding countryside, supplying sufficient drinkers to justify the presence of the Pig and Whistle. Whether sufficient holiday-makers ever passed this way to justify the cream teas was questionable.

Dawson parked and they went into the dim interior. Dawson immediately veered off towards the GENTS sign. "Back in half a tick."

A couple of rustic figures drank silently in a corner. The landlord, Geo. Potts, Prop., according to the requisite notice over the door, was propping up the bar. "Wotcher, ducks," he greeted her. "Wot can I getcher?"

Megan asked for pasties.

"Sorry, ducks." The landlord was an incomer, his accent dense as a London fog. "We only do 'ot pasties for the summer trade. I 'spect the old woman could run you up a nice sangwich, though. Gloria," he shouted over his shoulder, "can you do a couple of sangwiches?" An indistinct answer came from the rear of the premises. He turned back to Megan. "'Am and cheese do you?"

"Thanks, that'll be fine. A half of cider for me, and a pint . . . I'm not sure what he drinks. Better wait and see."

"Now wot's a copper up to in this neck of the woods wiv 'is ladyfriend this time of day, that's wot I'd like to know?" His expression wasn't quite a leer.

"I'm a detective officer," Megan said icily.

He threw up both hands. "Beg parding I'm sure. No offence

meant, orficer. Takes all sorts, that's wot I say. Last thing I want's to get on the wrong side of Old Bill. You're a 'tec, eh? Wouldn't've thought Bob Leacock'd need help from you lot to deal wiv a poacher."

"Leacock? He's in the village?"

"Up at Cedar Lodge." He gestured. "The big house over there. Squire thinks some bloke's been after his pheasants."

"Are they on the telephone? I must get hold of him at once and his car radio doesn't seem to be working."

"Yeah. Name's Dandridge. But we 'aven't got a phone. You'll 'ave to use the box."

"Right. Thanks."

"I'll tell your—um—pal in blue where you went."

"Thanks."

Unlike most urban telephone booths, this one had an intact directory. Megan found the number and dialled. The squire at the big house—She half-expected the phone to be answered by a butler. But a young foreign female voice said, *"Allo?"* and then quickly corrected herself and gave the exchange and number. Au pair, Megan thought.

She kept it simple and spoke slowly. "This is the police. I need to speak to PC Leacock, please."

"Please, here is policeman already, for the birds."

"Yes, I know. I must speak to him. Talk to him."

"He is talk Mr Dandridge. Do not disturb."

Megan was running low on both patience and change when Dawson came out of the pub, strolled over to the booth, and raised his eyebrows at her. She cracked the door open and hissed, "Foreigner. I can't make her understand."

"Leacock's there?"

"Yes, talking to the Big White Chief Who Is Not To Be Disturbed. Known locally as The Squire."

"We'd better hop on over there. I'll go tell the landlord we'll be right back, while you wind things up with the bird. My beer'll go flat," he added mournfully.

It was too late to "wind things up." They had been cut off. Dawson came back out of the Pig and Whistle, beckoned to her impatiently, and got into the car.

Megan went over. "It's that house just there. We can walk."

"I've got a better idea. Jump in."

As he turned off the street into the drive, he switched on the siren. They arrived *whoo-whoo*ing in a flurry of gravel. "I hope I haven't disturbed the Great White Chief," he said with a smirk.

Before flying gravel had stopped pinging against the flanks of the muddy panda car and the immaculate Rover already parked in front of the house, Bob Leacock erupted from the front door, helmet in hand.

"What's up?" he yelled. Then he took in Dawson's smug grin. "I just got the old sod to stop talking man-traps," he said bitterly, "and you come busting in—"

"Murder takes precedence over poaching," Megan interrupted, leaning forward. "Mr Scumble wants you to report in pronto."

"You should thank us for rescuing you," said Dawson.

"My radio quit again."

"He wants you on the spot," Megan told him, "at the shop, the LonStar shop in Port Mabyn, according to the HQ operator."

"Why? I didn't see anything that night, more's the pity, no matter how many times he asks me, and if anyone had told me anything useful, I'd've reported right away."

"I wasn't told what he wants. Reception's lousy here, but I gather they've been trying to get hold of you for some time, so I'd get a move on if I were you."

"All right," he said reluctantly. Then he brightened. "I'll have to leave you to explain to the squire. 'Bye!" Without further ado, he got into his car and rolled off down the drive.

Megan and Dawson looked at each other. Megan grabbed the radio transmitter. "I'd better tell them he's on his way. Don't keep the Great White Chief waiting."

"What exactly is a man-trap?" Dawson asked gloomily, opening his door.

"I expect you're about to find out. Hello, this is CaRaDoC L7 reporting . . ."

Dawson returned a few minutes later with all his limbs intact. He answered with a growl when Megan asked him about his interview with Dandridge, so she didn't persist. They departed from Cedar Lodge in another spray of gravel.

As a peace offering, she bought him a pint to replace the flat one awaiting him at the pub.

Starting on his third sandwich, he let her tackle El Alamein on her own.

Major Cartwright answered the door leaning heavily on a stout walking stick. Like all the others they had called on that day, he denied having donated anything of value to LonStar.

"Wish I could," he said gruffly, "but the pension doesn't stretch as far as it used to. Not that I'm complaining, mind. When I think of those poor blighters Mrs Trewynn is trying to help . . . And now it seems it's all our fault. The Empire and all, I mean."

He wasn't querulous, just puzzled. Megan produced a sympathetic murmur.

"A lot of chaps are saying so, so I suppose it must be true, but it's a bit bewildering for an old fogey like me. Thought we were helping them, don't you know. White man's burden, they called it in my young day. So I do what I can. Give Mrs Trewynn all my books. No use reading them again after you know the ending."

"Did you pack them up yourself?"

"Yes, indeed. I have them shipped to me from a London bookshop—I don't get about much any longer—so I just put them back in the boxes they sent them in."

"No one could have slipped something in without your noticing?"

"Not possibly. By George, this is just like stepping into a detective story. I read mostly detective stories," he added shyly. "I don't suppose they're really anything like real life—no lady police detectives, for one thing—but I enjoy 'em."

"And I know my aunt is very grateful for them, sir. They sell quickly."

"Your aunt?"

Megan's face grew hot. With Aunt Nell in the thick of this case, it was very difficult to keep the personal and the professional apart. "Mrs Trewynn happens to be my aunt, sir."

"No, is she? Wonderful lady!" the major enthused.

Aunt Nell had an admirer! How lucky that, with his difficulty in walking, he couldn't possibly be the villain of this particular detective story.

He was obviously dying for a chat, probably on the point of inviting her into his house. To Megan's relief, an impatient toot came from the direction of the inn.

"I've got to go. My partner's waiting. Thank you for your co-operation, sir."

"I hope you catch the rotter who put Mrs Trewynn through such a beastly experience," he said earnestly.

"We will, sooner or later," she promised, shaking his hand. Walking back to the car, she pondered his priorities. Apparently Aunt Nell's inconvenience weighed more heavily than the victim's lost life. No doubt he had read in the papers that the youth was a scruffy layabout. His first thought had probably been that a couple of years in the army would have set him straight.

Joining Dawson in the car, she reported, "A nice old boy, but no help." She checked the list and the map. "Only a couple more, but you'll have to turn around. We want to go on the way we were going."

Dawson put the gear into reverse and shot backwards along the street and into the drive of Cedar Lodge. Thence they continued their headlong career. Fortunately for Megan's nerves, the lane came out on a shoulder of Bodmin moor, and at least they could see their way ahead. To her vocal amazement, Dawson even deigned to slow down to chivvy occasional sheep and ponies off the road.

"Hey," he said, "do you know what the fine is for running over livestock?"

"No. What?"

"I don't know either, but I bet it's a whole lot more than dinging the nose of a tractor."

TWELVE

The gemologist from Castle Jewellers was short and tubby, with disproportionately short legs, crooked teeth, and a piebald mop of hair. Eleanor couldn't decide if it was naturally black and had gone white in patches, or whether it had gone white naturally and an unsuccessful attempt had been made to dye it black. Or perhaps it was a wig, a very peculiar one, though she'd seen much stranger fashions in obscure parts of the world: lengthened necks, stretched lips, bound feet, scarified faces and chests. If Mr Hobbes wanted to wear a small, shaggy dog on his head, then let him. She'd stick to a dab of lipstick.

Young people these days seemed to manage without lipstick, she mused, or used the palest shades. Heavy mascara was popular, though, along with vast quantities of eyeshadow.

"Would you mind, Mrs Trewynn," said DI Scumble in his exaggeratedly patient voice, "opening the safe, since Mr Hobbes has come some distance to examine the contents. You do recall the combination, I trust?"

Eleanor gave him a speaking look and turned to the safe. Such was the power of suggestion that for a terrible moment her mind went blank. Then she thought of Peter and at once knew the numbers, as well as she knew her own birthday. She unlocked the safe and swung the door open.

Hobbes darted forward with a squawk of horror. "Oh no, no, no, no, no!"

"What's the matter?" Scumble said sharply.

"Diamonds! Opals! Everything all jumbled together. Are you not aware that diamonds are the hardest substance known to man? They are capable of scratching even rubies and sapphires, while opals are extremely delicate. I'm afraid there may be extensive damage."

With the utmost delicacy, he started to disentangle the pieces.

In answer to Scumble's reproachful expression, Eleanor protested lamely, "They were like that when I found them. I just scooped them up and stuck them in there."

Her words elicited a moan from Hobbes.

Scumble put his finger to his lips, frowning. Eleanor gathered that he didn't want the jeweller to know any more than was absolutely necessary about the discovery of the hoard.

Extricating a bracelet, Hobbes brought it over to the table and carefully laid it flat. It was the lovely piece she had originally admired, woven gold wire set with violet stones. Amethysts? Judging by his extreme care, the expert must be pretty sure they were genuine.

One by one, necklaces, rings, brooches, and more bracelets spread across the table, glittering and gleaming. Scumble looked a trifle dazed. The safe was emptied at last. Hobbes sat down at the table, brought out his loupe, and stuck it in his eye. Eleanor held her breath, and she rather thought the inspector did, too.

Hobbes picked up a diamond and emerald pendant. "Light," he said irritably. "I need more light."

Eleanor switched on the ceiling light while Scumble dealt with her reading lamp. He tried to bring it over to the table, but the flex wasn't quite long enough. He turned on the light in the kitchen. Each new source of illumination brought more sparkles.

"Hmm." Hobbes moved on to the next piece.

He seemed to Eleanor to be working with excruciating slowness. Scumble looked as if he might explode any moment with suppressed impatience. At last Hobbes replaced a ring on the table, pushed back his chair, and removed the loupe from his eye.

"A few minor flaws, and the opals are scratched, as I feared, but not badly. All in all a superb collection."

"They're genuine?" Scumble burst out.

"Certainly."

"What are they worth?" Eleanor asked. She couldn't help it, though she wasn't sure she wanted to know. If they had to be returned to the owner, she'd only torture herself with might-have-beens.

"I couldn't possibly venture to give you even a rough figure, madam, without a thorough examination under proper conditions." He cast a disparaging glance at her reading lamp. "I understood the inspector required merely an opinion as to the authenticity of the gemstones. If you're interested in selling, you'll want to try the London market. We can't handle anything like this in Launceston."

"Would you mind writing out a list, Mr Hobbes?" Scumble requested, tearing a sheet from his notebook. "Not in great detail, just enough to be recognisable to someone who'd seen this collection before." He offered the paper and his biro.

Hobbes accepted the paper but rejected the biro with scorn. He took a fountain pen from his pocket and began to write. A few minutes later he handed a neat list to Scumble. "There you are. If there is nothing further I can help you with, I must be getting back to the shop."

Scumble ushered him out. In the doorway, the inspector turned back for a moment.

"I shall be wanting another word with you, Mrs Trewynn," he said grimly, as if he suspected she might scurry down the stairs and disappear through the back door while he was putting the jeweller into the police car for his return journey.

Eleanor was sorely tempted to take French leave—if it weren't for the constable still on duty at the back. Somehow she hadn't got around yet to telling Scumble about the briefcase. She had assured him nothing was missing from the flat or the stockroom. Where had she put it? She had brought it up here to empty it, she was certain of that. Impossible to carry all those bits and pieces safely in her hands. But the case would have been in the way in her sitting room. She must have taken it down again.

She closed her eyes and concentrated, trying to retrace her steps on Monday—

"Well?" The inspector, of course.

"In the passage!" she said, triumphant.

"In the passage! In the passage!" he exclaimed wildly. "What the devil do you mean, in the passage?"

"I assumed you'd want to know where I left the briefcase. Attaché-case, whatever you prefer to call it."

He dropped onto the chair by the table with such force that it creaked, every inch of him expressive of weary resignation. "All right, so there was a briefcase. I never even wondered what the jewelry was in until you said you scooped it up. Let's start again from when you started unloading your car."

"I let Teazle—"

"We'll take the dog as read. Where is she, anyway?"

"At the vicarage. She adores the vicar. He—"

"Mrs Trewynn!"

"You asked. I tipped the driving seat forwards and reached back for the clothes. As soon as I picked them up, I saw the brief-case. I didn't remember anyone giving it to me, but it was a nice one, black leather, so I assumed it was a donation someone I'd called on had put in the car when I wasn't looking. I took it out and carried it and the clothes back to the stockroom. It seemed heavier than if it were empty, so instead of putting it in the corner with the other new stuff, I set it on the table and opened it."

"It wasn't locked?"

"No. It had a lock, I think, a brass lock—no, keyholes in the latches, not a separate lock. But I didn't have a key, of course. If it had been locked, I wouldn't have tried to force it open."

"Naturally not." Was there a note of scepticism in his voice?

"I wasn't being nosy," Eleanor said with a touch of indigna-tion. "I'm in charge of collecting donations and Jocelyn expects me to know what I've picked up and from whom."

"Only in this case, you didn't know from whom and the what took you by surprise."

"It certainly did. More like shock than mere surprise, though I was sure they couldn't be real. And I knew Joce would be annoyed that I not only had no paperwork, I had absolutely no idea where they came from. Anyway, real or not, they looked quite valuable so I closed the case and took it upstairs."

"And scooped the jewelry into the safe. It was lying all higgledy-piggledy when you first opened the case?"

"Yes, but the case was lined with sort of cushiony black vel-vet, as if it had been made for jewelry. If it had been properly packed, I expect even the opals would have come to no harm."

"Aha! Now that's very interesting. Can you give me a more precise description of the exterior of the case?"

"Black leather. Good quality, as far as I could judge. A few scuff marks, but nothing a bit of polish wouldn't cover. About so big." She gestured to show the dimensions. "Hard-sided, like a small suitcase."

"In the passage?"

"At the bottom of the stairs."

"No way we could have overlooked something that size when we searched the place, though I suppose we'd better have another look around. Keyed brass latches, you said?"

"Yes. At least they had round knobs, buttons, the sort you press apart, if you see what I mean, with slots that looked like keyholes. I wondered why it wasn't locked, with all that in it."

"Not much point locking it. Opening it wouldn't give a thief much trouble."

"I suppose it wouldn't be difficult to break the locks. I expect it had brass hinges, too, but I didn't notice them."

"Could have been internal, hidden by the velvet. No maker's name on the latches?"

"Not that I remember," Eleanor said doubtfully. Wasn't there something—? Under the inspector's gaze, the harder she tried to remember, the blanker her mind.

"And no identification of the owner, inside or out, or you wouldn't have been in such a quandary. Wouldn't you think he'd put his business card inside in case he forgot it in a taxi? Well, that's a very clear description," Scumble congratulated her, then spoilt it by adding, "for once. And you put it down in the passage? Why was that?"

"The children arrived as I was coming down the stairs. I just put it down against the wall, where no one would fall over it."

"And it never dawned on you that we might be interested in it?"

"Not till last night. And I told Megan—Detective Sergeant Pencarrow—first thing this morning. I would have told you about it sooner, but all the fuss over the jewelry put it out of my mind. And then you obviously didn't want me to talk about it when Mr Hobbes was here."

"True," he conceded grudgingly. "Presumably the murderer took the case, to hide the evidence—afraid he'd left fingerprints, I expect—or even hoping the loot was still in it. He must have been in a tearing hurry to get away after killing the lad, perhaps too rushed to open it and check. Having left a body down below, he'll certainly realise that you've had police swarming here, but judging others by himself he might wonder if you've concealed the jewels, or some of them, from us."

"Mr Scumble!" Eleanor exclaimed, bursting with indignation.

"I'm not suggesting such a thing! And don't go telling Mrs Stearns I did. I'm just trying to read the mind of a murderous thief. One who knows who you are, or they'd never have put the stuff in the car and come here to retrieve it."

"You think he might come back again?" She shivered.

"There are plenty of my men around at present, but I'm going to have to persuade Superintendent Bentinck to spare a man or two to keep an eye on the shop for a couple more days at least. We don't want to scare him off again. No hiding in blackthorn bushes! Now, back to that briefcase. If he's got any sense at all, he'll have wiped it clean of prints and got rid of it, but we'll send out a description of it as well as of the jewels. If it's found, it might at least give us a clue as to which direction he's gone." He stood up and stared down at the neatly laid-out jewelry. "Meanwhile, we'll have to take custody of this lot. I'll have someone copy the list and give you a receipt."

"How are you going to take it away? You can't just stuff it in your pockets, after what Mr Hobbes said about damage."

"No," he agreed gloomily. "And I'd probably have my pockets picked. Any suggestions?"

"I've got a bit of tissue paper. If it's not enough, Joce is bound to have stacks." She went to her desk.

"You told Mrs Stearns about the jewelry, you said."

"Of course. As soon as I remembered it. I was just about to yesterday morning when I found the—the body and it put the jewelry right out of my mind. I told her in the afternoon. It appeared to be a donation, after all. She doesn't know it's genuine, though." Rummaging in the bottom drawer, she found a whole packet of tissue paper. "This should do. And Nick next door—the artist?—he has flat crates for shipping pictures. One of the smaller ones might work."

"The fewer people . . ." His voice trailed off as he saw her face. "That's right, you already told him. Who else?"

"No one else."

"And it was he who said you must report it to me."

"Yes. I did try to tell you last night—"

"And I cut you off. So you reminded me. My sincere apologies, Mrs Trewynn." He sounded more peeved than sincere. "Is there anything else you feel might be of interest to the police that you've had no opportunity to reveal?"

Eleanor's mind immediately went blank again. "I don't think so."

"Well, if anything should happen to occur to you, please let me know immediately, even if it's two in the morning. Ring Launceston and they'll get on to me."

"If you say so," she agreed, though surely she couldn't have forgotten anything sufficiently urgent to require waking him in the wee small hours! "When will I be able to move back home?"

"Are you sure you want to?"

"Oh yes. If he comes back again, I'm sure I'll be safe with

your men outside, whether they catch him or scare him off accidentally."

Scumble scowled. "Whenever you want, then. As soon as I get these sparklers out of your way. I'll go and make arrangements now. But please don't go anywhere. I want you to hear what Constable Leacock has to say about that car you claim he must have seen. If he ever turns up."

Naturally Bob Leacock turned up just when Eleanor had popped up to the vicarage to fetch her things. On her way back down the hill, after bringing Jocelyn up to date and having a bite to eat, she saw Bob's panda car parked outside his house. At least, she thought it must be his. With so many police cars hanging about the village these days, it was hard to be sure. Teazle at her heels, she hurried on down the street, fending off friends, neighbours, and presumed reporters with a "Sorry, can't stop." She missed Megan's protective escort.

As she approached the LonStar shop, a bellow echoed from within. "What do you mean, no one's answering the door? Where's the bloody woman got to *now?*" Scumble appeared in the passage doorway. "I told her she'd be needed," he snarled at the constable on guard. "Where the devil did she go?"

"You didn't tell me to stop her, sir. She—"

"Oh, there you are, Mrs Trewynn! I was under the impression I'd told you—"

"You told me I could return home, Inspector, so I went to collect the dog and my belongings from the vicarage. You also requested my presence when Constable Leacock reported to you. Here I am."

Scumble's mouth opened—and closed tightly on whatever rebuke he'd been about to utter. Bob Leacock and the other uniformed man repressed grins with obvious difficulty. Teazle barked, a puzzled note as if she couldn't understand why, having arrived home, they were standing on the front step.

"Come in," Scumble growled. He swung round, tramped back along the passage, and reached for the stockroom door.

"Don't worry," Leacock whispered, following Eleanor, "I only just got here."

She smiled at him over her shoulder. "Won't you come upstairs, Mr Scumble?" she invited. "We'll be much more comfortable."

"The aim of this interview is not to be comfortable!"

But Teazle was already at the top of the stairs, sitting waiting. Eleanor started up and the inspector came after her, with Bob bringing up the rear. Their combined tread made Eleanor glad she'd spent a bit extra to have the aged staircase reinforced when she bought the house. As she reached the top, she felt in her pocket for her keys, only to realise that she'd left them in the keyhole again.

With a bit of fiddling, she did her best to conceal the fact from Mr Scumble. Either she was successful or he couldn't be bothered to upbraid her. He said nothing as she opened the door. Teazle dashed past her ankles and went snuffling around the room. From her perspective, the place must be full of the fascinating odours of all the strangers who had been messing about in her house since she left.

The humans all sat down, Scumble after an invitation from Eleanor, Leacock with permission from Scumble. Rather wearily, Eleanor considered offering tea, but by her reckoning she and Jocelyn had by now contributed several gallons to the consumption of the county police force. Bob Leacock could always get a cup at home after the interrogation.

He might need something stronger if he hadn't noticed or couldn't remember the licence plate number of the grey car.

A peremptory knock on the door barely preceded the entrance of Nick Gresham. "What's going on, Eleanor? I heard a lot of shouting and reckoned I'd better come and see if you're in need of protection. Tut-tut, Officer," he said to Leacock, "attempting to intimidate a witness? I'd thought better of you."

"It wasn't my voice you heard, Mr Gresham," Bob assured him gravely, as though they hadn't played darts together at the Arms every Saturday for years.

"No one's trying to intimidate anyone, Mr Gresham." The familiar purple hue started to rise in Scumble's cheeks. "I merely want Mrs Trewynn's cooperation in corroborating Constable Leacock's report."

"Is that all? I think I'd better just stick around to make sure Mrs Trewynn chooses to cooperate, corroborate, et cetera." Nick dropped into the one remaining chair, where he lounged very much at ease.

"I suppose it can't hurt," Scumble conceded, his propensity for sarcasm once more in evidence. "You know far too much already."

"I shan't spill the beans to the reporters, if that's what you're worried about."

"As a matter of fact, in this matter we'll very likely be informing the press ourselves. I shall be obliged, Mrs Trewynn," continued the inspector with a stern look, "if you will refrain from speaking until I've heard Leacock's story."

Eleanor nodded but said nothing. Anyone would suppose he had reason to complain of her talking too much, whereas his grievance was that she hadn't talked enough, or at least not soon enough to please him.

He turned to the constable. "Well?"

"Sorry, sir," said Bob cheerfully, "but I don't know what it is you want to know."

"They didn't tell you? I told Launceston—"

"I didn't talk to Launceston direct, sir. My radio's out of order. Again. Now if you could see your way, sir, to putting in a word—"

"All right, all right! When it reaches the point of impeding a murder investigation . . . But you know they'll just start carrying on about the budget." Momentarily the two policemen found themselves in complete agreement.

"Miss Pencarrow and Dawson found me, sir, but they didn't know what you wanted, 'cepting for me to report in. Bad reception. It's the terrain, you see, and not enough relay towers."

"Don't tell *me*. You remember seeing Mrs Trewynn the afternoon before the murder was discovered?"

"Hey, what's all this about?" Nick protested. "You can't imagine—"

"It's all right, Nick," Eleanor assured him. "I told the inspector about it. I wasn't doing anything remotely sinister."

"You keep your mouth shut, Mr Gresham, or I'll change my mind about you staying." Turning back to the constable, Scumble said testily, "Let's have an answer quick, Leacock, before there's any more interruptions."

Bob gave Eleanor a puzzled look. "Yes, sir. Must've been a quarter past four or thereabouts. Mrs Trewynn had pulled her car into the lay-by where the public footpath goes off to Gorran Head and Pentil Cove. I stopped to make sure she wasn't having any trouble with it. She said she was just going to walk on the cliffs, so I drove on. It wasn't more than a minute I stopped."

"And then?"

"And then I went on, sir, like I said, down the hill. Just my usual rounds."

"You know your district well, I expect?"

"Pretty well, sir," said Leacock cautiously, as if he suspected a trap.

"You know or at least can recognise most people?"

"The residents, sir. Most of the regular summer people, after they've come down a year or two. But holiday-makers that come down, it may be—"

"I don't expect the impossible, man! What about cars? You know them as well as you do people?"

"Make and model, sir, and colour. I can't say as I know all their number plates by heart, but I take note of them that don't have Cornish registration. What exactly—Oh, would it be about the car that came up the hill just after I saw Mrs Trewynn?"

"That's the one. Mrs Trewynn didn't recognise it."

"That doesn't mean anything," Eleanor told Nick sotto voce. "I don't remember anyone's cars. Even my friends'. They always seem to buy new ones as soon as I'm used to them."

Leacock thumbed through his notebook. "Here we are, sir. A dark grey Hillman Minx, it was, not well kept up, dent and a bit of rust on the mudguard. Oldish, though I couldn't give the exact year." He gave the licence number, however. "London registration."

Scumble actually smiled. "Good man! Did you notice who was in it?"

"Two in the front, sir, but the sun was shining off the windshield and I can't say was they male or female, the way some grow their hair these days." He smoothed his own short crop self-consciously. "I couldn't describe 'em to save my life, let alone swear to their faces."

"Never mind. Could there have been more than two? Someone bent over in the backseat, out of sight, perhaps?"

"Well, sir, if they was out of sight, I wouldn't know. Maybe there was and maybe there wasn't."

"All right." The inspector jumped up, energy renewed. "At least we've got something solid to go on now. A lead to follow.

We can get the owner's name and start a search for the car. This is where the press can come in handy." He was halfway out of the door before he turned his head to call back over Leacock's shoulder, "Thanks, Mrs Trewynn."

As the door shut behind the two policemen, she said tartly to Nick, "Well! If I had further information for him, once again I'd have been cut off before I had a chance to pass it on. Nick, he says the murderer came back last night. You didn't hear anything?"

"Not a whisper. Earlier I had the *Symphonie Fantastique* on very loud, as you were away and old Merrick on the other side is deaf as a post. And later I slept like a log after all the excitement of the day. He didn't manage to break in, I take it."

"No. There was a policeman on guard who frightened him off."

"Does Scumble think he might come back again? Why don't you stay on at the vicarage?"

"Dearly as I love Joce," Eleanor said guiltily, "I don't think I can stand it. There will be guards again tonight. I'll be all right."

THIRTEEN

When the phone call came, Megan was attempting to turn Scumble's scribbled notes into a moderately coherent typed report. It was not an occupation she would have chosen, given her druthers. She had pointed out to the inspector that she was not a typist. However, the typists had both gone home for the night, and Scumble himself had to report in person to the superintendent.

Since the super was already half an hour late for a dinner party, on the whole Megan preferred her own task, however demeaning. But she was not a typist. She was searching in her desk drawer for the little bottle of Tippex white-out when the phone rang.

"Pencarrow here."

"It's CID Scotland Yard for the inspector."

"He's with the super. Scotland Yard! You'd better put it through to them, Nancy."

"Not bloody likely—pardon my French. I'm not going to be responsible for his majesty missing the soup as well as the hors d'oeuvres. Don't be wet, Megan, you can handle it. You worked for the Met, didn't you?"

"T Division, not the Yard."

"Close enough. Half a mo. Sir? DI Scumble is unavailable. I'm putting you through to DS Pencarrow, who's assisting Mr Scumble with the case."

"Pencarrow here," Megan said quickly, to prevent the caller assuming she was a man.

"Well, well, well, our little Meggie. Detective *Sergeant*, no less. Doing well for yourself down in the western wilds, are you?"

Only one person on the force had ever called her Meggie, first patronising, then teasing, then with affection—and then not at all. On the phone, it was hard to tell what his present tone meant. If anything.

Megan strove for casualness. "Quite nicely, thank you, Ken. And you've transferred to the Yard? Congratulations. You've got some information for us?"

"You seem to have found something we've been looking for. What's all this about a dragon's hoard of jewelry discovered in a charity shop?"

"We've got one. You want one?"

"Your description matches the proceeds of a robbery with violence, City of London jeweller's, last Friday evening."

"Friday!" Megan was concerned. Admittedly their list had been compiled only today, but someone here in Launceston ought to have noticed the similarity with the Yard's list of stolen property.

"Not to worry." He'd always had an irritating ability to guess what was on her mind. "Your lot hasn't dropped the ball. The jeweller—"

"Name?"

"Donaldson. Wilfred Donaldson. He was roughed up quite badly and couldn't remember what was taken till yesterday. Division did the rounds of London fences before handing the whole mess over to us. Our list was just about to go out when yours came in. What's your excuse?"

"Excuse?"

"Word is that a body was found in the same shop on Wednesday morning. This is Thursday night."

Megan had no intention of trying to explain Aunt Nell. If Aunt Nell was explicable, which she was by no means certain was the case. "We didn't find the loot till this morning," she said vaguely, "and then we weren't sure the gems were real. By the time we had a jeweller value them—"

"Yes, well, never mind. They'll have to be identified by Donaldson. We'll send someone to pick them up. There won't be any trouble over that at your end, will there?"

"Shouldn't think so. My guv'nor'll probably be glad to see them go. We haven't got your facilities for storing valuables. Did Donaldson manage to give you a description of his assailant? We're not absolutely sure the jewels are connected to the murder, but we have to work on that assumption."

"He said there were two of them. Masked, of course, the usual nylon stockings, so he couldn't identify them, but for what it's worth, they were both on the tall side and hefty, and well-dressed, gloves and all. Bully-boys in business suits. Apart from the stockings, that is. Well-spoken, but brutal. The doc suspects knuckledusters were used."

"Damn. What we've got looks more like a sneak-thief. And not a very successful one, at that."

"Pity. Looks as if he must have pinched the goods from our pair and run for it—and got caught. He must have hidden the stuff well for them to have left without it."

"Well, not exactly." Megan had no intention of telling him about Aunt Nell.

"No? You'd better send me a report."

"That's up to the super, Ken, you know that."

"Special favour?" he wheedled.

"It's up to the super. I'm sure he'll pass on all necessary info, and I'll tell the DI you'd like a full report. Who's in charge at your end?"

She took down the name of the detective inspector in charge of the robbery investigation. That meant Ken was still a sergeant. She couldn't help feeling a mean satisfaction. Still, he was only a couple of years older than her. Being a man, he'd probably make chief inspector while she was still a sergeant. She'd probably retire as a sergeant in twenty years.

"It seems we're on the same case again, Meggie—oops, sorry, Megan, just like the old days. You'd better have our direct number." He gave it to her, adding, "Keep in touch, won't you."

Professionally, of course. "We'll expect someone to pick up the jewels tomorrow, right? You'd better let us know his name in advance, once someone's been assigned."

"Will do. Or I might just come myself," he said, and rang off.

Bugger him, Megan thought. If he came, she'd make sure to be elsewhere.

She glanced at the wall clock. Not too late to ring the vicarage and give Aunt Nell the news about the jewelry. With luck Scumble would be stuck with the super for a while yet.

The Reverend Stearns answered the phone. "Good evening," he said courteously. "This is the vicar, or Mr Stearns, if you prefer. I really don't mind either way. Can I help you?"

"Good evening . . . er . . . Vicar. This is Megan Pencarrow. May I speak to my aunt, please."

"Aunt?" He sounded anxious and uncertain, as if he'd never heard the word before. "Ah, you must be one of Jocelyn's nieces."

Megan was sorry to spoil his pleasure in reaching this reasonable conclusion. "No, actually, Vicar. Mrs Trewynn's. She's staying with you."

"Oh, yes, but . . . I don't think . . . You'd better talk to Jocelyn. Oh dear, I think she's left for the Mothers' Union meeting . . . No, here she is." His voice continued more faintly as he turned away from the phone. "A Miss Pencarrow, Joce. Or Mrs? Mrs Trewynn's niece . . . ?"

"It's Megan, dear, the detective."

"Oh *yes*," said the vicar with heartfelt relief. "She asked for her aunt." Into the phone, he said, "God bless, my dear."

"Thank you, Vicar."

"Megan!" Mrs Stearns greeted her. "Didn't that man tell you? He let her go back to her flat."

"No, he didn't happen to mention it." Megan was annoyed, though not surprised. "I'm in Launceston. I'll try to ring to remind her to lock her door, but in case I don't have time—the inspector will be back any moment—or she's out walking the dog or something, would you mind—"

"Of course not. That's a good idea. In fact, I'll make sure Nicholas checks that she actually does lock up, downstairs as well."

"Thank you, Mrs Stearns." She hesitated. "She told you about . . . what was in her safe, didn't she?"

"Naturally," the vicar's wife said stiffly. "I had to know since it was connected with the shop."

"I'm not saying she shouldn't have. I just wanted to be sure. . . . The thing is, we've now discovered that the stuff was stolen from a shop in London. I'm afraid LonStar won't be able to keep it."

"That's no surprise. I never really thought we would. Eleanor was too sanguine. The unfortunate youth stole it, I suppose, and quarrelled with his confederates?"

"He wasn't actually one of the robbers, it seems. The description is quite different. But I mustn't say more, Mrs Stearns." She didn't actually know much more. "I just didn't want Aunt Nell to go on hoping it's a generous donation, so if you could break it to her . . . ?"

"I will, though not till the morning, I'm afraid. I'm just leaving for a meeting. But I'll have Timothy ring Nicholas about locking up."

"Thanks so much. I'm sure she'll be all right. It's just that—Oh, the inspector's coming. I must ring off. But Mrs Stearns, suppose they believe the loot is still on the premises? We have a couple of men out there but all the same, I wish her guard dog were a little larger!"

In spite of the Stearnses' kindness, Eleanor was happy to be back in her own flat. Stretching her culinary skills to the limit, she grilled a lamb chop for supper and ate it at her desk so that she could look out at the lighthouse blinking—two flashes, pause, three flashes, longer pause—against the last purple glow of sunset over the headland. Then she fed Teazle and took her downstairs for her final run.

The night was mild and clear. Overhead a million stars shone. The air smelt sweetly of gorse, with the musky scent of blackthorn blossom and a tang of seaweed. In the quiet, Eleanor could hear the slap of waves against the quay. Nick was in, his upstairs window a bright rectangle. He usually had music playing in the evenings, but perhaps he was turning over a record, she thought.

She strolled up the path, past the back of the row of shops and cottages, while Teazle scuffled around in the scrub. The dog gave one short, sharp bark. Perhaps she had found the lurking policeman, but if so, she quickly decided he was a friend. A few windows were lit, some with the eerie blue glow of televisions. Voices reached her, and snatches of music, but no one else was about. Coming this way, the burglars had faced little risk of being seen or heard.

At the end of the row she turned back. Teazle rejoined her as she reached her own back door. Nick was listening to the second half of Beethoven's *Pastoral* now. Eleanor had never had much opportunity for listening to classical music, but she did recognise that. The shepherds' hymn of thanksgiving after the storm exactly suited her mood—

—Until she heard her phone ringing upstairs. Cursing the tyranny of machines, in ordinary times she would have let it ring and assumed the caller would ring back later if it were important. In view of recent events, she hurried in and ran up the stairs, only to discover that she had relocked the flat door behind her when she went out, and left the keys in the downstairs door when she came in.

As soon as she started back down, the ringing stopped.

Teazle sat at the bottom, regarding her with a bewildered look. Sighing, Eleanor continued down, took her keys from the back door and closed it, returned upstairs, and unlocked her flat door. The dog stayed at the foot of the stairs, watching her as if uncertain of the next move in the game. Eleanor called her and she scuttled up.

During the course of these manoeuvres, Eleanor had been vaguely aware of Nick's telephone ringing next door. It stopped after a couple of rings, so she assumed he had answered it and thought no more about it.

A few minutes later came the sound of someone bounding up her stairs two at a time and knocking vigorously on her door. She was filling her hot water bottle, so she called, "Come in!" then wondered whether she had locked the door.

Nick came in, jingling her keys in midair. "My dear Eleanor, I've just received a frantic phone call from the vicar, who seems to be convinced the bad guys have got you."

"Oh dear, that must have been him calling." She squeezed the air from the hot water bottle and screwed in the top. "I heard the phone but couldn't get to it in time. But why on earth did he want to talk to me? I mean, rather than Joce."

"She's at some meeting or other, I gather. But don't change the subject. The bad guys, if so minded, could have got you easily. These were in the flat door up here, and you'd left the downstairs door unlocked."

"I refuse to believe that the vicar said anything whatsoever about 'bad guys.'"

"Well, no, not in so many words. I can't remember: Midianites? They were bad guys, weren't they? Or could it have been worshippers of Baal? Or simply the forces of evil, perhaps? At any rate, I was adjured to make all haste to rescue you from their toils."

"Much ado about nothing." Eleanor's friends had no conception of the dangers she had faced in troubled parts of the world, because she didn't like to talk about such things. In spite of the murder, she couldn't really believe she wasn't perfectly safe here in England, in the quiet village, in her cosy cottage. "I'd better ring up and tell him I'm perfectly all right. I don't really believe the burglars will come back again. Whatever Mr Scumble says, surely they must realise that the police have taken the jewelry."

"I would remind you that it wasn't taken into custody till today. "

"And the police are watching front and back."

"I presume Mrs Stearns doesn't know about them, or she didn't tell the vicar, or he didn't grasp the fact. In any case, he didn't mention it, and I haven't seen any sign of them."

"They're supposed to keep out of sight, so as not to tip off the bad guys."

"Then they're doing a good job of that, at least. The one at the back must be under a gorse bush. There isn't really anywhere to hide at the front, in the street, though, so he can't be close enough to be useful in an emergency. So if you wish your friends to retain their sanity, you will contrive to lock your doors until the police have caught these particular bad guys."

"I don't leave them unlocked on purpose."

"I know. That's why I've been sent to make sure they're secured."

"Well, since you're here, would you like some cocoa? I was just going to make a cup."

"I'd adore some cocoa."

"You'll have to make it. I'm going to pop this into my bed and then phone the vicar."

Nick laughed. "Yes'm."

"Everything's ready. Just find yourself another mug."

When she came down, she checked that he was keeping an eye on the heating milk to make sure it didn't boil over, then she dialled the vicarage. The phone rang several times before it was answered.

"Vicar, this is Eleanor."

"Ah, hm, Eleanor?" he said uncertainly.

"Eleanor Trewynn. You sent Nick Gresham over to make sure I was all right?"

"Ah, yes, Mrs Trewynn. And are you?"

"Am I . . . ? Oh, all right. Yes, perfectly, thank you. There's really no need to worry about me."

"Jocelyn had a telephone call from someone . . . a police officer, could it be? Yes, of course, your niece."

"Megan?"

"Er, yes. She seemed to be under the impression, if I'm not mistaken, that you were still staying here. At the vicarage."

Eleanor didn't want to confuse the poor man still further by asking why Megan hadn't rung her at home. No doubt she'd been in a hurry. But if she believed Eleanor was still at the vicarage, she wouldn't have had any reason to remind her to lock her doors, so her call must have had some other purpose.

Jocelyn had been in a hurry, also, to get to her meeting. Goodness knows how many messages had been lost in transit. She could only hope none were urgent. She was tired of the whole business.

She thanked the vicar once more for his concern and said good-night.

Nick brought her cocoa and sat down with his own on the other side of the fireplace. Eleanor had lit a small fire of driftwood earlier. Nick put another small log on. It crackled satisfyingly, flickering with multi-coloured flames.

"Lilac for potassium and green for sodium," Nick said reflectively, gazing into the fire. "Or vice versa. Or possibly neither. Chemistry was not my best subject at school."

"I'd have thought you'd remember colours, if nothing else."

"I remember coloured flames, just not their significance. People do expect one to remember the most uninteresting things."

"Like locking doors," Eleanor said dryly, "and where one put one's keys."

"Yes, but I wasn't getting at you, honestly. I have no difficulty understanding why you forget. Which isn't to say I shall leave without making sure you lock up. I promised the vicar, and by proxy Mrs Stearns, terrifying woman."

"I don't believe for a moment that she terrifies you."

"You'd be surprised. She'd never forgive me if the burglars came back and walked in without even having to pick the lock. Not that I think there's much danger of them returning." He sipped his cocoa. "You know, horrible as this has been for you, as far as I'm concerned it's been extremely good for business. People come in to ask me what's going on next door and, except for the reporters, most haven't the cheek to walk out without looking round. Having got that far, a few find my work irresistible, or more likely they want something to prove they weren't just being nosy. Mostly they've been buying the cheapest things they can find, the flower paintings, but I've sold five landscapes in two days."

"It's an ill wind—"

"And every cloud has a silver lining. It's a pity LonStar can't take advantage of it."

"I suppose so, though in some ways I'm glad we can't. But Nick, you haven't been giving people information, have you?"

"Nothing more than they can read in the papers," he reassured her, "recast in my own words. I don't want the Scumble descending on me like a ton of bricks, believe me. Even if they don't learn anything new, they like to hear it from the horse's mouth. And now that's enough proverbs and clichés for one evening. If you've finished your cocoa, you can just come down and let me listen to the sound of the back-door lock turning."

He took both mugs to the kitchen, put them in the sink, and ran cold water into them.

"Thank you," Eleanor said. "Stay, Teazle, you don't need another outing." She opened the door.

There was a jingling sound behind her and Nick laughed. "Here, haven't you forgotten something?" He handed her the keys.

FOURTEEN

In spite of everyone's worries for her safety, Eleanor slept much more soundly in her own bed than she had the night before at the vicarage. She woke to the clink of milkbottles outside and the sun glancing in aslant.

Even if it woke her early, she did like morning sun in the bedroom, she thought, lying there warm as an egg in its cosy. It was rare enough in this part of the world to be a treat.

"*Wuff?*" Teazle climbed over her knees and came to lick her on the nose.

"Time to go out, girl? All right, just let me put on my dressing gown and slippers."

Teazle scuttered down to the flat door and waited patiently. For once Eleanor found the keys right where they were supposed to be, on a hook in the kitchen. They went on down to the ground floor. Unlocking and opening the back door, Eleanor shivered in a brisk breeze off the sea. On the headland the sun shone, though. It was a perfect day for walking, and she hadn't had a proper walk in two days, only up and down the village street.

"We'll go to High Cliff later," she told the Westie's rear end, her front end being invisible under a blackthorn bush, still leafless but covered in white blossom. Somehow Teazle usually avoided getting scratched or pricked, though once she had come out with a thorn in her paw. "No one to see me practising, and plenty of rabbits for you."

At the word *rabbits*, Teazle backed out, stumpy tail wagging furiously. If a cold, stiff, thoroughly uncomfortable policeman was hiding in the thickets somewhere, she didn't bother to sniff him out.

They went in to breakfast.

Eleanor had just poured a second cup of coffee and was reaching for the telephone to tell Jocelyn her plans when it rang.

"Joce. You beat me to it."

"I've just heard from the police that we're allowed to reopen the shop today."

"That's wonderful. But you'll have to warn the volunteers." Eleanor explained what Nick had told her about the sensation-seekers. "You're the only one who actually has any inside information, but everyone had better be careful what they say."

"Luckily I'm on today," Jocelyn said austerely. "Mrs Davies may not know anything, but I wouldn't count on her to discourage gossip and speculation. On the other hand, it wouldn't surprise me if one or two don't want to come in today. Squeamish! Just let me see who's scheduled—"

"You'll manage everything perfectly as usual, Joce, I'm sure. I was thinking I might as well go out on my collecting round."

"Yes, you'd better. I was about to tell you, Megan rang last night to say that the jewels have been identified as stolen, so I'm afraid we have no claim on them."

"Not even if the thief had a change of heart and decided to give them to LonStar? No, I suppose not." Eleanor couldn't help being disappointed. With a sigh, she remembered her joy when she first saw what she had assumed was an exceedingly generous donation. "Well, it can't be helped."

"Speaking of the thief, or rather thieves, apparently the jeweller who was robbed gave a description of the men who attacked them, and they were nothing like the murder victim. Goodness knows where he sprang from."

"Poor boy! How worried his family must be! If he wasn't one of the robbers, perhaps he was trying to foil them."

"Hah," Jocelyn snorted. "More likely trying to double-cross them. I daresay he followed them down from London."

"Oh, London! It was stolen in London?"

"So Megan told me, and I suppose she knows."

"Well, that's a relief."

"A relief? Why is it a relief?"

"Oh, I don't know, Joce. Just that London's far away and somehow one expects that sort of thing to happen in big cities. I wouldn't like to think of someone local being involved."

"You can't possibly have forgotten," said Jocelyn, "that the murder took place in our own stockroom?"

"But if he followed the thieves from London—"

"That is pure speculation."

It was Jocelyn's speculation, not hers, thought Eleanor, but it wasn't worth arguing about. However illogical, she still felt relieved that the robbery had taken place in the distant city. "I'm glad it was a jeweller who was robbed."

"What on earth do you mean, Eleanor? What possible difference can it make?"

"Surely being robbed is an occupational hazard for jewellers. Suppose it had been family heirlooms that the owner was very attached to for personal reasons, not because of the value."

" 'Lay not up for yourselves treasures upon earth, where moth and rust doth corrupt, and where thieves break through and steal.' "

When Jocelyn started quoting the Bible, Eleanor refused to compete, though she was sometimes tempted when an apt line from the Bhagavad Gita, or a saying of Lao Tzu, or even an African proverb came to mind. "Did Megan tell you anything else?" she asked.

"No, she had to hang up because she heard that man coming."

"So it wasn't an official notification. We'll have to pretend not to know when we see Mr Scumble next or we'll get Megan into trouble. I take it the vicar didn't tell Nick, or he'd have told me last night."

"I didn't tell Timothy. It would only confuse him."

"I daresay. Nick said he's not telling inquisitive customers anything beyond what he's read in the papers. I'd better buy one and see what they're saying."

"You'd better borrow Nicholas's. If you walk into the news-agent's, everyone will be pestering you for the inside story."

"It all depends who 'everyone' is. I don't mind the neighbours. Are there still a lot of reporters about?"

"I think they all went off to the news conference that man held last night. I shouldn't think they'd be back. They must have just about all the pictures of the LonStar shop they could use in months. Not to mention the ones of you ducking behind Megan."

"Oh, Joce, no! When I think of all the times I've tried in vain to get the newspapers interested in what we do at LonStar! The news conferences where no one turned up! If any reporters come back and approach me, I'll refuse to talk about anything but LonStar's work."

"You can try. I must get going. Some of our volunteers haven't got telephones. Oh, Eleanor, will you leave a list of places you're going collecting, just in case the police decide they need to get in touch with you?"

"All right, though it won't be very exact. Unless people let us know they have something to be picked up, I often call in at random."

"Do your best," Jocelyn commanded. "See you later."

Eleanor went to her desk, found an old envelope, and did her best to make the required list. She hoped Jocelyn didn't expect precise directions. Some of the places she called at regularly were hidden away in folds of the country, on lanes that were little more than cart-tracks, not marked on any road map she had ever seen. Some, even the postman probably didn't know about; the inhabitants would pick up any letters at the nearest post office. Some, she suspected, were ancient cottages renovated without troubling the undoubtedly overworked county council for permits. She found them by chance or instinct, and returned to those that welcomed her by memory.

She had a good sense of direction and the lie of the land. Her memory was perfectly good for things that mattered, she thought, as she conscientiously locked the door of the flat behind her and the dog.

They emerged into the street and Eleanor again locked the door behind her. Few people were about so early in the day. Two housewives with baskets on their arms stood chatting outside the bakery opposite. Mrs Chin was sweeping the pavement in front of the restaurant. Farther down, Mr Dickinson was setting out boxes of local spinach and Jaffa oranges from Israel in front of his greengrocer's shop. A young mother with a pushchair came down the opposite hill, from the direction of the school, not so much pushing as hanging on tight to stop the pushchair running away from her.

"Heel, Teazle."

Mrs Chin gave Eleanor a shy wave as she passed, on her way up the hill to the newsagent's. She went in. Mr Chin was buying cigarettes. "And I'll take some Smarties for the kids," he said, "but don't tell the missus. Yeah, just a tube, not the box. Mustn't spoil 'em. Morning, Mrs Trewynn."

"Morning, Mrs Trewynn," echoed Mr Irvin, the shop owner. "Morning, Teazle."

"Good morning," Eleanor said with a nod to each man.

"What can I do for you this fine morning?"

"I'd like the *Guardian*, please, Mr Irvin, if you have one left."

"Sure you wouldn't rather have the *Sketch*? They got a good photo, and spelt your name right, too."

Eleanor blenched. "My photo's in the papers?"

"Course. Only nacheral when it was you found the body. Here." He took a copy of the *Daily Sketch* from the rack. "Page five, innit, Charlie?"

Mr Chin, born in Limehouse and christened Edward in honour of the Prince of Wales, was known to his friends as Charlie, in honour of the film character whose surname he didn't quite share. "Page four," he corrected, leaning against the counter.

"Right you are." Irvin folded back the paper. "Look here, Mrs Trewynn."

The blurred photograph could have been anyone from Myra Hindley to the Queen, except that the Queen would have been wearing a hat. Unfortunately, underneath was the caption, "Mrs Eleanor Trewynn, helping police with their enquiries." It had been taken when Eleanor was on her way from the vicarage to the flat to tell DI Scumble about the jewelry. Her arm was clearly in the grip of DS Pencarrow, and no one could have told from the picture that Megan was protecting her from the reporters rather than foiling an escape attempt.

"Oh dear!"

Charlie Chin pointed at another photo, lower down the page. "Here's the bloke you found. They're asking for anyone that reckernises him to come forward. Cleaned him up nice, they have. What I heard was, his mother wouldn't've known him."

He and Irvin both gave Eleanor interrogative looks.

"That's not true," she protested. "Though I'm glad his poor mother didn't see him. I hope someone recognises the photo and breaks the news to her before she sees it."

The two men stood in solemn silence for a moment, as if at a funeral.

The newsagent quickly regained his habitual cheeriness. "And here you are in the *Guardian*—No, I tell a lie. They didn't put your picture in the *Guardian* at all!" he said indignantly. "Just your name, spelt with an *i* and one *n*. Must be the *Telegraph* I was thinking of. Let's take a look—"

"Oh no, thank you, please don't bother. I'll take the *Guardian*."

"Go ahead and take the *Sketch*, too, on the house. Business ain't never been better since you found the dead burglar. You wouldn't believe the people that haven't read a paper in years coming in to get the latest. If you don't mind me asking, *did* you help the police with their enquiries?"

"Yes. Yes, as a matter of fact, I helped them quite a lot." Eleanor looked at their expectant faces and went on quickly, "But I can't talk about it. Sorry."

"Oh well, never mind, eh?" He turned to take a large jar off a shelf. "Here goes, Teazle, here's your aniseed ball." He tossed the reddish brown sweet.

Teazle missed the catch and it rolled across the floor like a small marble, the dog in hot pursuit, her short legs skittering on the slick floor. She cornered it under a display of magazines but couldn't get it out with either nose or paw. The men thought her antics uproariously funny.

This was a regular game the Westie always lost. Eleanor was pretty sure Irvin rigged it. He was the local darts champion and could probably have bunged the sweetie into Teazle's open mouth from twenty feet. Besides, she was usually good at catching.

Still, he had his fun. She didn't mind being laughed at. And she always got her treat in the end. Charlie, still chuckling, went over and fished it out for her and it went down with a couple of crunches that made Eleanor wince. She hated to think what it was doing to the little dog's teeth.

"Thanks," she said anyway.

"Oh, by the way," said Irvin as she turned to go, "when's the shop reopening?"

"Today. Mrs Stearns just told me."

"Good. I got some stuff for you."

"Summat that fell off the back of a lorry?" Chin asked derisively.

Irvin gave him a withering look. "Come off it, Charlie. I wouldn't land Mrs Trewynn in that kind of mess even if there wasn't swarms of coppers all over the place."

"Hey, just kidding. Tell you what, Mrs Trewynn, I'll make you up a couple of posters to stick up saying it's back to business as usual." As well as his expertise in Chinese cookery, Chin was a talented calligrapher—in the Roman alphabet. He had never learnt Chinese characters.

Eleanor was thanking them when the doorbell jangled and in came the two women who had been chatting in front of the bakery. Both put on unconvincing expressions of surprise. One said, "Oh, Mrs Trewynn, you're here!"

She wasn't acquainted with either beyond saying "Good morning" if they came face to face in the street. As far as she knew, neither had ever donated to LonStar or volunteered her time. All they wanted was the latest gossip about the murder.

But Eleanor was never one to let an opportunity pass. "I've just been telling these gentlemen that the shop will reopen today. I'm sure you'll be delighted that we're able to accept donations again. Now if you'll just tell me when it will be convenient for me to pick up—Oh, Mr Irvin, I knew there was something else I needed. One of those sixpenny notebooks, please."

She felt in her purse, but Irvin, grinning like the Cheshire cat, announced, "Consider it a donation, Mrs Trewynn. You'd better take the shilling one. It has a pencil attached."

With the men watching gleefully, she wrote down the women's names and addresses, grudgingly given, and the best time to call. "Perfect," she said. "How kind of you. Well, I really must be on my way now. I'm collecting in the country today."

"Back to work for me," said Charlie Chin, and escorted her out so that the women had no chance to question her.

As they stepped into the street, she heard behind her Irvin enquiring, "Now, what can I do for you ladies this morning?"

"Got 'em in a corner!" Chin congratulated her. "Them two, they're the gossipingest and the tightfistedest old cats in the village. You don't get anything out of 'em, you just let me know. I'll see they never hear the end of it."

"Oh no, Mr Chin, that would never do. You can't shame people into caring. It was very naughty of me to put them on the spot like that, but the alternative seemed to be to let them put me on the spot with questions I mustn't answer. Thank you for helping me to escape."

"Any time." With a wave, he crossed the street and disappeared into his restaurant.

Eleanor looked cautiously around before proceeding down the hill. Usually she enjoyed living in a small community where she was likely to meet an acquaintance every time she stepped out of doors, but it was a mixed blessing. At present she would have been happy to swap it for a large, anonymous town where no one would recognise her—certainly not from that terrible photograph in the paper!

She made it down as far as the LonStar shop without being accosted. Though she had intended to go up to the flat to study the newspapers, the *Guardian* at least, she decided to keep going while the going was good. Once she reached the car, she'd be safe.

The old stone bridge over the nameless stream was due to be replaced with concrete as soon as the funds were allotted. Built a hundred years ago, in place of a ford, it was little wider than the farm and fish carts for which it was designed. In the tourist season it caused endless back-ups of traffic. In quieter times, the wide walls were a popular seat for herring gulls and for elderly fishermen who had once battled the sea in mackerel smacks or crabbers.

When Eleanor reached it, old Mr Penmadden was there, wizened and weathered, basking in the early sunshine but bundled up warm in his reefer jacket over a seaman's blue jersey, peaked cap on his head. She couldn't pass him without a word.

Penmadden had a Cornish accent as softly opaque as a sea mist, but Eleanor had years of practice at understanding unorthodox English, besides having grown up in the Duchy. As long as he didn't stray too far into the wilds of dialect, she understood him perfectly well. Few people took the trouble.

"Lovely morning, Mr Penmadden," Eleanor greeted him.

He gave a sharp nod. "Aye, that it be. And a good thing, too. These lads nowadays—" He gestured contemptuously at the boats in the harbour, preparing to set out with the ebbing tide before they got stranded on the muddy sand. "They can't cope wi' a spot o' weather, for all their motors and their wireless radios! Least bit of a blow and they go running down to Padstow for shelter. In my day . . ."

Eleanor, realising she'd let herself in for a new *Rime of the Ancient Mariner*, sat down beside him. The stone struck chilly even through her tracksuit. He fixed her with a faded but still alert blue eye and said unexpectedly, "I heard tell as how you found a corpse."

"That's right, I'm afraid," she admitted, resigning herself to questions instead of reminiscences.

"Must 'a' bin a nasty shock for a nice lady like you."

"It was, a bit."

"Though living in furrin parts like you done, I daresay you seen the like afore. Ah, there's many a tale I could tell about pulling drownded corpses out o' the sea."

The Rime of the Ancient Mariner with an emphasis on corpses didn't bear thinking about, though Eleanor vaguely recalled Coleridge having a good deal to say on the subject. Wasn't there a working crew of dead sailors at some point in the poem?

Old Penmadden surprised her again. "But you'll 'a' had enough o' corpses for now. Going out in your little car, are you?"

"Yes. The police are letting us open the shop today, so I'm going out collecting."

"You come round our place later, my lover. I found a couple o' they glass ball floats t'other day. Harry up the Wreckers wanted 'em for his lounge bar. I told him he can buy 'em from your shop, same as any Christian."

Eleanor was touched, knowing that the pensioner could have sold the floats or exchanged them for several pints. Thanking him, she promised to listen to his stories of shipwrecks and men overboard at a later date, when the recent unhappy event had faded from her memory.

He winked at her. "Don't tell my girl. She don't like me talking about such. Digging up dead men's bones, she calls it. What I say is, they didn't ought to be forgot."

A good deal could be said for either point of view. Eleanor promised not to tell his daughter, who was her own age if she was a day, and went on her way.

On the far side of the bridge, upstream, the only flat piece of ground in Port Mabyn stretched along the bank of the brook for a hundred yards or so. It was safe from development because in the winter it was often under a foot or two of water. That was not a problem for the car park, as visitors were few and far between at that season. At spring tides with an onshore wind, or at a forecast of heavy rain likely to swell the stream, Eleanor would drive the Incorruptible up to one of the car parks at the top of either hill. At present the ground was somewhat soggy, but the daisy-starred turf was thick enough to reduce the hazard of getting stuck in mud.

Teazle scampered over to sniff at the rocks set along the edge of the stream. Eleanor had scarcely set foot on the grass when she was hailed.

"Mrs Trewynn, can you spare a moment?" called Mrs Davies.

Turning, Eleanor stifled a sigh. She wasn't afraid the Methodist minister's wife would start interrogating her about the murder, but there was no knowing what she wanted. A keen worker at the shop, she resented playing second fiddle to Jocelyn, although she hadn't half Joce's organising ability. Worse, she regarded the work as an extension of her or her husband's "mission." They had nearly lost several volunteers who objected to being asked to pass out a Methodist tract with every purchase. Eleanor had had to intervene between the vicar's wife and the minister's wife, an uncomfortable position she hated.

LonStar was a strictly secular organisation for any number of excellent reasons. They worked in countries with a wide variety of religious traditions, and the last thing they wanted was to have their efforts impeded by any suspicion of proselytising.

Likewise, many of their employees and volunteers were people of strong faith, who naturally would not put up with being preached at by those of differing faith. Nor did the non-believers among them care to be regarded as if their sincerity were suspect.

All in all, it was best to keep religion out of the picture, but there were always some, like Mrs Davies, who found it difficult.

"Huw and I have been praying for you," she said in a sombre tone. She was a young woman, not more than a couple of years older than Megan, but her mousy demeanour and her penchant for drab, old-fashioned clothes—cheap but new, not from LonStar—made her seem middle-aged.

"That's very kind of you. Don't you think, though, that the murderer is more in need of your prayers?" Eleanor immediately wished the words unsaid. Thank heaven at least she hadn't suggested prayers for the victim. It was only Catholics who believed in praying for the dead, wasn't it? She refused to become embroiled in a theological argument. "Did Jocelyn tell you yet?" she went on hastily. "The police are letting us open the shop today."

"Yes, Mrs Stearns telephoned. It's her day today. It's my day for visiting."

"You'll be at the shop tomorrow, though?"

"Y-yes. Oh, Mrs Trewynn, I don't think I can bear to go into the stockroom!"

"He was taken away long ago, you know. And if there are any signs at all left, I'm quite sure Mrs Stearns will clean everything up today. There will be nothing to see."

"No, but . . ." She shuddered. "He was struck down. What if his spirit . . ." Her voice trailed away.

"Oh dear, you believe in ghosts?"

"No, of course not. But just suppose . . . I mean, no one really knows, do they?"

"It's one of those unknowables, yes. Perhaps your husband

could conduct an exorcism?" Though what Jocelyn would say to that beggared the imagination.

Fortunately, Mrs Davies exclaimed, "Oh no! Methodists don't . . . You won't tell Huw I was talking about gh—spirits, will you?"

"Good gracious, no!" Eleanor promised. "The less said the better. I don't see why you need go into the stockroom for a while, though. You're in charge. You can send someone else back if anything's needed. You're supposed to have two people on the premises at all times." Which was another bone of contention, as the rule didn't apply to Jocelyn. But with luck, Mrs Davies's helpers would be less imaginative than she was. "Now, I'm on my way to get the car out. Can I give you a lift anywhere?"

"Oh no, thank you. I'm just going up there." She gestured at the houses spreading up the hill away from the street, inaccessible to any vehicle bigger than the vicar's moped.

"Goodbye, then. I'll see you tomorrow I expect. Come on, Teazle."

Ghosts! Just what she needed.

FIFTEEN

When Megan arrived at her desk in the Launceston police station on Friday morning, it was already covered with a blizzard of paper. As she dropped aghast onto her chair, Jennifer, the day-shift switchboard girl, brought in another two memos.

"Bloody hell, Jen, what *is* this lot?"

"You asked for it." She perched on the corner of the desk. "Every daily had the victim's photo in it," she said. "And most of 'em the car's licence plate, too, though we haven't had any calls on that yet. But I reckon twenty-five percent of readers all over the country think they recognise your bloke, and a quarter of those rang up their nearest cop-shop right away and another quarter will ring in the next day or two, and the other half won't bother."

"Thank heaven for the other half! At least, I hope they're not the ones who really do know him. I mean"—she waved at the desk—"these can't possibly all be right."

"Photos in the papers are always pretty bad, and it wasn't the greatest to start with, and he didn't have any warts on his nose or birthmarks on his cheeks. Most of these, the caller claimed to have seen him yesterday or the day before, so you can count them out. I tried to keep those on this side of the desk, but it's been a madhouse and the pile fell over twice—Oops, there goes the phone again. Have fun!"

"Thanks, Jen."

Megan stared at her desk, wondering where on earth to start. Then she heard Scumble's voice, speaking to the desk sergeant. It didn't matter so much what she did, she decided, as that when he walked in she should be doing something and give the appearance of knowing what she was doing. She reached for the heap Jennifer had told her were impossible sightings.

The inspector burst into the room. "Driscoll says the—Ye gods, every nut in the kingdom's called in! Hell, if the Great British Public were always this cooperative, we wouldn't have any crimes to solve. What are you doing?"

"I thought I'd start by winnowing out the people who claim to have seen the deceased on Tuesday or Wednesday, sir."

"They're forwarding—? Does every sodding copper in the rest of the country think the Cornish police have nothing to do?"

"Could be they just think we'll want to judge for ourselves?"

"Doesn't look as if we've much choice. When's this laddie from the Yard going to turn up to swipe our jewelry?"

"He didn't give a time, sir."

"Never mind. The super will want to deal with him. Maybe the CC, too. There were murmurs last night about handing over the case to the Yard."

"Oh no!" The prospect of being seconded to assist DS Kenneth Faraday, or worse, to act as liaison between him and DI Scumble, appalled Megan.

"Probably not. We're not doing too badly considering, and I shouldn't think they'd be interested. They have a finger in the pie, though, with this jewel robbery being in their territory. All right, this lot needs dealing with whether or not. Let's get on with it. If you're starting over there, I'll take these." His large hands scooped up a pile of memos and he retired to his own desk, where he sat rustling paper and muttering irritably.

Megan was surprised at how quickly they whittled down the heaps to a manageable level, in spite of a continuing trickle from Jennifer. Besides the obvious impossibilities, there were sightings in Liverpool, Durham, and other northern parts on Monday afternoon. Though these were highly unlikely, they were not quite inconceivable and would have to be kept on file.

Having thus increased the clutter on her desk by dividing one stack into two, Megan moved on to the next lot. She and Scumble worked steadily for some time. She had nearly finished winnowing her last lot when he sat back with a sigh, easing his back.

"Bet you a quid a good half of these didn't look past the long hair. They see that, they think *beatnik*, and the stereotype is all that sticks in their minds." He sighed. "I've got a couple of dozen that'll need to be gone into. How about you?"

She glanced through the remaining three memo sheets, set them aside, and picked up a pile about the same as his. "These seem possible—"

His phone rang and he picked it up. "Scumble here."

Megan could hear Jennifer saying, "Sir, Exeter thinks they may have found your car."

"May have?" Scumble snarled. "Don't they know how to read a number plate?"

"Fits the description—dark grey Hillman Minx in bad repair— but the plates've been removed. They say do you want to send someone over to search the area."

"I could go, sir," Megan suggested. Even slopping around in ditchwater—somehow searches always involved ditches—was preferable to facing Ken.

Maybe she sounded too eager. He gave her a suspicious look, waved at the papers they had just sorted and said, "I need you on the telephone. A couple of uniforms can do it. If it's really ours. Where is the car, Jennifer, and how long has it been there?"

"Exeter station, in their car park. This time of year they let it go for a couple of days before they start to give them grief. So sometime Monday night, Tuesday morning."

"Right. Peters'll have to go to do it over for dabs. Tell him and Farley I want 'em here pronto. But put Exeter through first. I'll have a word with them."

While he talked to someone at the Exeter police, Megan appropriated his final pile of sighting reports and quickly went through them. Based on what he considered worthy of further investigation, a few of hers could be moved to the back burner. By the time he got off the phone, she had whittled down the numbers to something that looked almost feasible. However, a dismaying number of the public-spirited citizens had not provided telephone numbers.

When she pointed this out to the inspector he said, "You'll have to ring back the station that sent us each report and ask them to get further details. If you have any trouble, remind them that this is murder, not a parlour game. Got it?"

"Yes, sir." Megan pulled the telephone towards her.

By lunchtime she had eliminated half the list, was waiting for call-backs on a quarter, had failed to contact several more individuals, and had two real possibilities.

"Both in Bristol, sir," she reported to Scumble. "Doesn't that make it more likely they're the real thing?"

"Could be." He scarcely glanced up from the report he was perusing. His desk, like Megan's, looked as if a blizzard had hit it.

"One's the proprietor of a pub. The other's a tobacconist. He's pretty sure it's a boy who comes—used to come in for cigarette papers but never bought tobacco."

That got his attention. "Sounds like our lad! I just read the forensic report—where is it?" He scrabbled through the detritus. "Traces of cannabis in his clothes, hair, and under his fingernails. The pathologist mentioned it, too, in his system. I didn't take much notice. So many kids smoke the stuff these days. But it's a link."

A pretty tenuous link, Megan thought, wondering what percentage of young men with long hair smoked pot. She didn't say so, nor did she propose that someone, namely herself, ought to go to Bristol and check the only leads they had to the victim's identity.

Her discretion was rewarded.

"Someone'll have to go and talk to these blokes," he growled. "I've got to stick around till this bright spark from the Yard turns up, so you're elected. Likely the tobacconist and the pub are on the wrong side of Bristol so take Dawson."

"I can manage on my own, sir."

"Take Dawson! That's an order, not a suggestion. Let's see, it's quite a drive. You'd better plan on spending the night, in case you actually get something useful out of them and have to follow up. But before you leave, send someone out for pasties for both of us. You stick by the phone in case any of those calls you're waiting for come through."

They were halfway through their pasties, and a couple of phone calls had knocked another two tips off the list, when a rumpus in the town square outside drew them both to their open window. The centre of the square—actually a triangle—was used as a car park, with narrow one-way streets on three sides. The street below the window was blocked by a large van, a rectangular, solid-looking vehicle that the constable on duty was urging to move along please and stop holding up the traffic.

A man in a dark grey suit jumped lithely down from the cab, announcing, "Police business," as he took something from his pocket and held it up for the constable to examine. They couldn't see much of him except his corn-gold hair, trimmed short but which Megan knew, if left to grow, would burst into wild curls.

"DS Faraday, sir."

"From Scotland Yard? Ye gods, they've sent an armoured car! What do the silly buggers think we've got here, the Crown Jewels?"

"We don't actually know what they're worth, sir," said Megan, realising too late that she was giving the inspector the false impression that she cared what he thought of Scotland Yard.

Below, the desk sergeant had come out and added his voice to the dispute. Scumble ignored them. He turned to Megan with a glint in his eye that she instinctively distrusted, though she couldn't guess what it might portend. "Know him, do you?"

"We worked together in T Division before I moved back to Cornwall."

"And now he's at the Yard," Scumble muttered. "Must be highly thought of."

Megan didn't consider it necessary to respond.

"Fancies himself, does he?"

"Well . . ." God's gift to women, that was Ken. ". . . I suppose so." What was the inspector up to? She didn't trust him an inch.

He leant out of the window and shouted down, "Get that bloody van out of the road. Now!" Without waiting to see if he was obeyed, he pulled his head back in, saying gloomily, "Now the super'll be getting complaints about language from all the old biddies."

"Shouldn't be too many about, sir. The shops are closed for lunch. The van's moving."

"You don't care about 'language'?"

He seemed genuinely curious, so she told him, "Compared to what I heard daily in London, it's nothing."

"Ah. We're old-fashioned, here in the country." His voice was more self-satisfied than discontented. He cocked his head at the sound of footsteps running up the stairs. "Here comes the boy wonder."

And that put Ken firmly in his place. Megan faced him without qualms as he knocked on the door and came in. He was as tall and broad-shouldered as the inspector, considerably slimmer, twenty years younger, and all too good-looking.

"DI Scumble? Sorry about that, sir." The boy wonder sounded not in the least repentant. And he had still not managed to get rid of his public school accent. "My driver's used to central London where there's never any parking spaces and we coppers stop wherever we need to. DS Faraday reporting. The Yard sent me to pick up the loot." He looked around as if he expected diamonds and rubies to be spread out on one of the desks. "Oh, hello, Megan."

She nodded in response, as Scumble said frostily, "In this part of the world we expect our drivers to do as they're told."

Before hostilities could progress, Superintendent Bentinck came in. Grey-haired, barely regulation height, thin as a whip, he had a casual manner. However, it was rumoured that the only officer ever to cross swords with him since he attained his present rank had subsequently sought political asylum in Outer Mongolia.

He perched on one corner of Megan's desk, careful not to disarrange her papers.

"This is Detective Sergeant Faraday, sir," said Scumble, "from the Met. He's come to fetch away that jewelry. Superintendent Bentinck," he added curtly to Ken.

"Afternoon, Sergeant. I'm afraid it's not so simple. I've been having a bit of a word with our CC. Given that the Yard's already involved, because of the jeweller who was robbed—What was his name?"

"Donaldson, sir," Megan and Ken both said at once. Ken had a confident, almost gloating gleam in his bright blue eyes.

DI Scumble was seething. It wasn't often he had a chance to get his teeth into a murder, and here it was being taken out of his hands, apparently to be given to a mere sergeant. Major Amboyne, the chief constable, always asked for and followed his superintendents' advice, so Scumble felt betrayed by his own guv'nor.

"We aren't certain yet that the jewels are the same, sir," he pointed out through gritted teeth.

"Very true, Inspector," the super agreed in his mild voice. "Mr Donaldson will have to identify them. But the descriptions do match quite closely, you know. We wouldn't dream of taking the case away from you, especially as the Yard can't spare anyone of appropriate rank—" That was one in the eye for Ken! "—at this point. So they're allowing us to keep DS Faraday as liaison and to assist you and DS Pencarrow in any way he can."

"Thank you, sir," said Scumble. The glint in his eye that Megan distrusted was back. "I'm sure we can make use of his experience."

Bentinck took Ken away to arrange the transfer of the jewelry to the armoured van in the custody of the two uniformed constables he'd brought with him and the private guard hired by Donaldson's insurance company.

"I'd better get going, sir," Megan said to Scumble, gathering up her shoulder-bag and rewrapping the remains of her pasty. "I'll eat this on the way."

"Not so fast! Forget Dawson. You can take Faraday with you."

"Sir! I'd much rather have Dawson."

"So would I. I want the boy wonder out of my hair, and you're the only excuse I can think of."

"But he doesn't know anything about the murder. He'll have to read all the reports."

"You've got the carbons. He can read them in the car, and you can answer any questions he has."

Wonderful, Megan thought gloomily, gathering a huge pile of blurry carbon copies. She'd not only have Ken on her hands, she was going to have to try to explain Aunt Nell to him.

SIXTEEN

"Tell me what this is all about, Meggie," Ken invited, leaning forward. He was stuck in the backseat of the Mini Cooper, thank heaven. The front seat couldn't possibly have accommodated both him and the box of copies of the reports. He had been annoyed when ordered to go to Bristol with her, and furious when he saw all the paperwork he was expected to study en route.

Negotiating traffic in the narrow streets, busy again after the lunch hour, Megan was silent. She wanted to get onto the eastbound A30 before she started what was sure to be a difficult conversation.

Ken apparently took her silence for displeasure. "All right, then, *Megan*. Fill me in on your murder. Please."

The end-of-speed-limit sign passed. "You've got all the info you can possibly need right there," she said.

"But you know what official reports are like. I'll make much more sense of them if I have a grasp of the big picture before I start."

He was right, unfortunately. Where should she start? If she told it right, maybe she could keep Aunt Nell's role out of it, at least until he read the reports. "Well . . . The call came in—"

"For pity's sake, don't make it sound like just another sodding report! Tell it like a story. You used to be good at that."

"And you used to say I ought to quit the police and go and write crime fiction!"

"Perhaps," he said softly, "perhaps I was wrong about that, Meggie—Megan. Perhaps I was wrong about other things, as well."

He couldn't help it, she thought. Put a halfway passable female in his presence and preferably no witnesses within hearing range, and the cajolery started up without any volition on his part. It was too bad it had taken her so long to discover the fact.

At least he wasn't trying to pull seniority on her.

"You can't possibly not have heard anything about it," she said, "so don't blame me if I repeat what you already know. A body was found in the stockroom of a charity shop, first thing Wednesday morning when the place was opened. We haven't managed to identify the victim yet—that's what we're going to Bristol for, we hope—but he was a boy or young man, late teens, scruffy, long hair, pot-smoker. He was found by the person who lives in the flat above the shop."

"That's Mrs Trewynn?"

"I knew you must have read about it! Yes, Eleanor Trewynn, who is not a suspect, I hasten to add. Nor is the manager of the shop, Jocelyn Stearns, the vicar's wife, who was also present when he was found. Far as we can tell, the victim was one of two or more intruders."

"He was killed by the traditional blunt instrument?"

"Not exactly." She explained about the dolphin table, though not the fact that it hadn't been discovered till hours later. He'd find out about the delay when—if—he got around to reading the reports.

"And the jewels are thought to explain his presence. What I don't get is what they were doing in the shop."

"Mrs Trewynn found them in her car. The theory is that the victim and a partner or partners dumped them there while she was walking her dog, perhaps because they were scared by the local constable driving past."

"Which suggests that one or more of them knew who she was, and therefore where to find the loot." No one ever suggested Kenneth Faraday wasn't quick on the uptake. "It also suggests that they may see her as a threat, able to identify them?"

"Yes. We've kept an eye on her and the shop, and one came back the next night, but he was scared off and hasn't been seen since. The trouble is, she knows a hell of a lot of people. Aunt Nell is . . ." Oh damn, damn, damn, exactly what she hadn't intended to say. "Mrs Trewynn does—"

"Hold on a minute! Aunt Nell? Mrs Trewynn is your aunt?"

"As a matter of fact, yes. Though it doesn't make any difference to anything."

"I suppose not, or you'd have been taken off the case. What do you mean by a hell of a lot of people? How many people can a little old lady living in a small Cornish village know?"

"She hasn't always lived there. She spent most of her life travelling all over the world. Asia, Africa—"

"I think Donaldson would have noticed if the men who beat him up and robbed him were Africans."

"I gathered they had stockings over their heads and wore gloves," Megan reminded him tartly.

"Touché." He was grinning, as a glance in the rear-view mirror divulged to her.

"Not that I have any reason to suppose they were foreigners. Aunt Nell's only been in Port Mabyn a couple of years, but she's very well known. For a start, there was an article in the *North*

Cornwall Times when she set up the shop. Two or three of the national dailies picked it up, and I think the *Observer*, too."

"Then there's every customer who's ever entered the shop."

"No, actually. She doesn't help in the shop itself. She's in charge of collecting contributions, goods to sell in the shop, that is. Not just in the village, for miles around. Which is why she was surprised but not absolutely stunned when she found the jewelry in her car. She assumed it was donated by stealth."

With a pause while she negotiated Okehampton traffic, she told him the rest of the story. She glossed over the matter of doors left unlocked, and Ken seemed to accept that as commonplace in the country. Also glossed over was the time-line. She wasn't going to give away Aunt Nell's dilatory disclosure of essential information—such as the very existence of the jewels.

"The car's been found in Exeter?" Ken said as they passed the city sign.

"They think so. Parked at the station."

"Let's go and take a look."

"No. It's bad enough driving through the city centre, without taking an unnecessary detour. From this direction the by-pass doesn't help much, not at this time of year when the centre is only clogged with shoppers, not holiday-makers. Once we get onto the A38 we still have seventy-five miles to go."

"I'll drive for a bit."

"You've got plenty to keep you busy with those reports. Besides, a couple of our chaps are on to the car already. I don't want to look as if I'm checking up on them."

"Perhaps they need checking up on."

"That's up to DI Scumble to decide. I wouldn't want someone telling him we were mucking about in Exeter when he sent us to Bristol."

"That's a point. He might pass it on to that redoubtable superintendent of yours. All right, I'll be good." With a sigh, he started digging into the box.

Along with the rustle of paper, mutterings came from the backseat, but Ken didn't comment aloud on Aunt Nell's vagaries, or anything else for that matter. It wasn't like him to fail to spot discrepancies, nor to miss a chance for a bit of one-upmanship. What was he up to? Megan was too busy wondering to enjoy the drive through the sunlit countryside.

Eleanor did her best to put the distressing events of the past few days out of her mind for the day. No ghosts followed her onto the sunlit cliffs. Seagulls and a lone buzzard were the only witnesses to her slow bends and stretches, her swift gyrations synchronised with sweeping gestures of her arms. The birds were no more interested than was Teazle, who had seen it all before and was herself lost in a paradise of a thousand different smells, ever familiar, ever fresh.

With the kinks worked out of her joints and her skills reinforced, Eleanor walked for miles along the cliff paths above the veridian sea, patched with lapis lazuli and edged with lacy white foam where it broke on the rocks.

Teazle's forays into the heather, bracken, and blackthorn thickets grew shorter as her little legs tired. Eleanor would have liked to persuade herself that she turned back for the dog's sake, but halfway down a steep slope, she had to admit that the rising hillside ahead looked quite daunting.

She was not, alas, as young as she had been.

By the time they got back to the car, she was tired. She castigated herself for allowing three days to pass without proper exercise, murder or no murder. She was also hungry, and Teazle was panting for a drink in spite of having gulped her fill from a freshet trickling down through a cleft in the cliffs.

"There's that nice café in Wadebridge, pet. They'll give you water, and some scraps, too, I shouldn't wonder. We'll just stop in at Penhaligon House on the way, to see if Mrs Destry has put anything aside for the shop. If we're lucky and she's not too busy, we won't have to go to the café."

Mrs Destry was the resident housekeeper at Penhaligon House. Her employers were often away, as Mr Wendell worked in London and the children were at boarding schools. At such times, Mrs Destry welcomed visitors, though when the family was at home she had far too much to do to sit and chat.

A long, muddy drive led to the old manor house, built of reddish brown granite by the Penhaligon family some three hundred years ago. The Penhaligons had fallen on hard times in the Depression, and lost two sons in the war to complete the family's ruin. Since the war, the house had changed hands two or three times. The Wendells had bought it about ten years ago, so they were still considered incomers by the local people, especially as they were absent much of the time.

However, they were regarded as quite decent people, as incomers go. They shopped locally, rather than arriving with crates of supplies from Fortnum and Mason. In fact, according to Mrs Destry, they even took fresh farm produce back to London with them, saying they couldn't get anything as good in town, which pleased the local farmers mightily.

There wouldn't be any gossiping with the housekeeper today, Eleanor realised as she reached the gravel forecourt and saw a muddy Range Rover and two sleek, expensive-looking cars, one dark green and the other dark blue. Perhaps it was just as well, as Mrs Destry was bound to want to talk about the murder.

Exchanging a wave with Bill Destry, who was enjoying the

sun as he buzzed round and round the huge lawn on his riding mower, Eleanor parked the Incorruptible in a shady, inconspicuous corner under an evergreen. With Teazle following strictly to heel, she went around the house to the kitchen entrance at the side.

The door stood open, and delicious smells wafted from something Mrs Destry was stirring on the Aga. Teazle's nostrils twitched. Muzzle raised, she sniffed in ecstasy, her tail wagging nineteen to the dozen.

"Oh, Mrs Trewynn, how nice to see you." Anyone anticipating a housekeeper on the lines of the villainess in *Rebecca* would have been disappointed by the plump, rosy-cheeked, cheerful Mrs Destry in her pink-and-yellow-flowered apron.

"I'm afraid I've arrived at an awkward moment."

"Not at all. This can simmer on its own for a few minutes. I'm afraid I haven't time just now to sit down for a cuppa and a natter, though. I've got a few things collected for LonStar in the scullery, and I'll put down a bowl of water in there for the dog. Come along, Teazle." She led the way into an old-fashioned scullery with a stone sink, wooden draining boards, and shelves holding earthenware crocks labelled flour, sugar, oats, and other staples. In one corner, incongruously, loomed a huge deep freeze.

"That's kind of you," said Eleanor. "We've been for a long walk and she's thirsty."

"Your Teazle's got such good manners. Here's a box for the shop, my lover, and now I come to think of it—I'll be forgetting my own name next—Mrs Wendell was saying she's got one or two bits and pieces for you. I'll just pop through and ask her."

Eleanor carried the box round to the car and returned to the kitchen. There she found a tall, slim woman in a tweed skirt, its hem barely skimming the top of her knees, with sheer nylons and high-heels, a lovat-green twinset, pearls, and slightly too much make-up. She looked like what she was, a Londoner playing the country lady. Since this involved furnishing the London maisonette with the latest fad, transferring slightly dated lamps, curtains, cushions, tablecloths, and other linens (Mrs Wendell wouldn't be caught dead sleeping between last year's candy-striped sheets) to the country house, and donating the lightly used objects they replaced to LonStar, Eleanor could only be grateful.

—Even though she now recalled that the hideous, hazardous, and eventually deadly dolphin table had emanated from this bountiful source.

"My dear Mrs Trewynn," cried Mrs Wendell, "I'm so happy to see you. Do say you'll lunch with us today."

Looking down at her tracksuit and trainers, Eleanor was in no doubt as to the reason for this sudden affability. "I'm afraid I'm not dressed for company," she pointed out.

"Oh, it's just my husband and I, and a couple of guests," said her would-be hostess airily. "We would so love you to join us."

"I have several more calls to make today."

"You won't need to do that. I've got lots of stuff for LonStar. We'll fill your car easily, and Lionel can bring the rest over to Port Mabyn in the Range Rover later."

Of course, Eleanor thought, the big vehicle explained how the table had reached the shop. "Nothing too large," she said cautiously. "We haven't got a lot of room."

"I promise, nothing too large. You will stay, won't you?"

Eleanor glanced at Teazle, who was sitting by the Aga gazing upward, her nose twitching hopefully. "I don't think—"

"The little dog will be quite happy out here with Mrs Destry. You'll find it some tidbits, won't you, Mrs Destry? Then that's settled." Mrs Wendell looked Eleanor up and down and blinked, as if, in her eagerness to grab a celebrity, however temporary, she hadn't really taken in before just what her guest was wearing. "Let me show you the cloakroom."

"I'll just get my handbag from the car." Though Eleanor didn't really care if she was a bit windblown, it would be only polite to comb her hair at least, especially as she had no intention of providing any information about the murder in exchange for lunch. She hoped she had a comb in her bag. She was fairly certain she hadn't brought a lipstick.

Though the front door stood invitingly open, she went back into the house through the kitchen. "Who are the other guests?" she asked Mrs Destry, hoping they might be local people she knew.

"Smart people from London. A Sir and a Lady. I think he works for the government. They're customers of Mr Wendell's, or clients, or whatever he likes to call 'em. He's some fancy kind of banker. They were invited to stop by for a couple of days on their way to the Scillies. It hasn't been going too smooth. Mrs Wendell tries too hard—well, I ask you, Russian caviar when I can get mackerel that come ashore this very morning! Never mind, they're leaving this afternoon."

"I bet they're enjoying your cooking at least! It smells wonderful."

"*Dob*, she calls it. I call it stew."

Eleanor found the cloakroom, went to the loo, and tugged the comb through her curls. Coming out, she followed the sound of voices to a long drawing room looking out over the gardens and the Camel estuary to the south of the house. As she appeared on the threshold, Mrs Wendell jumped up.

"Here's our unexpected guest. Lady Bellowe, Sir Edward, this is Mrs Trewynn. As I was telling you, Mrs Trewynn runs the charity shop where the body was found."

Georgina Bellowe, a massive lady with iron grey hair, dimples, and a double chin which could no longer be called incipient, alas, surged to her feet and advanced on Eleanor with arms held wide. "My dear Eleanor, too marvellous to see you again. It's been far too long." She clasped Eleanor to her well-fortified bosom.

"Gina, what a lovely surprise!"

"Oh," said Mrs Wendell weakly, "you know each other?"

Sir Edward, as spare as his wife was abundant, and looking much in need of a holiday from his duties in the Commonwealth Relations Office, came to clasp Eleanor's hand in both his and shake it heartily. "Mrs Trewynn, this is a lucky chance. You may be just the—"

"Later, Edward," his wife commanded.

"Yes, of course, dear." Sir Edward stepped back, leaving Eleanor wondering just what imbroglio he hoped to drag her into.

SEVENTEEN

Mr Wendell, who had hitherto regarded Eleanor with the lack of attention to be expected of a man sent to run his wife's charitable errands, greeted her with slightly more interest today. She couldn't be sure whether this was because of her connection with the murder or her friendship with the Bellowes, but she suspected the latter. Assuming he did business with the CRO, he was indeed a "fancy kind of banker." Perhaps he thought she had some sort of influence in the awarding of contracts for overseas development aid. If so, he was far out in his reckoning.

At lunch, as delicious as the kitchen aromas promised, Eleanor deflected Mrs Wendell's questions about the murder by announcing that the detective inspector in charge had forbidden discussion of the case.

However, Scumble couldn't protect her from her hostess's attempts to pinpoint her place in the social hierarchy. Some enterprising reporter covering the murder had delved into Eleanor's background. Peter, before his death, had been Director of Field Managers, an imposing title which meant he spent most of his time flying around the world making sure LonStar projects ran smoothly and troubleshooting when they didn't. Eleanor had rejoiced in the still more impressive title of Ambassador at Large. In this guise, she had hobnobbed not only with village elders but with heads of government. Unfortunately—from Mrs Wendell's point of view—they were foreign heads of government, and mostly not even European. Still, she had to adjust her view of Eleanor, who was no longer, in spite of her tracksuit, just the little woman who ran the charity shop.

Not that Mrs Wendell was so lacking in social savvy as to say this outright, but Eleanor was amused by her all too obvious efforts to come to grips with the problem.

"But I don't run the shop," she insisted. "Mrs Stearns, our local vicar's wife, is in charge. Do you know her? No? Such a delightful and thoroughly practical person. When the police have sorted everything out, I'll give you a ring and you must come and meet her. As you're so interested in LonStar, I'm sure she'll manage to fit you into her volunteer schedule."

Alarmed, Mrs Wendell started to babble about children and unreliable au pairs and spending so little time in Cornwall. She welcomed with relief Mrs Destry's entrance with elegant glass bowls filled with a heavenly lemon soufflé. Georgina Bellowe deftly turned the conversation into less disruptive channels.

The Bellowes' bags were already in the hall as they had to depart immediately after coffee to catch the helicopter to St Mary's. The Wendells were in even more of a rush to pick up their offspring off the London train. Mr Wendell carried two of the Bellowes' suitcases out and set them on the gravel behind their car. Teazle, who had found her way outside and was guarding the Incorruptible, gambolled over to Eleanor with a happy bark.

The Bellowes offered polite, though hardly enthusiastic thanks for hospitality received, to which the Wendells responded with equally unenthusiastic murmurs of "Must stop over again next time you're down this way." Then the Wendells dashed off in the Range Rover.

Sir Edward had brought out a third suitcase and an official-looking briefcase. Unlocking the boot and heaving in the first two, he said, "Wendell's good at his business, but I think we won't come again, Gee."

"It was a mistake," his wife agreed. "That was very wicked of you, Eleanor. Somehow I simply can't see the woman helping behind a counter, even in a good cause."

"No, and somehow I can't see Jocelyn appreciating the introduction either. Sir Edward, what did you mean by 'a lucky chance'?"

"I'm going to ask a favour of you," he said, "as I expect you've guessed. There's some nasty intertribal troubles that seem to be brewing in Nigeria. A coup d'état, possibly, or secession, either leading to civil war. I've got a couple of chaps, one a Hausa, one Ibo, coming to our house in the Scillies to see if we can't sort things out amicably. I think you may know one or both." He told her their names.

"I've met both of them," Eleanor said. "I wouldn't say I know either well."

"However, you're an expert at making people believe in other people's good intentions. We don't want to make a big song and dance of it by bringing in a horde of diplomats—"

"But one little old lady shouldn't raise any eyebrows?"

"Exactly!"

"Edward, that's hardly gallant!"

"Gallant be blowed. What I need is competence, charm, and discretion. Not that you don't have all those, my dear, but your competence is in making people comfortable. Mrs Trewynn's is in making them see eye to eye." He turned back to Eleanor. "Will you come?"

"If you really think I can help . . . The only thing is, I'm rather tied up by the police at the moment. I seem to be caught in the middle of this investigation, and I doubt Detective Inspector Scumble will be happy if I trot off—"

"Scumble?" Sir Edward took out a notebook and wrote down the name. "Cornish police, or Scotland Yard?"

"He's CaRaDoC."

"Caradoc?"

"That's what the Constabulary of the Royal Duchy of Cornwall call themselves." Eleanor was pleased with her command of the vernacular. "My niece is a junior detective. Scotland Yard is involved, too, but I think only peripherally."

"Never mind, I'll sort it all out. Could you come on Tuesday? The CRO will pay your fare, of course, and you'll stay with us. Our house is on St Mary's, so it's just the helicopter ride from Penzance."

"And your dog is welcome, too," Georgina put in. "You'll be comfortable, I promise. After all, my own husband admits making people comfortable is my forte! Come along, Edward, or we'll miss the helicopter."

Sir Edward picked up the last of their luggage, his briefcase, and placed it carefully in the boot. The sun caught the letters stamped in gold on the side, OHMS, and the monogram by the handle: *E* for Edward and *B* for Bellowe thoroughly mixed up with what could have been an *R* for his middle name, whatever it was.

It reminded her of the monogram on the jewelry case. Had she mentioned it to DI Scumble? No, she distinctly recalled describing the case to him and having a feeling she was leaving something out. With his customary impatience, he had interrupted her train of thought and rushed on to something else. If only she could remember what the letters of the monogram had been. Like Sir Edward's, they'd been hard to disentangle. She hadn't been sure—

"So we'll see you on Tuesday?" Sir Edward's voice pierced her abstraction.

"What . . . ? Oh, yes, if you make it all right with the police. And send me directions."

"Here's our phone number." He tore a sheet from his notebook. "Reverse the charges, of course. Let us know which flight you're taking and one of us will meet you at the heliport. Yes, Gee, I'm coming."

Eleanor waved as the Bellowes disappeared down the drive, then she turned to the Incorruptible. Bill Destry, man-of-all-work, was leaning against the car.

"You didn't lock up, Mrs Trewynn, so I've stuffed in as much as'll go in. The boss'll bring the rest to Port Mabyn later, or tomorrow, seeing as I don't drive nowt bigger'n my mowing machine."

"It looks like fun."

He grinned, his leathery face crinkling. "That it is, and no worries about anyone getting in my road."

"True! Thanks, Bill. Please say thanks and goodbye to Mrs Destry for me. I need to be getting home." Surely by the time she found Scumble to tell him about the monogram she would remember the letters! "Hop in, Teazle."

"*Dyw genes*, Mrs Trewynn."

"Goodbye." She knew the Cornish phrase, but having been brought up speaking the King's—now Queen's—English, she felt it would be presumptuous to use it. Ridiculous, really, considering the number of languages in which she had in her time said goodbye and thank you without being able to speak another word.

Eleanor didn't want to dwell on the prospect of civil war in Nigeria, so as she drove homeward, she sang "Green Grow the Rushes-oh" from beginning to end, and "Ten Green Bottles," and all the other time-passing songs from her school days. Teazle didn't care if she was out of tune.

The Incorruptible was heavily loaded and struggled up the steeper hills. Leaning forward to urge it on, Eleanor sympathised. Like her, the poor thing was not as young as it had been. At last they reached Port Mabyn. She drove up to the shop and parked as usual with two wheels on the pavement. It was just after three o'clock, so the helpful children wouldn't be out of school for a while. Nick didn't pop out to lend a hand. He must be back in his workroom, painting. The flood of sensation-seekers pouring into his shop had slackened after the first couple of days, though the weekend would doubtless bring a new lot.

Eleanor let Teazle into the passage and told her to go upstairs. Then she popped into the shop. A couple of visitors were browsing the bookshelves, watched with an anxious eye by Mrs Drover, an elderly incomer whose retired husband spent all his time on the golf links.

"Oh, Mrs Trewynn, you're back already. Mrs Stearns is in the stockroom, pricing. Isn't she brave?" Mrs Drover added in a whisper.

"How is it going today?"

"I haven't been here very long. Mrs Stearns said it was very busy this morning, with lots of people asking about . . . you know." Again she finished in a whisper. "But I don't know anything so it's no good them asking me."

"I'm very grateful to you for coming in, Mrs Drover."

"Oh, I couldn't let Mrs Stearns down." *Wouldn't dare*, her voice and expression suggested. No doubt she was more afraid of Jocelyn than of mere ghosts.

"I must have a word with her. I've got a carload of donations outside."

Eleanor went back to the stockroom, nodding hello to the

strangers, aware as she passed that they put their heads together and looked after her. She shut the door behind her.

No one was visible.

"Joce?"

Jocelyn stuck her head through between the clothes hanging on a rack. "Eleanor, you're back early. No luck?"

"On the contrary, the Incorruptible is bursting at the seams. I'll tell you later. I must see if Nick can help me unload before Bob Leacock gives me a parking ticket."

"I'll give you a hand if he can't, but there's a tremendous lot to do here after not being allowed in for two days. Not to mention the mess the police left! I've cleared some space for you by the back wall."

Where she had found the body, it seemed like eons ago.

"I'll shout if I need you."

Eleanor went out by way of the passage and the back door to avoid the book-browsers in the shop, in case they had summoned up the audacity to approach her in hope of lurid details.

She found Nick in his studio. He was painting a pair of choughs pecking for insects among the wiry sheep's fescue on the brink of a cliff, with a view of the sea and a towering headland beyond, in the background. The birds were unmistakable, with their red legs and bills. He was just adding touches to make their glossy black feathers shine.

Black feathers. Black birds.

"Nick, what other black birds are there? Crows, rooks—"

"Black birds? Why on earth?"

"There was a monogram on the briefcase with the jewelry, and I can't remember what the three letters were but somehow I associate them with black birds."

He laughed. "That probably means they actually spell something connected with blue birds. You know how it is. A word is on the tip of your tongue and you're quite sure it begins with *P* and then it turns out to be *T*. *T I T*, bluetit? *N U T*, nuthatch? I can't see how you can turn kingfisher into three letters, though, and I can't think of any other blue birds. Not English ones, at any rate."

"Not blue, black," Eleanor insisted. "I just can't think of anything in three letters."

"Plain common-or-garden blackbird. Coot. Cormorant. Black swan. Raven. Oystercatcher."

"Not black and white, black all over. Raven . . . No, jackdaw!" she said triumphantly.

"Seven letters."

"Often known as a daw. *D A W*. That's it. I can picture them now, all wound together. I must tell Mr Scumble. Dearest, kindest Nick, could you come and help me unload, and then I'll ring the police."

"Give me five minutes to finish off this bird." He dabbed with a delicate brush. "What have you got in the car this time? Any mysterious objects?"

"I sincerely hope not! I don't actually know what's there as someone else loaded up."

"Much more fun that way," Nick said absently, reaching for a rag.

"As long as they're not going to present us with another dolphin table!"

"Hmm?" He wasn't listening.

Eleanor left him in peace. She considered ringing DI Scumble while she waited for him, but she might be stuck on the phone for ages while he was looked for, or finished whatever he was doing, or upbraided her. Instead, she went upstairs and let Teazle into the flat (which she had remembered to lock, *and* the keys were in her pocket where they belonged), filled the kettle ready for a cuppa later, and went back down to start unloading.

She took a bag in. Returning through the passage, she met Nick, invisible behind the pile of boxes in his arms, but instantly recognisable by the paint-stained jeans.

Standing aside to let him pass, she said, "It's all so well packed, I still don't know what we have."

"Makes life interesting. Any briefcases?"

"If we find one, I'll return it unopened!"

"Good idea."

When they had finished, Eleanor said, "If you don't have to hurry back to your choughs, come up and have a cup of tea. Joce can't leave the shop."

"The choughs can wait, and I left a note next door saying I could be found here. Just in case there should be a sudden swarm of people wanting my pictures. I'll take the Incorruptible down while you boil a kettle, shall I? Then I'll come back and hold your hand while you ring the Scumble."

"Oh bother! I'd managed to forget that temporarily. Nick," she said in a sudden panic, "what were the initials?"

"*D A W.* Jackdaw. I'd definitely better come and hold your hand."

He returned just as the kettle boiled, and made the tea while Eleanor dialled the Launceston police. To her dismay, she was told that DI Scumble was already on his way to Port Mabyn.

"What on earth does he want now?" Nick asked crossly.

"They didn't say. They're going to tell him on the car radio that I want to speak to him. *Botheration!* I'd much rather deal with him at telephone's length."

"I won't desert you." He glanced at the window, where the sunny day was dissolving in a sea mist. "No one's going to stroll about in this looking for the perfect painting for their sitting room wall. You know, I'd like to paint Port Mabyn on a misty day, but all the tourists want is sun, even if it rained every day of their holidays."

Eleanor thought of the inspector driving from Launceston. Sometimes mist at sea-level left the moors in sunlight. Sometimes it enveloped the higher land in fog that rivalled the pre–Clean Air Act London pea-soupers.

She wouldn't wish a Bodmin Moor fog on anyone, but wouldn't it be nice if Scumble was sufficiently deterred to turn round and go back to Launceston!

EIGHTEEN

It was nearly five o'clock when DI Scumble at last arrived. He was not happy. He had indeed hit fog on Bodmin Moor. His cretin of a driver had missed the turn to Port Mabyn. They had been wandering about unsignposted back lanes for most of an hour before finding the B road again, and then had been unsure whether they needed to turn north or south.

"Tea, Mr Scumble?" Eleanor suggested soothingly. "I'll make a fresh pot."

"I won't say it wouldn't be welcome, ma'am," Scumble conceded.

"What about your driver?" she asked, filling the kettle.

"He and the other two idiots I brought with me are doing some house-to-house. Going from door to door, asking a few questions," he clarified.

"I hope they don't get lost in the fog," Nick said, in what seemed to Eleanor a purely inflammatory spirit.

The inspector glared at him. "And what exactly are you doing here, Mr Gresham?"

Before Nick could add fuel to the flames with the remark about protecting her from police harassment that she saw hovering on his lips, Eleanor said quickly, "Nick helped me unload the car and came up for tea."

"Another load of donations? Any mysterious briefcases?"

Nick burst out laughing, and after a moment, Scumble grinned. "As a matter of fact, Inspector," Nick said, "we kept a careful lookout for anything of the sort. No such luck."

"No such *bad* luck," said Eleanor, opening a packet of chocolate digestive biscuits. "What did you want to see me about, Mr Scumble?"

"That can wait. What did *you* want to see *me* about?"

"I . . . um . . . remembered something." She put the plate of biscuits on the table at his elbow as a peace offering.

"Hey!" said Nick. "How come I only got plain digies?"

"I know how you go through the choccy ones, Nick, so I never open a new packet just for you. Would you make the tea while I tell Mr Scumble? Restrain yourself!" she added as he nabbed a biscuit in passing.

"Well?" the inspector demanded impatiently, his notebook at the ready.

"It's about the briefcase, actually. When you asked me to describe it, I forgot about the monogram."

"A monogram! Do you realise that if you'd told me at once—?"

"It wasn't very obvious," Eleanor excused herself. "Embossed, not gilt or . . . or anything that stood out. And it was difficult to make out. Those curlicue-ish sort of letters, you know, all intertwined."

"*What* letters?"

"*D* and *A* and a *W*."

"*D A W*? In that order?"

"Not exactly." She could picture it now. "Superimposed. There was a big D, with a W inside it, and the A was formed by a cross-bar in the centre of the W."

"Can you draw it?"

"Heavens no. I'm hopeless at drawing. I actually managed to fail art at school."

"That would take some doing," said Nick, setting down the tea tray. He whipped Scumble's biro from his fingers and bent over the official notebook. "Something like this, Eleanor?" He held it up.

"Yes, sort of."

Scumble retrieved his pen and pad and studied Nick's drawing. "So it could equally well be *W A D?*"

"I suppose so. Is that what you're looking for?"

"It's not important," he said dismissively. "Call it useful, perhaps, but not vital. We're already ninety-nine percent certain who the jewels belong to. The monogram makes it ninety-nine and a half. And it'll confirm that the case is his, if we find it."

"Oh." All that angst for nothing. "Whose are they?"

"Now, now, Mrs Trewynn, you know I'm in the business of asking questions, not answering them."

"So, what was it you came to ask me about?"

Leafing slowly back through his notebook, Scumble said, "It's a bit of a discrepancy we have here. You claim you've never seen the deceased before?"

"Not to my knowledge. I said I didn't recognise him. He may, for all I know, have crossed my field of vision without my noticing him. But whatever my failings, I have an excellent memory for faces. If I had ever had anything to do with him, I'd remember him, very likely his name if I had heard it, and probably whatever it was that brought us into contact."

"Then how do you explain that five people are ready to swear they've seen him several times helping you carry goods from your car into the shop?"

"Megan said no one recognised him."

"My men have asked a lot more people since then. So? Your explanation?"

"That's easy. I'd be astounded if a single one of them actually noticed anything more than a thin boy with long hair and shabby jeans. It's like policemen: How many people really look at the face under the helmet? What they see is a bobby, in the one case; a hippy, or a slacker, or some similar pejorative label in the other." Eleanor warmed to her thesis. "If a tall African man were to walk down the street outside, and the next day you took round a photo of a completely different tall African man and asked if people had seen him, how many do you suppose would realise it wasn't the same person?"

"All right, all right, you've made your point."

"What's more, I bet I can give you the names of at least two of those people who've told your men they saw the dead boy helping me."

"There's no need for that!" Scumble said hastily. "I gather you don't deny having had a 'thin boy with long hair and shabby jeans' helping you?"

"Of course not. In fact—" She looked round as the door opened. "Oh, Joce, you're just in time. Mr Scumble—"

"Back *again*, Inspector? I hope you've come to tell us you have arrested the murderer?"

"I might have by now," Scumble growled, "if everybody had told me all they know right away instead of doling it out like . . . like Oliver Twist's porridge!"

"Nicely put, Inspector," said Nick. "You must have seen the musical. Tea, Mrs Stearns?"

"I read the book at school," Scumble said acidly, turning back to Eleanor. "You were telling me about the victim's double."

"*Not* his double, Inspector. Joce, you remember when I found the body?"

"I'm hardly likely to forget it!"

"You remember," Eleanor persisted, "at first I thought it was someone else?"

"You thought it might be Trevor. But as soon as you looked at his face, you knew it wasn't."

"A very superficial resemblance, Mr Scumble. Skinny, long darkish hair—"

"Scruffy jeans, yes. You know what they say, though: Birds of a feather flock together. There's likely some connection. After all, someone knew whose car they put the loot in. It's a great pity the sun was shining on their windscreen so that you couldn't see them."

"Not at all, Inspector," Jocelyn protested. "Surely Eleanor would be in danger if she were able to identify them."

"It doesn't make much difference," Nick pointed out, "as long as they think she can."

"In any case," said Scumble, "I'll have to follow up this Trevor of yours. What's his surname?"

Eleanor and Jocelyn looked at each other and shook their heads.

"He didn't mention it, and we had no reason to ask."

"Never look a gift horse in the mouth," said Nick blandly.

Scumble gave him a black look. "You must know something more about him. I assume he didn't live locally, or people would know him. Did he stay in the area often, or were all his appearances within a short period, a holiday?"

"I'd say on and off over the past couple of years," said Jocelyn. "You're the one who talked to him, Eleanor."

"He's not a talker. I gathered he came to stay with an uncle hereabouts, but whether the uncle's a resident or a summer visitor, I've no idea."

"And I suppose you don't know the uncle's name."

"I'm afraid not. He never referred to him by name."

"Nor where the boy's home is," Scumble said without hope.

"I'm afraid not," Eleanor repeated. "He's a nice boy, though. I'm sure he can't have had anything to do with the jewel robbery."

"Assuming the uncle lives outside Port Mabyn, how did Trevor get to the village? Car? Motorbike?"

"His uncle may have given him a lift sometimes for all I know, but he did mention walking and hitchhiking."

"So you don't know whether he could drive."

"Sorry, no idea."

The inspector sighed.

"Did you find the car, Inspector?" Jocelyn asked. "The one Eleanor saw that may have been the jewel thieves'?"

"Now what did I just say to Mrs Trewynn? I'm the one asking questions, not answering them. And my next is: Is there anything else she's told you, Mrs Stearns—or Mr Gresham, come to that—that she hasn't yet got round to telling *me?*"

"How can we know, Inspector," Nick enquired pointedly, "unless you tell us everything you've found out so far?"

"I'm not that desperate yet," snapped Scumble.

Megan was zipping down the north slope of the Mendip hills into the valley of the Yeo when Ken Faraday emerged from a sea of paper.

"Nice driving," he said appreciatively, then ruined the compliment by adding, "Very much improved. I didn't have to grab the edge of the seat once. Of course, in this toy car I couldn't fall off it if I tried."

"You never fell off when I was driving in London."

"I always gripped the edge of the seat. You must have been practising. Have you got yourself a car of your own?"

"No, but I'll have to splurge soon if Dr Beeching keeps wielding his axe in the name of economy. They're threatening to close down every railway in Cornwall, even the main line from Plymouth to Penzance!"

"Disgraceful," said Ken with a grin.

"It is. Most people can't afford a car, and we don't want any motorways. Ah well, *revenons à nos moutons*. Have you read all the reports?

"Just about. Your chaps seem pretty thorough, but there's one thing . . . Meggie—oops, Megan—who's this starving artist type who keeps popping up? Grisham—no, Gresham. He seems to be very much in the thick of things, and I gather no one has investigated him thoroughly."

"He's a friend of Aunt Nell's."

"Oh, an old fogey."

"Not at all. He's about our age. I wouldn't say he's starving. He appears to be doing better than merely keeping body and soul together."

"'Appears to.' Many a crime's been committed for the sake of keeping up appearances."

Megan laughed. "I can't imagine many people less likely to care about keeping up appearances."

"Scruffy is he? Like the victim?"

"Not at all. Paint-splotched, usually, but he cleans up nicely."

"He would have cleaned up, presumably, to take your aunt out to dinner. That's odd, isn't it? That he should invite an old lady out? Gay, is he?"

"I have no idea," Megan said coldly. "He's Aunt Nell's neighbour and friend."

"Or trying to ingratiate himself with a childless elderly widow."

That made Megan laugh again. "If you mean, with an eye to a legacy, you're way off target. Aunt Nell put every penny she owned into buying the cottage and getting the shop going. She's living on a pension, and I think there's a small annuity her husband set up."

"All right, so they're friends. But he knew she'd found the jewelry in her car—"

"Not till the following day."

"So they claim. And he very neatly got her out of the way while a murder was committed on her ground floor. Living next door, he must have known the dog would rouse her if there were intruders in the night."

"Ken, you're flogging a dead horse," Megan said, exasperated. "Let's concentrate on identifying the victim. Then we'll have half a chance of working out who topped him and why. Now shut up, would you? I need to concentrate on driving. Have you got the directions handy?"

They found their way through the city to the main police station, where they were expected. The desk sergeant had a street map waiting, with the tobacconist and the pub, the Sailors' Rest, marked on it.

"It's not the nicest part of town," he said, addressing Ken but looking at Megan. "Down by the docks. Going to be redeveloped soon. You want a couple of our lads along?"

"No, thanks. We're not looking for aggro."

"Yeah, but is aggro looking for you?"

"Doubt it. We'll find out, won't we."

"Up to you, mate. You get your blocks knocked off, we'll give you a nice funeral."

"Kind of you," said Ken sardonically. "Thanks a lot."

When they reached the dockyards, they understood the sergeant's remarks. The area was indeed uninviting, to put it kindly. Most buildings were dilapidated, many obviously unused, with a shuttered look, just waiting for demolition. Every flat surface was covered with graffiti.

Behind and among the warehouses stood cheerless rows of stevedores' dwellings and sailors' rooming houses, opening directly onto the pavement. Those that were still occupied gave an overwhelming impression of dinginess. Most of the residents were probably on the dole. Almost all ground-floor windows of the abandoned houses were broken. Shards of window glass and shattered beer bottles flashed in the incongruous evening sunshine as Megan and Ken drove by. Litter scurried and swirled before a brisk breeze.

The only people they saw were a shabby boy kicking a rusty tin along the street and an equally shabby couple of men standing on a doorstep arguing. The pubs were open by now. No doubt they were full.

All the shops they passed were boarded up until they came to the corner where *J. Bradshaw, licensed to sell tobacco,* eked out a meagre living. Megan stopped at the kerb right outside. There was no competition here for parking space. It was impossible to see inside through all the bits of paper pasted in the windows, offering everything from a bedsitter at a ridiculously low rent to "French lessons" for not much more.

Though Megan had seen sights just as dismal when she worked in London, the contrast with Launceston and Port Mabyn was shocking. There might be poverty in the country, but at least one had the scenery to take the edge off.

"I hate to leave the car unguarded," she said. "Some yobbo'll have the wheels off it in seconds."

"We should have borrowed a marked car. You stay here. I'll go in."

"I'll go in. I'm less likely to make him nervous, don't you think? He's bound to be doing *something* illegal, if it's only fiddling his taxes."

"You think the poor sod makes enough to owe taxes?"

Looking at the shop, Megan conceded, "No. Unless it's immoral earnings off the adverts in his window. He can't be too worried, or he wouldn't have contacted us."

"True."

"Look, I saw the body. If he's iffy about the photo, perhaps I can remember something that'll help."

"I suppose it's possible. Okay, you go in. Leave the door open so you'll hear me shout for help if I'm assaulted."

Megan bit her lip, remembering why she had once been . . . fond of him. That self-deprecating sense of humour and his occasional kindness had—for a while—masked the innate arrogance and the roving eye.

For a while. She hurried across the littered pavement into the shop.

NINETEEN

The man behind the counter of the tobacconist–newsagent–sweet shop was short, spare, and almost completely bald. A burly customer leant against the counter, holding the *Evening Standard* folded to the sports page. They stopped discussing football when Megan came in, and the burly man turned to look at her. His dungarees were well worn but not quite shabby. Still in work, Megan guessed.

"Born in a barn, was you, darlin'?" he enquired truculently, with a pointed glance at the open door. The shopman muttered something to him. "Huh! Right you are, Jim. No offence meant," he said to Megan, ingratiating now, "and none taken, I 'ope. See you, Jim." He went out, skirting Megan as though she had the plague, and leaving the door open.

"Mr Bradshaw?" she asked, going up to the counter. She knew she had been identified as a rozzer. Some people had a sixth sense about it, though it often failed when they were faced with a woman officer.

"That's me."

"DS Pencarrow, North Cornwall police." She showed her

warrant card. "You telephoned in response to our request for information about a murder victim."

"'Sright. I couldn't swear to 'im, mind."

"Newspaper pictures aren't too good. I have a proper print here, if you wouldn't mind taking a look."

"Gruesome, is it?" He put out his hand and regarded with disappointment the bloodless photo she put into it. "Not a mark on 'im, but you can tell 'e's a goner, can't you? That's 'im, all right."

"You know his name? Or where we can find someone who knew him?"

He shook his head. "Sorry, miss, or should I say officer? All I can say is I seen 'im in the shop maybe four or five times. 'E's one of these squatters, see. Leastways, that's what I reckon. He come in with a couple of kids just like 'im once. Never had a job, most of 'em. Dirty 'abits, drugs, long hair." He smoothed a hand over his bare scalp. "They break into unoccupied houses, don't care the water and electric's been turned off. Doss there till it gets too smelly even for them, then they go find another one. So even if I knew where he'd been staying, which I don't, them he was sharing with likely moved on by now."

"But you're sure he was in this area."

"Got a good memory for faces, I 'ave. And I keep an eye on 'em seeing I've caught a couple nicking fags—or sweets. Wet behind the ears, some of 'em. Ought to pack it in and go home to mummy."

"Could you identify any of those you've seen with him?" She tapped the photo, which he'd laid down on the counter.

"You show me photos, or line 'em up in front of me, I could. But you got to catch 'em first, haven't you?"

"Yes," Megan agreed ruefully. "Can you by any chance put a date to the last time you saw him?" Again she tapped the picture.

"Last weekend," Bradshaw said promptly. "He bought a paper.

The *Mirror*, was it? No, I tell a lie, it was Sunday, the *News of the World*. And I never seen him buy a paper before. Which ain't to say he never did, but I'm the only newsagent still open hereabouts."

"It doesn't sound as if he was a frequent reader."

"Though the truth is, they don't buy much of anything," the newsagent went on. "Turning the place into a slum, they are. I'm not saying it was ever smart hereabouts, but it was a decent place, plenty of work and respectable people, mostly, 'cepting Sat'day nights when the pubs let out. Nowadays the ships are too big to come up the river. They're going to clear the rest of us out when they get round to it, but the more run-down it is, the less compensation they'll be paying. So if you lot was to clear out them squatters, there's none would lift a finger to stop you."

That explained his cooperation. "I'm afraid that's up to the Bristol police," Megan reminded him.

"Yeah, but if you tell 'em the squatters 've got themselves mixed up in murder now, maybe they'll get up off their fat arses and do something. Pardon my French."

"Thank you for your cooperation," Megan said. "It's possible someone may have to contact you again."

"'S all right by me." He waved at his deserted shop. "Ain't got so much to do I can't spare the time. Gets boring dusting the stock."

Megan went out, closing the shop door behind her against the cold wind. In the back of the car, Ken was still lounging, reading reports by the light of a torch, but he had the window open in spite of the breeze, so she knew he'd been listening in case she ran into trouble. It was getting dark. Most of the street lamps were smashed, or simply not working.

He rolled up the window as, with a shiver, she returned to the driving seat.

"Well?"

"Positive identification. But no name, neither his nor his friends, and he doesn't know where he's been squatting."

"Better than nothing. At least we know where to start looking. Anything else?"

She relayed her interview with Bradshaw, rant and all. "And that's about it. It sounds as if he was checking for news of the robbery, doesn't it? But how was he involved? He certainly doesn't sound like—and didn't looked like—the sort anyone in their right mind would entrust with the proceeds of a major heist."

"My guess is he was the bully-boys' get-away driver, and somehow he got-away with the loot."

"But someone else had to be in it, too, someone who knew Aunt Nell's car and the shop."

"Who's either the murderer, or told the bully-boys where to look for him."

"He might have been forced to tell."

"He might. And he could well be dead, too. Come on, let's hit the pub."

She reached for the keys, then paused. "Just a minute. Something Bradshaw said . . . No, it wasn't *what* he said, it was the way he said it. 'Go home to mummy,' in a mincing voice."

"Putting on an upper-class accent?"

"No, not exactly. Not as posh as yours, anyway. More middle-class."

"A lot of these kids are not yobbos, they're runaways."

"What on earth do they live on?"

It was a rhetorical question, but he answered it. "The dole. Odd jobs, off the books. Begging, and a bit of theft, though most aren't serious thieves. They don't want to draw our attention. In London, the cleaner ones, those with any talent, do a bit of busking, but I don't know if that's on the cards down here. Then there's often a few quid now and then from 'mummy,' that she's saved from housekeeping on the sly. Some are just rebels, but some are escaping pretty nasty home situations. A lot of the girls end up on the game, and some of the boys, too."

Megan wished she hadn't asked. "You should be a social worker," she said.

"Not bloody likely. But I don't go out of my way to harass them. Come on, we'd better get over to the pub."

The Sailors' Rest was not far away but appeared slightly less run-down than the tobacconist's. At least, a lively noise came from inside when they pulled up in front.

"Friday night. I don't think you should go in here on your own," Ken said, "but I don't like to—"

"Look, there's a car-park sign. Pointing round the back."

The sign was faded almost to illegibility. "All right, we'll give it a try," he agreed, his voice full of doubt.

No car much wider than the Mini could have squeezed through along the side of the building. They emerged in a tiny yard, enclosed by the pub on one side and walls on the other three. Double gates in the back wall suggested an alley, no doubt used for lorries unloading. The headlights gleamed on a padlock. Theirs was the only vehicle present. The only light was a low-wattage bulb over a door with another faded sign reading BAR. Beside it an arrow pointed to GENTS.

"Looks safe enough. All the same, we don't want some half-pissed lout looking for valuables mucking about with these reports. You'd better park in the darkest corner, farthest from the door and the loo."

"None of it's exactly floodlit." Megan pulled the car into the far corner. They got out and locked the doors.

"We'll walk round to the front," Ken said. "Better not give

anyone even a hint that there may be something worth nicking out here."

Inside, they discovered that much of the noise came from a dart game in progress. Megan was relieved to see three women among the cheering onlookers. Even now, in this day and age, there were pubs where female intruders were bitterly resented. On the other hand, nor was it the sort of pub where strangers are welcomed. As the door clunked to behind them, everyone not totally absorbed in the game turned and looked at them.

Neither of them was dressed to fit into this milieu. Megan was certain a good proportion of the clientele guessed they were police. She didn't exactly feel threatened, but she was glad Ken was with her.

Not turning a hair, he walked straight towards the bar, so she followed. A large man who was sitting on a stool, talking to the barman, stood up and moved as if to block Ken's path. The barman leant over and put a hand on his arm, saying something in a soft voice. The man scowled, picked up his pint, and moved away. He was in fact no taller than Ken, broader but middle-aged and out of shape. Megan glanced around and noticed that almost everyone in the room was middle-aged or older . . . except for a group over in the far corner.

The light over there was dim in contrast to the brightness over the bar and the dart players, but they looked young. And unkempt. Very like the dead youth.

Megan turned to draw Ken's attention to the young people. She touched his sleeve, but he was focussed on the barman.

"Mr Redditch?"

"That's me."

Ken put his hand in his breast pocket to retrieve his warrant card, but Redditch said in a fierce whisper, "No need to wave it around in here. You come about that lad that was murdered?"

"That's right. I've got a much better photo than was in the paper to show you."

"Order summat, and slip it to me with the cash."

"Half of cider, Autumn Gold if you've got it, and a pint of bitter."

Megan couldn't decide whether she was pleased or annoyed that he'd remembered what she preferred to drink in pubs. In some odd way it felt like an intrusion. It was none of his business anymore.

"I'll pay for my own."

"Don't be silly." He had already laid a pound note and the photo on a dry spot on the bar. "Expenses."

"Ken, those people over there . . ." She swung round as she spoke, to point them out to him. They were gone. "Hell! That's where the back door is. Shall I go after them?"

"Who?"

"A bunch of scruffy kids. Just the sort we're looking for." She took a step in the direction of the back door.

"Out the front. You stay here." As he spoke he was running to the street entrance.

"Hoy!" Redditch set two tankards on the counter with a thump that sloshed liquid over the side. "Your pal want the info or not?"

"Yes. He'll be back shortly, but in the meantime you can tell me."

"You a 'tec, too? No, don't bother with that," he added hastily as Megan reached for her card. "The boy came in here a couple of times, with friends."

"Do you know his name?"

"Nah."

"You didn't check his age?"

The barman shrugged. "I ask. They tell me they don't have a

student card or a driving licence, what can I do? He said he was over eighteen, so I served him."

Underage drinking in Bristol was none of her business, especially as she needed his cooperation. "Those young people who were over there when we came in, have you seen him with them?"

Another shrug. "Couldn't say. They're all much alike. Him I remember 'cause he was kind of cocky, full of himself."

Ken returned. "Too late. It's pitch dark out there." He took a deep swig of his beer. "I think I saw a couple disappearing round a corner but there's no sense following them. They'll have gone to earth by now. This area is a warren and they know it. We don't. What's the story?"

"Mr Redditch recognises the victim but can't tell us much about him. He says he was the cocky type."

"Yeah, and he had a nasty look in his eye, like, when I asked his age. I wouldn't've wanted to cross that one."

"What about the rest of his crowd?" Ken asked.

"Mellow—isn't that the word they use these days? It's that muck they smoke does it, I reckon. No get-up-and-go."

"Unfortunately," Ken pointed out, "they got up and went. You have any idea where they're hanging out at present?"

"Not a clue. They don't come in here often, them just now or others like 'em, and when they do they're not chatty. And that's about all I can tell you," he said pointedly, with a sweep of his cloth across the bar. "I got other customers to see to."

Ken thanked him. They finished their drinks and went out the back way to the car. As far as they could tell by torchlight, it was undamaged by the departing young people.

They got in, Ken in the front passenger seat.

"A nasty look in his eye," he reflected. "That's something to think about."

"I'm glad Aunt Nell wasn't at home that evening. Where to now?"

"The hotel." The Bristol police had booked them a couple of rooms at a modest place near the nick. Ken waited until Megan had negotiated the tricky exit from the so-called car park before he said casually, "You know, we could save your department some money by sharing a room."

"Not bloody likely!" Megan was furious. It was typical of him to assume he could waltz into her bed after waltzing out of her life without a backward glance. If only he'd stop thinking with his gonads . . . But saying so would just provoke a lecture on her out-of-date ideas of morality. They were hers, and it would be a cold day in hell before she changed them to suit him, even if she could make herself believe he would thereafter cleave only to her. Which she couldn't.

She drove in stony silence to the hotel.

TWENTY

As Megan parked the car, Ken said, "Sorry. You know, we ought to discuss what we've found out and what to do next. I'll buy you a decent dinner. Not on expenses."

"I have to ring the guv'nor."

"So do I. Let's sign into our rooms first. Then I'll phone the Yard to report and to find out whether the jeweller has positively identified the stuff as his. If he says it's not—not likely but always possible—I'll be off your case, and you'll want to tell DI Scumble."

"That's a point. I'll wait till we know."

"And dinner afterwards?"

"Yes. Thanks. But I didn't bring anything special to change into. Just my overnight bag. And I'm not sure what's in that. I don't exactly need it often in Cornwall, not like you Yard types."

"You can borrow my toothpaste, but not my toothbrush. What you're wearing looks fine to me. I'll ask the receptionist for suggestions. Let's go."

The hotel served breakfasts but not dinners, so the plump blond receptionist was quite happy to recommend a couple of restaurants nearby that were "nice" but didn't expect their customers to dress up.

Megan eyed the very public telephone next to the stairs. It was not the sort of hotel that has a phone in every bedroom. "We'd better make our calls from the nick," she suggested to Ken.

"Definitely."

"It's only a couple of minutes walk, I think. Let's drop off our bags and go over."

She had spoken in a low voice, but the girl overheard. "You're with the police, aren't you?" she asked. "They booked for you."

"From Scotland Yard." Ken showed her his card.

Her eyes rounded. "Gosh, fab! Wait till I tell Mum we had Scotland Yard detectives staying in the hotel. You're a detective, too, Miss—" She glanced at the register. "—Pencarrow?"

"Yes." Megan didn't think it necessary to specify that she was merely from Cornwall.

"Fab! If there's anything you need, just let me know. I think there's a magnifying glass in the manager's office."

"Don't tell anyone who we are," Ken told her solemnly.

"Not even Mum?" she asked, disappointed.

"Oh, I think you can tell your mother," said Megan, "but not until after we leave, all right?"

"All right! Fab!"

They went up the stairs. On the landing, they exchanged a look, said together, "Fab!" and burst out laughing.

Megan's room was small but adequate, the mattress sagging a bit but not lumpy. The wash-basin had running hot water that was really hot, and the bathroom and loo were nearly opposite, not hidden away down miles of corridors. Unpacking her night things, she discovered her toothpaste in her sponge bag and was glad she wouldn't have to borrow Ken's—or more likely do without. Underneath was a clean pale blue blouse that was not too creased. She hung it over the basin while she washed, in the hope that the creases would be diminished by the steam.

. . . Well, it was worth a try. She hadn't time for a nice hot steamy bath. When she put the blouse on, it didn't look too bad with the dark green suit, which would definitely have to go to the cleaners next week.

She brushed her hair and was applying her usual peach-coloured lipstick when Ken knocked on her door.

"Coming!" she called, annoyed to find she was looking forward to having dinner with him.

He had taken off his tie and changed from his dark suit into a tweed jacket and fawn slacks. A sudden thought struck her.

"Why did you bring your overnight bag?" she asked accusingly. "You were supposed to collect the jewels and go back to London."

He grinned. "As a matter of fact, my super and yours had already had a confab before I left town. But yours had to consult your CC, and he didn't want to alert DI Scumble to the possibility of working with the Yard in time for him to think up objections. I rather think Scumble won the second round, though, shipping me off to Bristol."

"He may be a misogynistic pain in the neck, but he's not stupid. I knew he was planning something tricky. He got both of us out of his hair in one swell foop."

"I hope he's pleased with the result. Let's go and report."

"I just hope he doesn't want *us* to do a house-to-house down by the docks."

"Horrors! We'd better be extra charming to the Bristol people and with any luck they'll agree to send uniforms."

It was a pleasant evening. The wind had died down and the air was balmy. On the way to the Bristol nick they passed both the recommended restaurants and both looked "nice." One was Italian, the other Indian.

"Which do you prefer?"

Megan picked Indian. "One thing I do miss in our rural fastness is a choice of restaurants."

"Pasties or fish and chips?" Ken said sympathetically.

"Not quite that bad! Even Port Mabyn has Chinese, and we have an Italian place in Launceston. Your choice of spaghetti bolognese or ravioli. Oh, and minestrone, of course. I have to admit that my mother makes a better spaghetti bolognese."

"Your parents live in Cornwall too, don't they, as well as your aunt? I had forgotten."

"Yes, near Falmouth. It's quite a trek on our roads, but I get down there once a month or so. Here we are."

They were accommodated with a small office containing a desk, a file cabinet, two chairs, and a telephone. Ken sat down behind the desk, pulled the phone to him, and dialled the Yard.

Megan didn't listen as he talked his way towards whomever he was supposed to report to. She was too busy reading over her notes and preparing her own report in her mind. Then his exasperated tone broke through her absorption.

"What the hell d'you mean, 'something's happened'?"

She couldn't hear the person on the other end.

Then Ken said, "All right, all right, so no one told you and no one left a message for me. Get me a typist and I'll dictate my report." He put his hand over the receiver and hissed at Megan's enquiring look, "'Something's happened'! Apparently only God and my guv'nor know what, and the guv'nor's gone home to bed. Do *not* suggest that we try . . . Yes, Faraday here. Ready?"

His report was admirably concise yet complete. Megan took it down word for word in shorthand. Unless DI Scumble was still at the station and wanted to discuss what to do next, she would just repeat Ken's account.

Ken hung up. "At least my guv'nor left word he'd be in tomorrow and I should ring at nine. Your turn." He shoved the phone across the desk.

Megan had even less luck. She spoke to the desk sergeant in Launceston, who told her he was the only copper in the station. He had no idea when DI Scumble would be in on Saturday morning, if at all. He would leave a message for the inspector to ring DS Pencarrow at Bristol HQ.

"But if he gets in before nine, to try my hotel first, please. *Number?*" she mouthed at Ken, and was impressed when he knew it. She passed it on to Sergeant Welham. "And please tell him—"

"Keep it short, Pencarrow. I'm expecting another call."

"Tell him the victim was definitely seen in Bristol but we haven't got a name or address yet." So much for her planned miracle of comprehensive conciseness. She hung up.

"Another misogynist?" Ken asked.

"Welham? Not really. The bastard is just as bloody-minded with everyone. Including the public we're supposed to serve."

"That's why they put that sort on the desk, didn't you realise? Keeps away all but the most determined of the public."

"Most of ours are all right, actually."

"Call it a wild generalisation. Well, we've done what we can to appease our lords and masters. Let's go and eat."

Over an excellent meal, they discussed how they might set about finding the people who had known the victim, if they were required to do so. Their dispiriting conclusion was that it would take a large number of officers to draw a net around the entire area.

"CaRaDoC's not going to supply them," Megan said with certainty.

"Nor's the Yard. Caradoc?"

"Constabulary of the Royal Duchy of Cornwall."

"I can see why you shorten it!"

"Caradoc was a Celtic prince. I think he fought the Romans. He was Welsh, strictly speaking, but all us Celts have to stick together. *Onen hag oll* is Cornwall's motto. Kernow's, I should say."

"Should you?"

"'One and all,' it means."

"Let's hope Bristol feels that way about lending us a hand."

"What we need is lots of hands," Megan pointed out.

Ken sighed. "Which probably means bringing out the big guns, otherwise known as the Assistant Commissioner. Who will not be happy."

"How about offering a reward?"

He brightened. "Now that's an idea. Having a concrete proposal to suggest will look a whole lot better than admitting we can't do our job without calling out the entire Bristol force. Nothing we can do about it tonight, anyway."

And by the morning, Megan suspected, it would have metamorphosed into his own idea. Never mind; that was just the way he was.

Her move from London to Cornwall had been dictated as much by the desire to escape her helpless attraction to Ken as by the promotion to sergeant and her preference for rural over urban life. She was grateful to Scumble for sending him to Bristol with her. Seeing him again had exorcised a ghost. Now, she hoped, they could be friends.

In the morning, they fortified themselves with eggs, bacon, sausages, fried tomatoes, and fried bread, not to mention toast and marmalade, before walking over to the Bristol police HQ.

To their dismay, they were directed to the office of the superintendent of the local CID.

The presence in his office of a uniformed inspector and a shorthand writer didn't make them feel any better. Megan wondered whether, in spite of having their plans okayed by the Bristol force, they had transgressed against some local shibboleth. She came to attention beside Ken—and a little to the rear. Cowardly, perhaps, but he was the man from Scotland Yard and she was merely from Cornwall.

"DS Faraday and DS Pencarrow reporting, sir."

Superintendent Oakhurst looked them over without any sign of either approval or disapproval. "I've been talking to your respective superiors," he said, in the clipped accent of South African English. "I gather you've found a link between Bristol and the charity shop murder. Inspector Everett here is very familiar with the area you expressed an interest in."

"I can mebbe give you a hint whether your informants are reliable." In contrast to the superintendent, the inspector had the slow, soft voice of a West Country native. "Give us a report, Sergeant, with a bit more detail than you phoned in last night, please."

Ken did so, including the group of young people who had skedaddled from the pub when they weren't looking. "I didn't actually spot them," he admitted. "DS Pencarrow drew their departure to my attention."

The superintendent's and inspector's attention thus drawn to Megan, she explained that the youths had vanished through an unnoticed back door while she was waiting for a suitable moment to interrupt DS Faraday's questioning of the informant.

Oakhurst looked as if he was about to utter a reprimand, but Inspector Everett said placidly, "Silent as shadows and slippery as eels, those squatters, when they want to be. They'd have disappeared into their holes before you got outside to go after them."

"That's what I reckoned, sir," said Ken, "having had some experience of the type in London. It seems to me it will take considerable manpower to find the ones we're looking for."

"You won't be one of them," the superintendent informed him. "You're to take the first train back to London. I understand you're needed at Scotland Yard. The presumed owner of the stolen goods the Cornish force recovered"—he nodded at Megan—"was released from the hospital yesterday morning and he seems to have disappeared."

"What!"

"An officer went to his home to take him to the Yard to identify the jewelry. He wasn't there. Nor was his car garaged. The next-door neighbour's out of town and no one they've contacted has seen him or has any idea where he might have gone. They seem to think you might be able to find him, Sergeant. Or perhaps it's just that they can't spare anyone else to look." Everett glanced at the electric clock on the wall. "You'd better get going. Temple Meads station is just a few minutes walk."

"I need to discuss the case with M—my Cornish colleague, sir. The parts that aren't relevant to your force."

"DS Pencarrow's superior is expecting her to ring him, and we need her cooperation with regard to these squatters."

Superintendent Oakhurst intervened. "A few minutes is neither here nor there, except when it comes to catching trains. We won't have men to spare till Sunday."

"Both Bristol teams have home games," Everett put in gloomily.

"Or even Monday, if your lot don't want a huge bill for over time. You may go with Faraday to the station, Miss Pencarrow, but make your discussion quick and come straight back." He nodded dismissal.

"Sir."

Ken held his tongue till the door was safely shut behind them, then he burst out, "What the hell does it mean? Disappeared! Did the robbers snatch him and do him in for fear he might be able to identify them? Or has he scarpered for fear they might? Oakhurst didn't give me much info to build theories on."

Megan stopped to ask the desk sergeant for directions to Temple Meads station.

"The disappearing jeweller is really none of Oakhurst's business," she pointed out as they went out to the street. "His only part is to help to identify our victim. I doubt he bothered to find out more than he told you."

Ken mimicked the South African accent: "'An officer went to his home to take him to the Yard to identify the jewelry. He wasn't there. They seem to think you might be able to find him, Sergeant. Or perhaps it's just that they can't spare anyone else to look.'"

Megan laughed. "That final dig was uncalled-for. I expect he's just fed up at being asked to lend his men for at least several hours for a case that's not his problem. It's a nuisance they can't get onto it till Monday. Too bad both Bristol City and Rovers have home fixtures this weekend."

"Yes. I hope the kids who knew him won't have taken fright by then to the point of leaving town."

"Like Donaldson. Are you going to try for a warrant to search his house?"

"I suppose so. At least I might be able to tell whether he left voluntarily. Though I doubt they'll grant a warrant till he's been missing a bit longer."

"I take it he's not married, since no mention's been made of a wife. He probably has a daily. She might know something useful."

"Good point. But with any luck he'll have turned up by the

time I get back." They entered the station and studied the departure board. "Damn, I've just missed a train."

"That was a slow one, look. The next is an express. You'd better buck up and get your ticket."

"Yes." Ken checked his watch against the station clock. "Meggie—Megan—do you ever think of transferring back to the Met?"

"Never. I love Cornwall."

"Pity. We'd make a good team."

On the job or off it? she wondered. "We didn't do too well at the pub, letting the people we wanted get away."

"True," he said ruefully. "But you have the makings of a good detective. Don't let your guv'nor get you down. Well, if you ever come up to town for a weekend, give me a ring."

"I'll think about it." But not for very long.

In a most unprofessional manner, he dropped a kiss on her cheek. "See you later, alligator."

"In a while, crocodile."

Watching as he joined the queue at the ticket window, she gave a little wave as he turned his head to glance back. Good-looking, charming, intelligent, competent—and doubtless dating some gorgeous leggy blond model, his preferred type of female. Megan left the station and headed back towards police headquarters.

She was less than a hundred yards from the building, walking briskly, when a girl darted out of an alley and caught her sleeve.

"Oh, please," she gasped, "are you a policeman? A policewoman, I mean? A police officer?"

"I am."

"That's what Jake said."

"Is there something—?"

"I've got to talk to you!" A slight figure, nervous but determined, she peered at Megan through National Health glasses and a long fringe—raggedly cut but neatly combed—of lank, mousy hair. She wore faded plimsolls and grey bell-bottom trousers two or three sizes too large, cut off at ankle height and badly hemmed, cinched at the waist with a worn leather belt over a tight top in a psychedelic design of pink and orange. "I don't care what the others say, it's not right!"

TWENTY-ONE

Megan guessed the girl was sixteen or seventeen, certainly not much older. Skinny and pallid, she looked badly in need of good food and fresh air. "I'll be happy to hear what you have to say," Megan affirmed, and gestured towards the police station. "Let's go in."

"Oh no, not in there. All those old men . . . I'm not talking to them."

"All right. I just passed a café, let's go in there."

"I haven't got any money."

"I'll treat you, okay?" She turned back, and the girl trailed after her. "I'm Megan. What's your name?"

"Cam. Camilla, really. Isn't it awful? I like Megan."

"It's not bad, but I hate being called Meggie."

That surprised a laugh out of her. "I wouldn't think anyone'd dare. I mean, what with you being in the police and all. You're a detective, aren't you? Not wearing the uniform. Do you like it? Being a detective?"

"Mostly. Except when another officer calls me Meggie! It's

like any job—there are things I have to do that aren't much fun, but most of the time I like it, or I wouldn't do it."

"You're a grown-up. You can do whatever you want."

Megan waited to respond until they were seated in the café. It was a pleasant, old-fashioned place with rubber plants in the windows, real tablecloths, and waitresses in frilly aprons. The service was correspondingly slow.

While they waited for menus, Megan asked, "What would *you* like to do?" Pop star, film star, model? she wondered.

"Work on a farm. My dad's a farm-worker and I help . . . I used to help him in the holidays. I love working with animals. But he says it's a dead-end job, like my mum's, charring. He never had a chance for a proper education so he wants me to get my A levels, even go to university. I tried, honestly. I got ten O levels. I stuck it through the autumn term in the sixth form, but I spent all my time swotting. I just can't face another two years, let alone five, reading boring books. I'll puke if I ever have to read another book by Dickens or Balzac, I swear it."

"How about science?"

"My best marks were in science, 'specially biology. It's interesting."

"Have you considered working towards being a vet?"

"A vet! Girls can't be vets."

"Girls can be anything they want to be, if they want it badly enough and are prepared to work for it. I'm not saying it's not harder than for boys. But plenty of people told me girls can't be detectives."

"Really?"

The waitress arrived at that moment and handed them menus.

"Are you still serving breakfast?" Megan asked.

The waitress glanced at the clock. "No, madam."

"All right, we'll call it an early lunch. Do you like omelettes, Cam?"

Cam nodded, eyes gleaming through specs and hair.

"It's only morning coffee at this time, madam."

"I'll have coffee. This young lady will have an omelette and toast and a glass of milk."

"The luncheon chef hasn't come in yet," the waitress told her haughtily.

"In that case, make it scrambled eggs. We don't want to be difficult."

"Luncheon isn't served till—"

"You don't know how to scramble eggs?"

"Of course—"

"That's all right then." Megan beamed at her. "Thank you, you're most accommodating."

The waitress's mouth opened and closed, and she flounced off.

Cam giggled. "Do you think she'll bring it?"

"I expect so. She'll decide it's easier than arguing. Not that I was arguing."

"You weren't?"

"Not at all, I was presenting alternatives, in a polite and reasonable manner. There are ways and ways of getting your way, and some ways are better than others. Now, while she's trying to work out how to make toast, why don't you tell me what you wanted to talk to me about?"

"It's that boy . . ." Cam said hesitantly. "The one who was found dead in Cornwall? I think . . . But it's awfully hard to be sure from a newspaper photo. It was wrapped round the fish and chips and got a bit greasy, too."

Megan took out a print of the photo and placed it on the table.

Cam drew in a sharp breath. "It is! That's him. He . . . Was it taken after . . . ?"

"Yes. Whatever they do, it's always obvious." She picked up the picture as Cam, with a shudder, shoved it back across the table at her. "Who was he?"

"His name was Norm. Norman Wilmot. Mostly we just go by christian names but he—It was weird. He never called his dad Father, or Dad, or Pa, or anything, always 'Doctor Wilmot,' in a horrible sarcastic voice. Not a medical doctor, a PhD. His parents are entomologists, bug-people he calls—called them. They went away for years and years, to Borneo or New Guinea or somewhere like that, and left him in boarding schools he hated. You know, fagging and caning and stuff, and what-ho for the jolly old cricket team. He hated all the team games. Boxing was the only thing he liked. He failed his A levels."

"He must be at least eighteen, then?"

"Eighteen or nineteen, I s'pose."

"Did he mention the name of the last school he attended?"

"Not that I remember. He called it 'that place.' "

"Was it a public school, do you know?"

"Like Eton, you mean? He never said, but he did talk kind of la-di-da. We don't talk about stuff like that much, though. I mean, where we come from and that. We're sort of squatters, that is, we *are* squatters. I know it's illegal. You aren't going to . . . ?"

"Arrest you? No. You're being extremely helpful. What's more, your friends won't have such a hard time of it now that you've given me this—Ah, here's your scrambled eggs, if I'm not mistaken."

The eggs looked done to a crisp, and the toast was burnt around the edges, but Cam set to ravenously, so Megan let it be.

Drinking her coffee, surprisingly good, she looked back over the notes she'd been taking. She hadn't written down any of Camilla's personal details. She'd have to try to get an address from her, though, preferably somewhere she could be found when needed as a witness. That meant her parents', which meant persuading her to go home. Megan had already made a start on that, she hoped.

She remembered kidding Ken when he talked about the squatters, saying he ought to be a social worker. Now here she was trying to sort out Camilla's life. Perhaps it went with the job; she just hadn't realised it before. On the other hand, perhaps it was a weakness that would prevent either of them rising to the top of their profession.

She shrugged. She would just have to wait and see.

Cam finished her meal and looked anxiously at Megan. "Thank you," she said. "That was . . . good."

Megan grinned. "Come now! Filling perhaps, edible I assume since you ate it all, but good?"

"We-ell . . . I was hungry. We had some bread back there, but I was too upset to eat."

"Upset about talking to me?"

"I didn't know how to find you, not without asking the . . . the police. The others kept saying we shouldn't get mixed up in it at all. They all said we couldn't be sure it was him and it was none of our business anyway, and nobody liked Norm much, either."

"Why was that?"

"He was a bully. We're supposed to be all about peace and love and that sort of thing, but he was a creep. But I thought, even if his parents were bug people and deserted him for years and years, they ought to know what happened to him. Don't you think?"

"I do," Megan said gravely. "When did you last see him?"

"Monday. I worked it out when we read about him in the chip paper. He was killed Tuesday night, wasn't he?"

"Yes. Did he spend much time with your . . . group?"

"On and off. People come and go. But as I said, no one was mad keen on him. He was Trev's mate, mostly."

"Trev—Trevor?" A second name, Megan thought with satisfaction. Trevor and Jake. It ought to be possible to track down the group. "Do you know his surname?"

Cam shook her head. "He's nice, really nice. He gets an allowance from some relative or other. Not much, but he always shares. If you ask me, that's why Norm was matey with him. Or wasn't nasty to him, at least."

"I need to get in touch with him. I realise you don't want to tell me where you and your friends are staying at the moment, but could you ask him to meet me here, or wherever—"

"I would, honestly, but I haven't seen him since . . ." She broke off, looking horrified.

"Since Tuesday?" Megan demanded urgently. Camilla gave a reluctant nod. "He left with Norman?"

"He *couldn't* have anything to do with the murder! You mustn't say that. He *wouldn't*!"

"I'm not saying he did. But Cam, listen to me, if he was with Norman, and Norman was murdered, he may be in danger."

"D'you really think so?"

"I do. We need to find him, quickly. What does he look like?"

The girl made a helpless gesture. "Just ordinary."

"Have you ever heard of IdentiKit?"

"No." She hesitated. "I don't think so."

"It's a way of making a picture of a face when you have someone who knows a person but can't describe him very well. You just keep changing the shape of the eyes and nose and so on, until your witness recognises it as the person you're trying to find. Do you think you could do that for Trevor?"

"I don't know. Maybe. Do you really think he's in danger?"

"How can I be sure? What I do know is that if I wait until I'm sure, it might be too late for him."

"Oh."

"Do you think you could do that, for Trevor's sake?"

"I . . . Would I have to go into the police station?"

"I may be able to arrange for the expert to meet you here—or their artist if they don't use IdentiKit." The Met did, or had the facilities at least, but CaRaDoC didn't. Bristol was an unknown quantity. "The trouble is, I'm not local—I'm from the Cornish police—and I'm only a detective sergeant, so I haven't got much pull. Besides, if I leave you here while I go and ask, could I trust you to wait?"

"I don't think *she'd* let me." Camilla jerked her head towards the waitress, who was starting towards them with a purposeful air.

"She'll have to if I order coffee and a selection of cakes for you and pay in advance."

"I don't much like coffee."

"Tea? Never mind, you don't have to drink it." Megan turned to the waitress, now bearing down upon them bill in hand. "A pot of tea and some cakes for my friend. I have an errand to run, but I'll pay for everything before I go."

"I'll have to write up a separate bill," the waitress grumbled.

"All right, just tell me the total."

"Depends how many she eats."

"Bring four. If she doesn't eat them all, she can take them with her. I'm sure you'll be able provide a pastry box, won't you?"

Wondering how much she'd be able to claim on expenses, she paid what seemed an exorbitant amount. The waitress stalked off to fetch the tea and cakes.

"I'll wait for you," said Cam. "I promise. You won't be long, will you?"

"I'll be as quick as I can. Eat slowly, but for pity's sake don't eat so many cakes you make yourself sick!"

Hurrying towards the Bristol nick, Megan knew she was taking a big risk in trusting the girl. If she was wrong, she would be in a lot of trouble, perhaps even demoted to uniform. She didn't even know Camilla's surname, having been afraid of scaring her off. But she couldn't see what else she could have done. The mysterious Trevor was either the murderer or conceivably in deadly danger. They had to find him.

She could have forced Camilla to come with her, but producing a portrait with an uncooperative witness was as good as impossible.

Halfway up the steps, she heard a voice behind her call, "Wait! Please wait!"

She turned as Camilla panted up, a square white cardboard box swinging from her hand.

"What's up?"

"That bitch! The waitress. She didn't bring me a pot of tea and plate of cakes, she brought this, already packed up, and gave me the money for the tea, and told me, 'We don't serve the likes of you.' So I nearly told her what she could do with her stupid cakes, but I thought you wouldn't like that, so I told her ever so sweetly, 'Thanks for making the scrambled eggs for me,' even though they were rotten. Then I just walked out."

"Good for you."

"And I thought, the fuzz can't be any worse than her. So here I am."

"Thank you for coming, Cam. You've saved my bacon."

"Really?" said Camilla, looking pleased.

"Really. Come on."

The desk sergeant showed no surprise at Megan arriving with a tatty young girl in tow after leaving with a sleek male colleague. "Your guv'nor phoned again," he told her, with a commiserating glance. "Inspector Everett's office." He jerked a thumb towards the right-hand corridor.

"Thanks. Have you got an IdentiKit, here, or an artist? This young lady can provide a description of a chap we're going to be looking for."

"I'll deal with it. You run." He gave Camilla a fatherly smile and said, "Good of you to come in, miss."

"Just do your best, Cam," Megan said, and ran. Scumble at best was not a patient man. Scumble kept waiting for a couple of hours didn't bear thinking of.

TWENTY-TWO

Megan found a door with Inspector Everett's name on it and knocked. In response to his "Come in," she entered. He was seated behind a desk covered with paperwork, reading a report. Looking up, he said nothing but gestured at the telephone on his desk.

He returned to his work as she dialled the Launceston nick, but she had a feeling he was listening.

She was put through to DI Scumble.

"Pencarrow here, sir."

"Where the bloody hell have you been, Pencarrow? Your aunt . . ." He took an audible breath and let it out in a bellow: *"Your aunt has remembered yet another fact she forgot to tell us!"*

Megan wondered what the bloody hell she was supposed to say or do about it. Cautiously returning the receiver to her ear, whence she had removed it to preserve her eardrums, she ventured to ask, "What has she remembered, sir?"

Having blown off steam, he achieved a more normal voice. "First tell me, did you ever mention the jeweller's name to her? Or to her side-kicks?"

"Side-kicks, sir?"

"The artist and the vicar's wife. Well?"

"No, sir, I'm sure I didn't."

"Then, if you didn't put it into her head, I suppose she really is remembering. She says there was a monogram on the case the jewelry was in. *D A W*, she thinks, but the letters were superimposed and it could equally well be *W A D*."

"Wilfred Donaldson!"

"It's not absolute proof, but it's another link. We're not going to get a positive identification of the jewels from the jeweller for a while. Did the boy wonder tell you he's disappeared?"

"Yes, sir. DS Faraday's gone back to town to look for him."

"Good. We'll leave the Yard to handle that end of things." The satisfaction in his voice made Megan relax, so she was unprepared when the bellow came again. "So where the bloody hell have you been, Pencarrow? I've been waiting for your report for hours. On a Saturday! I hope you have an excuse for the delay, and something to show for your jaunt to Bristol?"

Thank heaven she did have something to show. "The victim's name, sir. Norman Wilmot." She explained about the squatters and Camilla's unexpected approach. "That's why I was late phoning, sir. I had to talk to her right away or I'd have lost her."

He grunted a grudging approval. "Norman Wilmot, eh? Just his name?"

Megan passed on what little more she had learnt about him. "There must be a society of entomologists, don't you think, sir? Dr Wilmot would surely be a member, and they'd know where he went."

"Which jungle? Very helpful!"

"How to contact him, perhaps?"

"I suppose we'll have to try. You've not done too badly, Pencarrow."

Would it hurt the sod to say she'd done well?

On second thoughts, yes, it probably would hurt him. Still, he had yet to hear the rest of Camilla's revelations. "I have another name, sir. Just a Christian name, but it may be useful. Apparently a friend of Wilmot's was coming and going with him last weekend, a youth by the name of Trevor—"

"*Trevor!* Bloody hell, Pencarrow, your aunt . . ." His voice died away in a gobbling noise.

Megan hoped she wouldn't be blamed if he was having a fit. She saw that Inspector Everett was all ears, no longer pretending not to listen. "My aunt, sir?" she asked cautiously.

"Your aunt, apparently, when she first saw the body of the wretched Wilmot, before she saw the face, jumped to the conclusion that it was a youth known to her by the name of Trevor."

"Good heavens!"

"Good heavens indeed. It will not surprise you that neither she nor Mrs Stearns saw fit to mention it to us."

"But sir," Megan dared to argue, "when they discovered it wasn't him, why should—"

"It's for us, Pencarrow—and that 'us' presently includes you— to decide what information is relevant. The sooner you learn that any and all details a witness can provide may prove vital, the more likely you are to remain one of 'us.'"

"Yes, sir." She was seething, on her aunt's behalf as well as her own. She was ninety-nine percent sure that if Aunt Nell had told the insufferable Scumble about her mistaken first impression, he'd have informed her in no uncertain terms that he had no interest whatsoever in her erroneous guesses.

"I have here a sketch that artist chappie drew from the ladies' description of Trevor."

"The girl who told me about him, sir, assuming it's the same

Trevor, is helping a police artist here to produce a sketch."
Megan crossed her fingers for luck, praying that Camilla was still
cooperative and able to provide a good enough description for
the artist or IdentiKit man to work with.

If the inspector managed to force himself to utter a word of
appreciation, she missed it. "The sooner we can compare the
two the better," he said. "Bring it back here as soon as it's done.
This girl, could she have killed Wilmot?"

"I don't think so, sir. She's a skinny little thing. If it was a
matter of hitting him over the head with a weapon, perhaps,
but bashing his head on that table would take much more
strength."

"I had worked that out for myself, Pencarrow. Well, if that's
all you've got to report, put me through to Inspector Everett."

"Yes, sir." Megan covered the receiver with her hand and
turned to Everett. "DI Scumble would appreciate a word with
you, sir. I'll just go and—"

"No, stay. I want to hear all about your aunt." He was grinning. "And I'll need to talk to you about finding these squatters."

"I'll come back, sir." With any luck he'd have lost interest in
Aunt Nell by then and want to talk only business. She handed
over the phone. "I've got a rather nervous witness, you see. I
think I'd better go and hold her hand a bit."

He nodded and waved her away. As she closed the door behind her, she heard him say, "Everett here, Mr Scumble. Tell me
about DS Pencarrow's aunt."

Talk about red flags to a raging bull! Whether Scumble complied or not, Megan didn't want to hear. She went to find
Camilla.

The artist was a uniformed sergeant, a policewoman. Megan

was annoyed with herself for having assumed it would be a man. If women had such low expectations for each other, how could they demand anything better from mere men?

Camilla and Sergeant Winston were getting on like a house on fire. Megan recalled thinking that an unwilling witness would be totally useless in producing a likeness. It followed that a police artist must have the skills to make people want to cooperate, along with the artistic ability.

All the same, Camilla looked relieved to see Megan.

Megan introduced herself to the sergeant. "How's it going?" she asked.

"I think people might recognise Trevor from the picture," Camilla said doubtfully.

"But it's not quite right yet," said Sergeant Winston. "Eyes, nose, chin?"

"I'm not sure."

"May I?" Megan requested, reaching for the sketch. She knew at once one aspect that was wrong. The question was how to phrase it without sounding rude or upsetting the girl. "I wonder, Cam, could it be that you're used to seeing him somewhat less . . . tidy?"

Camilla at once raised her hand to stroke her chin. "Could be."

The sergeant took back her work. With a touch of shading and a few squiggles, she produced a faint stubble and tangled locks. "How's this?"

"Oh yes! That's much better. It looks quite like Trevor."

Sergeant Winston looked at Megan and shrugged. "Good enough? All right, I'll get it duplicated for you."

"Many thanks. Inspector Everett will want copies, I expect. I've got to go back to see him. Could you leave my copies with the desk sergeant?"

"Will do. Goodbye, Camilla. You were a great help."

They parted in the passage, Megan and Cam turning back towards the lobby.

"Megan . . . Miss Pencarrow—"

"Megan will do fine."

"Megan, do I have to talk to Inspector Everett, too?"

"I haven't had a chance to discuss with him what you've told me." But what little time she'd had to think had convinced her that in spite of Camilla's help they still needed to question her friends, if they could be found. Their testimony could confirm or refute the girl's recollections of Trevor's and Norman Wilmot's movements. "I think he'll want to talk to you."

Camilla sighed. "In for a penny, in for a pound, I suppose. All right. But you promised my friends'd be in less trouble because I told you about Norm and Trev."

"I said they wouldn't have such a hard time. You see, with the information you've given us, they can't deny knowing those two, so instead of having to bring them in and keep at them till they admit that much, we can get straight on with asking them *what* they know about them."

"I see," Camilla said doubtfully, then clutched Megan's arm. "Only, they'll know I split on them. I can't go back to the squat. Everything's so awful!" She started to cry.

Megan put an arm around her shoulders and felt for a hankie. "That's one of the terrible things about murder. It messes up the lives of a lot of people who don't really have anything much to do with it. Here, blow your nose. Look, there's a ladies' room. Go and wash your face and comb your hair—"

"I haven't g-got a comb!"

"Here's mine. I need it, so please don't run away with it. I want you to go to the desk sergeant—the man in the lobby?—and wait for me there. Will you do that? I promise I'll sort things out for you somehow. I won't desert you."

"All r-right," sobbed Camilla, and once again Megan just had to hope she meant it.

Eleanor had been baking. She enjoyed the process, but the results were rarely what she hoped for. Her life had provided little opportunity to exercise the domestic skills until very recently. But every now and again she tried.

She liked to provide some sort of treat for the volunteers who gave up their Saturday afternoons for LonStar. Usually they had to make do with shop biscuits or cake, from the bakery opposite if she was feeling extravagant—which wasn't really "making do," she reflected, as the bakery's products were excellent and her home-made often were not—otherwise ordinary packaged stuff. However, Mr Scumble and Nick had between them demolished the entire packet of chocolate digestives, and Eleanor had been too busy this morning to get to the shops before they closed.

Only tourist-oriented shops, such as Nick's gallery and Brian and Mavis's Ye Olde Cornysh Piskie Curio Shoppe, stayed open on Saturday afternoons. Jocelyn had decided LonStar qualified, though many of their customers were local people.

Hence, Eleanor had been baking for the volunteers.

Shortbread sounded easy enough. Only four ingredients, and Jocelyn had said she didn't really need to use rice flour, which she didn't have. She had just increased the amount of ordinary flour instead. Not self-raising, Jocelyn had stressed, and it must be butter; marge wouldn't do. Castor sugar, not ordinary gran, she'd done that. So why was her table covered with broken bits that couldn't possibly be offered to the volunteers? Something to do with the way she had turned it out of the pans onto the racks, perhaps, or perhaps she had kneaded too little. Or too much.

With a sigh she put one of the smaller fragments into her mouth. It was delicious! Suppose she took the large bits and cut them into neater shapes—

The phone rang. Her fingers sticky, Eleanor grabbed a tea-towel to pick up the receiver and gave her number, a bit indistinctly through the crumbs. The phone beeped and she heard the clink of coins.

"Aunt Nell?"

"Megan, dear. Don't tell me Mr Scumble has thought up a whole new lot of questions for me!"

"No, this is nothing to do with . . . At least, it is, sort of. I've sort of landed myself with a witness—"

"Megan, so far I haven't the slightest idea what you're talking about. Am I being very dense?"

"Not at all, Aunt Nell. It's sort of hard to explain because Mr Scumble'll kill me if I tell you too much, but the end result is that I have a young girl on my hands who has no money and not even a toothbrush. I'm hoping to persuade the inspector to give her funds from petty cash for that and a nightie at least, but the shops are shut. And she has nowhere to stay. I'd take her home, even though I've only got the bedsitter, but I'm going to be working tomorrow and I simply can't leave her on her own."

"Of course she must come here, dear, at least till Tuesday. I probably have an extra toothbrush somewhere, or Jocelyn will, and I certainly have a clean nightdress. I hope it fits. Or we can always get one from downstairs."

"I can really bring her to you?"

"But only till Tuesday. I must go to the Scilly Islands on Tuesday, come what may. I do hope you won't feel obliged to tell Mr Scumble, because he'd have to arrest me to stop me."

"This is a very bad line. I'm ringing from a public box. The only thing I heard is that I can bring Camilla to stay with you. The rest we'll have to sort out when I see you. Thanks, Aunt Nell, you're an angel. We'll be there about six, I hope."

Thoughtfully, Eleanor popped another broken bit into her mouth. She tidied up the larger pieces, arranged them on a plate, and went downstairs, leaving Teazle staring up hopefully at the counter.

In the stockroom, she found four women and one elderly gentleman. Only one was a regular volunteer. The others she knew only to say "Good morning" to in the street. She was fairly certain they didn't appear on Jocelyn's roster. Mrs Davies must have recruited a troop of irregulars to make quite sure she didn't have to enter the haunted stockroom herself.

Jocelyn would be furious if she found out. Ought Eleanor to tell her? Though, obviously, it was important that only trustworthy people work in the shop, these were surely all members of the faithful flock at the chapel—which wouldn't endear them to the vicar's wife but guaranteed their respectability as far as the minister's wife was concerned.

They did seem to have done a good deal of sorting, tidying, and cleaning, and one was busy ironing clothes.

What Jocelyn didn't know couldn't upset her. Eleanor decided to have a quiet word with Mrs Davies later, pointing out that as Jocelyn bore ultimate responsibility for the shop, it really wasn't fair to bring new people in without consulting her.

In the meantime, the irregulars were delighted with the shortbread, "so original to shape them like crazy paving," instead of the usual rectangles or triangles. Someone went to put on the electric kettle and the one regular among them invited Eleanor to join them for a cup of tea.

"Sorry, I can't. I'm expecting an unexpected guest, if you see what I mean, and I have to get things ready. Just leave the plate on the table here and I'll fetch it later."

She went upstairs. Teazle was in exactly the same position, staring hopefully, nose twitching, so Eleanor put some crumbs in her dish. "Not too much, or you'll get fat, my girl."

Considering the debris, she ate another scrap herself. A witness, she thought, a young girl with no money, no luggage, nowhere to go, she probably wouldn't turn up her nose at fresh shortbread just because it wasn't beautiful. The pieces big enough to pick up went into a cake tin, and Eleanor tossed the crumbs out of the back window for the birds.

No luggage, no toothbrush—better ring Jocelyn. Surely she must be home by now from lunch with the bishop in Truro.

Jocelyn had just walked in the door as her phone was ringing. "A witness?" she asked, intrigued. "Witness to what?"

"I don't know, and I'm pretty sure Megan won't tell me."

"She can't have been in the storeroom when the boy was killed. They couldn't be sure she didn't do it, and Megan would never land you with a possible murderer. All the same, I'd better come over and—"

"No, Joce. You'd never be able to resist interrogating her, and I'm sure Megan will have told her she's not to answer any questions. It wouldn't be fair. I just rang to ask if you happen to have a spare toothbrush you could let me have for her."

"A toothbrush! She really has nothing at all? Well, it all sounds very odd to me, but yes, I've got a toothbrush you can have. I always keep a spare because Timothy occasionally uses his to clean out the fiddly parts of the Vespa. Are you *quite* sure you wouldn't like me to—"

"Quite sure," Eleanor said firmly. "If Megan's bringing her here, she must be all right. I'll be up in a couple of minutes for the toothbrush."

As she put on her jacket and found the dog's lead, she reflected on the fact that her notion of an "all right" person was probably quite different from Jocelyn's. Life was so much simpler if one took people as they came. All the same, she hoped Megan would be able to give her at least a hint as to why her guest had no possessions and no home.

TWENTY-THREE

However suspicious of the unknown guest, Jocelyn provided not only a pristine toothbrush still in its cellophane wrapping but a warm dressing gown. "I thought you've probably only got one. My sister left this last time she stayed. She said not to bother sending it on. I keep meaning to bring it down to the shop. You really don't want me to be there when she comes?"

"Really. In the circumstances, it would be astonishing if the poor child were not in a fragile emotional state. The fewer strangers she has to cope with the better."

"I daresay. But if you need me, or anything else for the girl, just ring and I'll come straight down."

When Eleanor reached home, the shop had closed and Mrs Davies was locking the front door.

"Oh, Mrs Trewynn," she said, "I'm so glad you came home. The passage door isn't locked and I wasn't sure whether you had your keys. I didn't want to lock you out."

Eleanor felt in her pockets. Toothbrush, no keys. "I must have left them behind. I just popped out for a moment to see Mrs Stearns."

"You didn't . . . I mean, she doesn't . . . You haven't told her . . . ?"

"About the ghost, if any? Of course not. Did any of your helpers see one?"

"No," admitted the minister's wife, shamefaced. "I suppose I let my imagination run away with me."

"All too easy when such a horrible thing happens. All the same, Mrs Davies, it's not a good idea to bring in people Mrs Stearns doesn't know, who aren't on her schedule. I'm grateful for their help, but please, in future, when you recruit new volunteers be sure to notify her before they start work."

"You didn't tell her . . . ?"

"I didn't. But if it happens again—"

"It won't, I promise. I did go in there, last thing, to make sure everything was as it should be. I didn't see anything." She lowered her voice. "Or even feel any horrid—"

"Eleanor!" It was Nick.

Mrs Davies said a hurried goodbye to Eleanor, gave Nick a distant nod in passing, and hurried off.

"Even in this modern age," he said mournfully, "art equates with sin in the nonconformist imagination."

"Don't talk to me about imagination!"

"All right, I won't. I've just had a telephone call from . . . er . . . Detective Sergeant Pencarrow, with an extremely confused, not to say confusing, message for you. She seemed to think you'd know what she was talking about. What it boils down to, as far as I can see, is that she can't get away till much later than planned so could you please ring her back at the Launceston police station to let her know if it's all right if she arrives late. When I asked how late, she could only say, 'it depends.'"

"On Mr Scumble, I expect. Oh dear, that poor girl! I know, I'll drive over to Launceston and fetch her."

"Who? I mean, whom?"

"I'd better not tell you what little I know, dear. Megan was a bit mysterious about her. But she's coming to stay with me, just for a couple of days. It's bad timing, I'm afraid. I'm going to the Scillies on Tuesday."

"You're taking a holiday at last! The Scillies in April are wonderful."

"Not a holiday," Eleanor said gravely. "It's a last-ditch effort to prevent a civil war—"

"Between the Scillonians and the mainland?"

"It's not funny, Nick. Somewhere in Africa. I ought not to be more precise. A person in authority thinks I may be able to help, so of course that takes absolute priority. I must go and ring Megan. Did you happen to notice yesterday how much petrol there is in the car?"

"The needle swung wildly between empty and three quarters on the way down the hill, so, going by precedent, you have about half a tank. Enough to get you to Launceston and back. But Eleanor, most schools broke up yesterday for the holidays. The roads will be aswarm with Easter emmets, holiday-makers who left London or Birmingham this morning to invade us. It'll be a hell of a drive."

"I'll be going in the opposite direction."

"Not coming home."

"Then I'll take the back lanes. I've learnt every twist and turn on my scavenging expeditions."

"By then it'll be getting dark. And there may be fog on the moor. I'm coming with you. Go and ring Megan, and for heaven's sake bring a warm coat. The Incorruptible has more draughts than my attic. Don't forget the car keys. I'll just get my anorak."

Eleanor didn't protest as he disappeared into his shop. She disliked driving at night even without fog and traffic to contend with. No doubt Nick was actuated by curiosity as well as kindness, but he was bound to meet the girl anyway in the couple of days she'd be staying. Eleanor must impress on him that he wasn't to ask questions.

Nick was waiting for her when she came down, his jacket slung over his shoulder. She had brought an extra woolly for the girl, who now had a name.

"Camilla," she said as they walked down the hill, "but Megan says she prefers Cam. I don't know why, it's a very pretty name."

"Old-fashioned," Nick suggested.

"No more so than Nicholas! Think of St Nicholas. Wasn't he an ancient Greek?"

"Something of the sort. And then there's Old Nick."

"True. Odd, isn't it? Megan's very grateful to you for accompanying her aged aunt, by the way."

"Is that what she said?"

"Not exactly. She's grateful to me for offering to pick Cam up, but she wouldn't have let me if it meant driving on my own."

"That sounds much more likely!"

Nick drove. He stuck to the main road once they reached it. As he had foreseen there was quite a bit of tourist traffic coming towards them on this first day of the Easter holidays, though nothing like the swarms that would clog the roads in the summer. At least the road works were closed down for the weekend. Whatever one's opinion of the devastation caused by ubiquitous widening and straightening of the roads, it had become necessary since Dr Beeching slashed so many branch railways to such devastating effect.

On the way, Eleanor told Nick what little she knew about Camilla. Megan had said even less on their second phone call, presumably because Scumble was present. Eleanor could hear him giving orders in the background.

"She did say the inspector would be glad to have her safely out of the way. Perhaps gratitude will make him more friendly next time I see him."

"I wouldn't count on it."

"No. But very likely I shan't be there anyway."

"Does he know you're going to Scilly?"

"I asked Megan not to tell him."

"Brave woman!"

"If you had ever seen the consequences of civil war, you'd know there's no question of my not going."

"Sorry. I didn't mean to sound flippant."

"And I didn't mean to snap. Dear me, Mr Scumble's attitude must be rubbing off. I do hope Megan doesn't end up with the same manners."

"Or lack thereof. Why on earth did she join the police?"

"You'll have to ask her sometime."

"I will. Quite apart from his manner, do you think Scumble is any good at his job? It's nearly a week since the boy was killed and we don't even know his name yet."

"We don't, but they may. And it's only five days. Four, really. Give the man a chance. In any case, his name doesn't matter so much as who he was, how he got mixed up in the robbery in the first place. That's what puzzles me. The news says the police are looking for two tall, well-built men, and no one could describe the dead boy as tall and brawny."

"No, you said he was a scrawny pipsqueak."

"I never called him a pipsqueak! Though I rather like the word."

"That's what he sounded like."

"Well, I couldn't really tell how tall he was. He certainly wasn't brawny, but that doesn't mean he was a weakling, necessarily. Everything goes slack when . . ." Eleanor decided not to pursue that line of thought. "I wonder whether the jeweller is a scrawny pipsqueak, so that his assailants looked bigger to him than they actually were."

"Surely the police would have taken that into account. It wasn't up to the Scumble, was it. That was Scotland Yard's end of things. They wouldn't miss something like that."

"Perhaps he exaggerated their size because he felt silly for giving in to a couple of pipsqueaks."

"Unlikely. It was two against one, remember, and it sounds as if he put up a fight. He was pretty bashed about, they said. Besides, he'd want to give the most accurate description possible to give the cops every chance of recovering his jewels."

"In fact, it sounds as if the boy in the stockroom wasn't one of the robbers."

"I doubt he was one of the two who attacked the jeweller," Nick agreed. "He might have driven their getaway car. Somehow he got hold of the loot and scarpered with it. He got nervous when he saw Bob Leacock's car and stashed the stuff in your car. The actual robbers caught up with him when he broke into the shop to retrieve the jewelry and bonked him on the head because he'd double-crossed them."

"That's an excellent theory as far as it goes, Nick."

"But?"

"It doesn't explain how he recognised my car, how he knew who I was, and where I'd take the stuff. He can't have been familiar with Port Mabyn, or someone local would have recognised him from the photo. I mean, really recognised him, not that nonsense about having seen him helping me."

"That's a point," he conceded.

"And it doesn't explain why these ruthless robbers didn't proceed to ransack the shop and my flat. They just tamely picked up the empty attaché-case—which wasn't locked, so it wouldn't take more than a moment to find out it was empty—and disappeared into the night. It doesn't sound to me like a pair of bold, brawny, brutal villains."

"Hmm. Let me think."

It took them a good hour to get to Launceston as the Incorruptible objected to doing over thirty-five miles an hour except downhill. When they reached the police station, Nick still hadn't come up with a convincing scenario to fill in the gaps. Eleanor remembered the DI's remark about "birds of a feather" and his request for Nick to draw a portrait of Trevor. It seemed to her that the only viable explanation involved the boy as a thief and probably a murderer. She didn't want to believe it.

"We won't talk about the murder on the way home," she said as Nick parked in the square. "If she's spent the day being bullied about it by Mr Scumble, the poor child won't want to—"

"Child! How old is this waif we're rescuing?"

"Megan said a 'young girl,' which translates to 'child' from the heights of my great age."

"Teenager, I should think. I hope she's not one of these impossible modern adolescents whose motto is 'never trust anyone over thirty,'" he said from the heights of his great age. "We'll see. Do you think I should wait in the car? The Scumble may not be pleased to see me."

"What, and miss the chance to wallow in Megan's gratitude?"

"That's a point. Here I come."

"Bring the cardigan from the backseat, would you, Nick?"

The desk sergeant directed them to a small room, painted institutional cream and dark green, furnished with a battered table and a few hard chairs. Here they found a spruce WPC and a crumpled, drooping, disconsolate slip of a girl.

The policewoman stood up, looking relieved. "Mrs Trewynn?"

"Yes, and this is Mr Gresham. We've come to fetch Cam."

Eleanor smiled at the girl, who managed a faint smile in return and started to rise.

"If you wouldn't mind waiting a moment, ma'am, DS Pencarrow should be on her way. She'd like a word before you go."

Cam subsided wearily. Nick went and sat down beside her. He eyed with disgust the two thick white china mugs half filled with scummy tea.

"Revolting!" he said.

"Isn't it? They keep plying me with tea and sandwiches. I'm not hungry."

"If the sandwiches are anything like the tea, I'm not surprised. But I bet you would be, faced with decent food. I know I am. We'll stop for something on the way home."

"Who are you?" she blurted out.

"Nick. Mrs Trewynn's next-door neighbour. It's no fun driving over the moors at night alone, especially in an old rattler like her car, so I came with her. I'm an artist."

"Really? I don't think I've ever met an artist before. Not a real one."

"I'm as real as they get. Ah, here's Miss Pencarrow."

The WPC exchanged a word with Megan as she entered, then took herself off. Camilla jumped up eagerly. "Megan, can't I stay with you? Please?"

Megan looked almost as worn as her pet witness. "Sorry, Cam. I'd love to have you, but it's just not on. We're running about back there like chickens with our heads cut off, though with more purpose, I hope. I don't know what time I'll get away, and I'll be working tomorrow. Aunt Nell will take good care of you, I promise."

"Oh, all right. But I'll see you again, won't I?"

"Yes, of course. Monday, if not sooner."

"Fab!"

"Aunt Nell, Cam's been an enormous help to us. You absolutely mustn't ask her anything about that, though. Nor you, Nick—Mr Gresham. I wish I could tell you more, but DI Scumble won't hear of it. Cam, for heaven's sake remember, don't you dare breathe a word about what Mr Scumble told you not to talk about."

"I won't, honestly."

"Good. Otherwise, you won't see me on Monday because he'll have cut off my head or sent me to Siberia or something. You know how reluctant he is to let you out of our clutches."

Camilla giggled, but she took a firm grip on Eleanor's sleeve. "I won't forget, Megan. And I won't be any trouble, Mrs Trewynn, honestly," she added anxiously.

"I'm sure you won't, my dear. Nick has a warm cardy for you, if he hasn't put it down somewhere." She retrieved it from over the back of a chair. "Here you go. You'll probably think it's terribly old-ladyish, but it's quite chilly out. Oh dear, I'm afraid it's rather dog-hairy." She brushed at the blue cable-knit, but in the miraculous manner of dog-hair, it had woven itself into the wool.

"I don't mind. I love dogs. Did you bring yours with you? What kind of dog is it?"

"She's a Westie, a West Highland terrier. Teazle. Yes, she came with us, and it rather looks as if she slept on this in the backseat."

"That's all right. She can sleep on it again on the way home, on my lap. If she likes me."

Nick turned away from his conversation with Megan to assure Camilla, "Teazle's a friendly little thing. There's nothing she likes better than a lap to sit on." In an unexpected fit of gallantry, he held the cardigan up to help her to insert her arms.

Eleanor glanced at Megan and read a certain degree of cynicism in the gaze she fixed on Nick. Could Nick possibly be displaying his plumage, demonstrating to Megan what an attentive mate—boyfriend—he could be? With a touch of "there are other fish in the sea," of course. And if so, was he doing it consciously or unconsciously?

"Duty calls, I must go," Megan said. She kissed Eleanor's cheek. "I'll ring tomorrow, Aunt Nell. 'Bye, Cam. 'Bye, Mr—Nick, and thanks."

How wonderful it would be, Eleanor thought, if they should take a fancy to each other, once the investigation was out of the way. They were perfectly suited to each other . . .

Or perhaps not. An artist and a policewoman? Eleanor sighed. Perhaps not.

In any case, courtship had changed since Eleanor's youth and she wasn't sure she knew how to recognise it nowadays.

TWENTY-FOUR

Eleanor, Nick, and Camilla went out to the car park. The girl was eager now to see the dog. Nick pointed out the Incorruptible. "It's not locked," he said, and she hurried ahead.

"Nick!" Eleanor teased, "not locked?"

"It didn't seem necessary under the windows of the police, with your guard dog inside." He stuck his hand in his pocket and presented Eleanor with four five-pound notes.

"What . . . ?"

"A gift from CaRaDoC. Megan somehow talked the powers that hold the purse-strings into providing for their vital witness. She handed the dosh over to me because she was afraid you might spurn it. Here, you should be able to outfit the child from the Lon-Star shop, and take us all out for a bite right now before I take a bite out of a policeman. How about that chicken-in-a-basket place on the way out of town? It's not too infra dig for you, is it?"

"My dear Nick, when did you ever see me stand on my dignity?"

"I bet you could if you tried," he observed.

They reached the car and he opened the passenger-side door

for her. Camilla was already in the back, cuddling Teazle, who was licking her face.

Climbing in, Eleanor said, "I've never quite understood why they can't put the chicken on a plate like everyone else, but I'm hungry enough to eat it out of a bucket, as they do in America."

"Out of a *bucket?*" Nick bent down to peer at her. "Are you sure?"

"Yes. I never tried it but I remember some sort of military man—a Major something?—who sells fried chicken by the bucket, all across the country."

"Extraordinary people, the Americans!" He closed the door and went round to the driver's side.

"Have you really been to America, Mrs Trewynn?" Camilla asked.

"Yes, two or three times."

"Fab! To San Francisco?"

"I'm afraid not. Just New York and Washington."

"Mrs Trewynn has worked all over the world, though she's a Cornishwoman born and bred. Now, how do I get out of here? It's too much work to pedal my bike over the moors, so I usually take the bus if I can't get a lift. I haven't a clue how the one-way system works."

"Left, I think, dear. Or is it right?"

"Do you know, Cam?"

"Sorry, I've never been here before."

"I thought there was more Somerset in your voice than Devon or Cornwall. Let's try turning left, and if a minion of the law comes after us with a whistle, I'll let you explain, Eleanor. Somerset?"

"I come from near Taunton, but I've been living in Bristol. Only I don't think Megan wants me to talk about that."

"All right," said Nick, cheerfully buzzing the wrong way

round the town centre, as Eleanor realised when she spotted a one-way arrow pointing in the opposite direction. Luckily central Launceston was not exactly a hotbed of activity on a Saturday evening, at least until the pubs let out. "Forget Bristol, we'll talk about Taunton. Where the cider comes from."

"That's right. The farm my dad works on has cider-apple orchards, but it has animals, too. That's what I like best. I wanted to work on the farm like him, but Megan says . . ." She hesitated.

"What does Megan say?" Eleanor asked.

"You see, Mum and Dad want me to better myself, and I understand, honestly I do. They've worked so hard all their lives and all they've got to show for it is a tied cottage they could be turfed out of when Dad retires. I did quite well at school, and they want me to do A levels and go on to a secretarial course, or teacher training, or maybe . . . maybe even university. But I don't want to be a secretary or a teacher, I want to work with animals."

"And Megan said?" Eleanor persisted.

"She said if I'm clever enough and work hard enough, I could be a vet."

"Would you like to be a vet?" Nick asked, pulling into the last space in the parking area in front of the floodlit Chicken-in-a-Basket restaurant.

"Oh yes!" Cam hugged Teazle so tight she squeaked. "But you have to take science, and there's no A level science at my high school. They think science is for boys. Even if they'd take me back, which they prob'ly wouldn't after I ran away."

"That is a problem, but problems are made to be overcome," said Eleanor encouragingly. "We'll think about it while we eat. I'll just take Teazle along the verge for a few yards first." They were on the outskirts of the town, beyond the reach of pavements and street lamps.

"Let me! Please! Did you bring her lead? She shouldn't go loose on the main road." The lead was found on the floor at Eleanor's feet. "If you give me the keys, I'll put her back in and lock up, and you can go in and find a table."

Nick had handed the keys to Eleanor, who passed them on to Camilla. She and Teazle disappeared along the road.

As they entered the crowded restaurant, Nick said thoughtfully, "Do you think that was wise?"

"What?"

"Giving Camilla the keys. We don't actually know anything about her except that she ran away from home. Suppose she decides to flit again, taking the Incorruptible with her?"

"Then we'll have to walk back into town and ignominiously confess to Mr Scumble that we've lost his witness."

A hurrying waitress paused to say, "Sorry, love, there'll be a bit of a wait for a table. Saturday's our busy night. Shouldn't be too long."

"That's all right," Nick assured her, and she scurried on.

Eleanor continued their discussion. "But I don't think Cam's been lying to us. Do you?"

"Not about running away from home and wanting to be a vet, no. The Exeter poly's probably the answer to that."

"Poly?"

"Polytechnic College. I know a chap who teaches art there. I'm sure they take A level students. She could live at home and take the bus in, if she's willing to go home. But that's assuming she's not in league with jewel thieves and murderers."

"Not in league with, Nick. Under the influence of, perhaps, without realising what sort of people they are."

"Megan wasn't too happy about Scumble not letting us know what's going on."

"I can't help feeling we could be more helpful if we had more information. But who can guess what goes on in the inspector's mind?" Eleanor asked rhetorically.

"Not I, for sure! The trouble is, as Camilla's not allowed to mention whatever she's witness to, you can't test your infallible lie-o-meter on the subject."

"My *what*? Ah, here she comes. At least she was telling the truth about that."

Just as Camilla joined them, the waitress returned and showed them to a cramped table. Baskets of chicken and chips quickly arrived—as it was the only food item on the menu there was no time wasted over deliberations—along with fizzy orange for Camilla, coffee for Eleanor and Nick.

Eleanor had no objection to eating with her fingers. She had done so in many parts of the world where only the rich owned cutlery. In many of the same parts of the world, only the rich ate chicken. She had never understood why in order for chicken to be affordable for the masses, it had to be deprived of all flavour, but it seemed to be a fact of life. The chicken in the basket was of the curious modern breed that tastes of cardboard, but the young people had no memories of pre-war chicken, so they were happy enough. At least it wasn't too greasy and the chips were good. Eleanor was a glutton for chips on the rare occasions she indulged.

The place was too noisy and closely packed for private conversation. Not until they returned to the car and an ecstatic Teazle—even more ecstatic when she discovered each of them had secreted a morsel of chicken for her—were they able to talk about Camilla's affairs.

A car in the dark was an excellent place for confidences, Eleanor thought, as the Incorruptible laboured up from the valley to the moors. Camilla sounded a bit weepy when she told them how much she missed her parents, in spite of their disagreement over her future. If she'd been face to face with Nick she might have been embarrassed, but to her, he and Eleanor were just dark silhouettes against the patch of road illuminated by the headlights. There was no sign of fog.

"I'm pretty sure Mum and Dad would be happy if I went home," Cam said. "And I *did* send them postcards, though I didn't say where I was. All the same, it seems a bit thick just to waltz in and say, 'Hello, I'm back.'"

"Telephone first," Nick suggested.

"We're not on the phone."

Eleanor liked the sound of that *We*. "You ought to write a letter," she said, "but there won't be time for them to get it and reply before I go away."

"You're going away?" Camilla asked in alarm.

"I have to leave on Tuesday, and it can't be put off. Don't worry, Megan will take care of you if we haven't settled things by then. But I think it may be best if I drive you over to Taunton tomorrow so that I'm there to smooth the path if necessary."

"Would you really? That would be perfect!"

Nick said, "Will your parents be pleased that you want to try for your A levels?"

"Oh yes. Dad always wanted me to. If only there was a way!"

"There may be. I know a bloke who teaches at the Exeter poly. I can find out from him what you need to do to get in to take A level courses in the sci—"

That was the last he said. As they reached the top of the hill at Cold Northcutt, a blast of wind struck, howling like a hobgoblin. The little Morris veered and shook. Nick gripped the wheel so hard his knuckles gleamed white in the beams of occasional approaching headlights. Eleanor thanked heaven she wasn't driving. She could never have kept the Incorruptible on the road. She kept quiet so as not to distract Nick. She thought she heard Teazle's anxious whine, but if Camilla spoke, she couldn't be heard.

At the highest point of the journey, where the A395 met the A39, they turned southward and the wind hit them broadside instead of head on. The two and a half miles to Camelford were alarming. After that they started descending towards St Teath and soon the car stopped shuddering.

"Whew!" said Camilla. "I thought we were going to be blown backwards all the way to Launceston."

"If Nick hadn't offered to drive," Eleanor told her, "we probably would have been."

By the time they reached Port Mabyn, Eleanor was feeling her age. Nick stopped outside LonStar.

"I'll take the car key off the ring and park the Incorruptible for you," he said.

"Thank you. With this gale blowing, you'd better go back up to the top car park."

Eleanor, Camilla, and Teazle got out. The wind whistled along the street, but the buildings afforded protection from the worst buffets. Inside felt cosy in comparison, especially after Eleanor lit the fire.

Quite at ease with Camilla now, Eleanor treated her as a young family member, showed her where the clean sheets were, and left her to make up the bed in the spare room. She went downstairs to put on the kettle for hot water bottles and a pan of milk for cocoa. Before pulling down the blind, she peered out through the kitchen window to see if Nick was on his way.

No sign of Nick, but she noticed a man coming down the other side of the street. He took shelter from the wind in the recessed doorway of a shop a short way up the hill. Dressed in a dark overcoat and hat, he merged into the darkness.

Though she hadn't seen his face, she couldn't help thinking

there was something familiar about him. Someone local, she assumed; no doubt he had come from the Trelawney Arms and stepped out of the wind to light a cigarette.

She pulled down the blind and turned just in time to stop the milk boiling over. As she made the cocoa, Nick came in with the car key.

"Did you see the rozzer lurking across the road?" he asked in a low voice.

"A policeman? Bob Leacock?"

"Now would I refer to Bob as a rozzer?"

"No, but I thought I recognised something about him when I saw him walking down the hill."

"They all walk the same way. Legacy of years on the beat. Their car was just arriving at the car park when I walked out."

"Their?"

"Two of them. The second will have gone round the back. I came down this side of the street, out of the worst of the wind, and that chap out there followed me down on the other side."

"What on earth are they doing here? I thought they'd stopped watching the shop. I wish we knew what's going on!"

"Presumably the Scumble's protecting his witness—though I can't imagine who could know she's here—or more likely he's afraid she'll do a flit and leave him witnessless." As he spoke, he strode across to the sitting-room window, parted the curtains, and looked out. "Too dark, I can't spot him, but I bet he's there."

"Oh, for heaven's sake! I've given up trying to fathom the inspector's mind."

"He's so bloody close-mouthed, we really haven't a clue what's going on."

"I do wish he'd be a bit more forthcoming. But his men will catch pneumonia and I'll have their deaths on my conscience. Go and tell them both to come and keep watch in the passage, will you? At least they'll be out of the wind, and the rain which I'm sure is on the way. They can sit on the stairs."

"I'll tell them on my way home," said Nick, cheerfully callous. "Let them suffer a bit first."

Camilla came down. As they drank their cocoa, she started yawning. She offered to scrub out the milk pan, but Eleanor sent her up to bed. Nick didn't stay long. Eleanor reminded him to invite the policemen in.

"If you insist," he said, yawning in his turn.

Eleanor put on the kettle again to make coffee for the men while listening to the weather forecast on the wireless: heavy rain before midnight and gale force winds off the Atlantic. She was not going to be driving to Taunton tomorrow, she decided. She could only hope the winds would drop before she was supposed to take the helicopter to St Mary's.

When she took the coffee down, she found DCs Wilkes and Polmenna damp and very grateful. The rain had already started. She told them about the forecast.

"Yeah," said Wilkes gloomily, "we heard it as we followed you over. I just hope it doesn't mean they won't be relieving us in the morning."

Nick was right, Scumble was keeping an eye on his witness. Why? Was he afraid Cam might run away, as Nick had speculated? Or, far more alarming, did he suspect that the villains were after her?

TWENTY-FIVE

On Sunday morning, Megan arrived at the Launceston nick feeling like a drowned rat, and looking like one, too, to judge by the desk sergeant's grin. Her oilskins had been little protection against torrents of rain blown sideways by boisterous gusts. She usually biked in from her bedsitter on Tavistock Road, but this morning she hadn't dared. On the moor and over on the coast, the wind must be truly terrifying.

"Lovely weather for ducks," said the sergeant.

"If they have any sense, they're huddled in the rushes for fear of getting their feathers blown off."

He laughed. "Bit of a blow," he conceded. "I'll have a paraffin heater taken up to your room, love."

"Thanks." She didn't like the "love," but he was old enough to be her father, so she let it pass. "Mr Scumble here yet?"

"Came in a couple of hours ago. He's been asking for you."

"What? The bastard! He told me not to come in till noon and it's only half eleven. He could have rung me at home."

"I wouldn't remind him, if I was you. He's like a bear with a sore head."

"When isn't he?" Megan asked bitterly and hurried upstairs.

The phone on her desk rang as she entered Scumble's room. She grabbed it without sitting down, not wanting to drip all over her chair. "Pencarrow here."

"At last," snarled the inspector not quite sotto voce from across the room.

"I've got Scotland Yard on the line for you. DS Faraday."

"Just a moment. It's the Yard, sir. D'you want to talk to him?"

"The boy wonder, is it? You can handle him."

"Put him through, please." She managed to escape her cape and sou'wester before Ken's voice came on.

"Megan? You haven't blown away yet? Or washed away? They say the Southwest's getting hit pretty hard."

"We're used to it. Any news?"

"Of a sort. Not much help. I've talked to most of the neighbours, and none of them saw Donaldson come home from the hospital or leave again—"

"Hold on a mo. I never got the full story on your end of things, just what was in the papers, and you people were pretty cagey. We were too busy talking about this end. Give me a quick run-down."

"You know he was robbed at home? He doesn't have a shop, as such, just offices in the City."

"Ah, that must complicate matters."

"We'd certainly move faster if the City force weren't so touchy about its rights and privileges vis à vis the Met," Ken said dryly. "It wouldn't hurt, either, if our own Fraud boys would get off their lazy bums and do a stroke of work at the weekend. The insurance people, too. It's impossible even to get hold of anyone in authority till tomorrow."

"Did he put in a claim already? From the hospital?"

"No, but we found his policy and notified them. They were

investigating last week, but more on the lines of what the hell was Donaldson doing taking stuff home."

"And what was he doing taking stuff home?"

"His line is showing specially selected jewelry privately by appointment. Not common, but not an unknown way to work, I gather. When he has an appointment on a Saturday, he almost always takes the stuff home with him so that he doesn't have to go into the City to pick it up. There's a small-print clause inserted in his insurance policy to cover it, as long as he takes certain precautions, locks and alarms and so on."

"Methinks some lowly underwriter's going to get the sack," said Megan, taking notes.

"Wouldn't surprise me. Anyway, Medlow Insurance was looking into whether he had taken the proper precautions, not easy when he was in hospital under sedation. They hadn't really got started on the possibility of fraud, and won't now until tomorrow."

"So he took the goods home and the villains broke in—"

"They didn't have to. Nabbed him on the doorstep and hustled him inside. No one else saw or heard a thing. He lives in Richmond, in one of those detached Victorian villas hidden in a thicket of laurel and rhododendron. His nearest neighbours are in Majorca, lucky sods."

"No wife, right? Who found him?"

"The beat bobby actually. They do have their uses. A bright lad who'd noticed that Donaldson's front gate was always latched and went for a look-see when he saw it hanging open. He seems to have been a bit of a recluse, apart from his business contacts. We got onto his char and she said he's never home when she goes to clean—five mornings a week and she leaves him something to heat up for his supper. Sometimes on a Monday she'll find someone's been staying over the weekend."

"Lady-friend?"

"Male, she's sure. Separate bedrooms and no sign of any funny business. No one turned up last weekend or this. We also talked to his assistant and his secretary. I spoke to both of them again yesterday. The assistant says Donaldson has mentioned a place in the country but he's never said where it is. He's probably just retired there to recuperate."

"He ought to have told you, though."

"He's not—as far as we're aware—a criminal. He can go wherever he wants. Sorry I can't tell you any more. I'll get back to you as soon as I have solid info but it'll probably be tomorrow. There's something on that car, though. The Hillman that was dumped in Exeter. Where did your chaps find the plates, by the way?"

"Under some bushes by the railway tracks. Just chucked there, no serious attempt to hide them. Why?"

"The car was sold for cash the morning of the robbery, by a very dodgy dealer in the East End. The previous owner saw the licence number in the paper and went to his local nick to say he'd sold it to this outfit earlier in the week. One of our chaps went round. They had a record of the number plate, and sketchy ledger entries of what they paid for it and what they claim they sold it for, but that's about it as far as paperwork goes."

"Did your man show them the pics of Norman Wilmot and Trevor?"

"We didn't have Trevor's yet. Nor did the *Observer* or the *Sunday Times*, not the early editions, anyway. Incidentally, how did you get—No, I haven't got time now, tell me later. In any case, the salesman who sold the car wasn't there yesterday. What's more, I very much doubt if he'll admit to remembering anything about the buyer. Definitely a shady lot. We'll try again to get hold of him of course. No dabs?"

"No, they seem to have been canny enough to put on gloves and keep them on. The briefcase was near the licence plates and there was nothing on that, either. Not even the jeweller's finger-prints." Only Aunt Nell's, but he didn't need to know about those.

"It was a chilly evening when he was robbed. He was wearing gloves, too. You're sure it's his? Not just proximity to the plates?"

"There's the monogram. *W A D.*"

"Good enough. Anything else I need to know?"

"I think that's all."

"Right. Got to go. 'Bye, love."

Megan said goodbye, hung up the phone, hung up her oilskins, and reported to Scumble. At the back of her mind as she spoke, she wondered whether the *love* was a term of endearment, or only the equivalent of *ducks*, or *dearie*, or the Cornish *my lover*. Except that, judged by Nancy Mitford's class-based categories, all those were definitely non-U, and Ken was about as Upper as a junior policeman could be.

"Trevor could be anywhere," Scumble complained. "The Cotswolds, the Lake District, a Birmingham squat. Still, we can be pretty sure it's Donaldson's stuff we recovered since your aunt came clean about the monogram." He paused, as if waiting for her to protest this characterisation of Aunt Nell's story. Though indignation bubbled inside her, she managed to hold her tongue. "Right, you'd better ring your pal in Bristol and see if they've got anything for us."

"They said not till Monday, sir. Besides, Mr Everett's an in-spector. I'm sure he'd prefer to speak to you."

"I daresay. But you know at first hand what he's dealing with, the area, the people. You should be able to understand what he's talking about better than I can, and ask the right questions. If you put your mind to it. And maybe they'll get moving with the job if you ask nicely. Get on with it."

Megan flipped through her notebook, found the number, and dialled. She held on for two or three minutes, hearing nothing but buzzes and clicks. Her finger hovered over the cut-off button.

Scumble looked up from his paperwork. "Can't read your own writing?" he enquired nastily.

She was about to press the button and redial when a recorded voice came on. "Telephone lines are down in the Bristol and north Somerset area due to floods and gale-force winds. Available lines are reserved for emergency services. If this is an emergency, please ring 999. Normal service will be restored as soon as possible."

Megan put down the receiver. "They've got flooding in Bristol, sir. The area we're interested in is the waterfront. The Bristol police'll be too busy to worry about our request."

"Damn!"

"I can't get through unless I claim it's an emergency."

"Well, it's not that," he conceded. "With any luck, the floods'll stop up the rats in their holes till they can get to them. I'd really like confirmation of your girl's story."

Amazing how anything problematic immediately became *your*. "Camilla? Don't you believe her?"

"Do you?" He was watching her.

"I believe she was telling the truth as she remembers it," Megan said carefully. "She chose to come forward about her recognition of the photo as Norman Wilmot. The others didn't."

"So maybe she made it up, thought you'd be a soft touch and get her out of a situation that wasn't to her liking."

"I suppose that's possible. But her description of Trevor is borne out by the similarity of the portrait to Mr Gresham's version—"

"From your aunt's description."

"And Mrs Stearns's."

"True."

"And neither had seen the other. It's too much of a coincidence! Two boys called Trevor who look so much alike?"

"Quite a coincidence. But when you've been in this game as long as I have, you'll have seen plenty stranger. How about what the girl said about Trevor? Him being chummy with our victim and going off with him? You reckon that's true?"

"I don't see any reason to doubt it, sir," Megan said stiffly.

"She wasn't just getting her own back after he dropped her, maybe?"

"No, I'm sure she wasn't. She wouldn't have told me about that if I hadn't told her Trevor might be in danger from whoever killed Norman Wilmot."

"Ah, so that's how you got it out of her. Tricksy!"

"Well, he might."

"Or he might have killed him. You didn't tell her that."

"Of course not, sir."

"She could have worked it out for herself. It leaves open the possibility that she has it in for him."

"I think she's truly fond of him."

"If so, suppose he finds her: Whose side is she going to be on?"

Megan had no answer. "If that's what you think, that she might side with Trevor even if she finds out he's a murderer, then why did you send her to stay with my aunt?"

"It was your idea. Look, I realise you hadn't much choice but to bring her with you. I can't just let her wander loose either, and I've got no grounds whatsoever to hold her. I wouldn't have sent her with Mrs Trewynn if I'd been able to come up with any better alternative. Can you, now you've had time to think about it?"

"No," she admitted. "Except taking her home, and she wouldn't tell me where her parents live. Nor even her surname."

Scumble shrugged. "So there we are. For what it's worth, I tend to believe her story, and the chance of Trevor finding her seems remote. But I have to remember the fact that we both *want* to believe her. You found her; you have a stake in her. She's my only witness to the identity of the victim; I can't count on the Bristol coppers finding someone else willing to name him, or on any more useful tips coming in. If she's not telling the truth, we're stuck."

"There doesn't seem to be much we can do whether she's lying or not."

"This is where we go through all the reports, looking for patterns, or details that don't mesh, or statements that sound a bit off, or any bloody hint at all of what to do next."

"I'd better ring my aunt first, hadn't I, sir?"

"You haven't talked to her yet today?"

"I thought I'd better wait to see if we got any new information overnight that might affect her. And you said, sir—" She paused to listen pointedly to the clock on St Mary Magdalene's tower, just across the square, chiming twelve. "—you said not to come in till noon."

"Did I?" he asked blandly, reaching for one of the piles of papers on his desk. "Well, let me see what was waiting when I arrived. The CRO says none of the dabs in the Hillman are on record."

"Either they're new to crime, or they've never been caught."

"More likely they're the salesman's and the previous owner's, as everyone else seems to have been very careful to wear gloves. Whichever, it's not of any interest to Mrs Trewynn."

"And not much help to us."

"Not that the Criminal Records Office has ever been much help to us poor bloody provincials. More to the point, another call came in, a schoolmaster, private school in the Midlands. Last week, end-of-term stuff kept him too busy to read the newspapers. Yesterday evening his wife, who never reads the papers, used an old one to wrap some potato peelings, noticed our photo of the victim, thought she recognised him, and drew it to Mr . . . Here it is, Mr Chewly . . . to Mr Chewly's attention."

Megan was certain he was throwing all this unnecessary detail at her just to be annoying. "And?" she said.

"He's an old boy, a rather unsatisfactory old boy, by the name of Norman Wilmot."

"Cam *was* telling the truth!" What's more Scumble had known it perfectly well when he asked her opinion of the girl's credibility.

"So it would seem."

"Which makes it the more probable that she told the truth about Trevor. That he was Wilmot's mate." Megan reached for the phone. "I must warn Aunt Nell."

"No!" His voice was so adamant, she let the receiver drop back into its cradle.

"Why not? Suppose he turns up—"

"Highly unlikely. You can't plead ignorance of the weather after coming in here and leaving a puddle on the floor. Bristol's not the only place that's got gales and flooding. If the men I sent to follow your aunt last night—"

"You did? Why didn't you tell me?"

"I didn't want you imagining I thought she was in any danger. I don't. I just don't want the girl hopping it, and supposing Trevor had turned up before the weather got so bad, I wanted him nabbed. I was going to relieve them this morning, of course, but when they radioed in, they said they'd rather take it in turns sleeping on old rugs in the stockroom than try to drive back over the moor in this." He gestured at the rain lashing down the window.

"In the stockroom? Haven't they been keeping obbo outside?"

"Your aunt and the artist spotted them, and she invited them in."

"She would," Megan said with a grin. "All right, she's got guards, but I don't see why I shouldn't warn her about Trevor, all the same."

"Think about it," Scumble advised, and returned to his paper-work.

Megan thought. He had a point, though she didn't altogether agree. Still, if Aunt Nell knew about Trevor, she might let it slip to Camilla, and they couldn't be absolutely sure Camilla was not in league with Trevor.

On the other hand, forewarned was forearmed—but the DI was dead set against it, and he was the boss.

TWENTY-SIX

Eleanor and Camilla were peeling potatoes when the phone rang. Eleanor hastily dried her hands and went to answer it.

"Aunt Nell, are you all right?"

"Yes, dear, perfectly. No slates off the roof, no rain seeping through the window frames."

"Oh . . . Good. And everything else?"

"Now let me see, what other disasters might we anticipate? The phone lines haven't blown down, obviously. The lights have flickered a few times but for the most part the electricity is working. Fortunately, as Cam and I have some unexpected guests for lunch."

"Yes, I'm sorry about that, Aunt Nell. I only just found out about them. You weren't supposed to be taking care of them."

"That's all right. Cam is helping me cook. She's much better at it than I ever was or will be. The stuffing she made for the chicken smells divine."

"She's all right?"

"She gives every appearance of enjoying herself. Do you want a word with her?"

"No, no, never mind. It's just that I feel sort of responsible for her."

"I'd say you've made yourself responsible for her. But there's nothing you can do for her at the moment. I'll tell her you asked after her."

"Please. You will be careful, won't you?"

"If it's still blowing like this in the morning, I'll take one of your policemen to the shops with me to hold me down."

Megan's laugh was half-hearted. "Yes, make use of them. But promise you'll ring right away if . . . anything happens? I'm at the nick, the Launceston police station, for the foreseeable future."

"I'll ring, unless what happens is that the phone lines go down."

"Bless you, Aunt Nell. I—Sorry, I've got to go. 'Bye."

Eleanor hung up thoughtfully. She was sure Megan had wanted to tell her something, restrained no doubt by the presence of Mr Scumble. Ah well, if it was important, no doubt she'd find out in due course.

Lunch for five was enough to worry about for the moment. She had just returned to the potato-peeling when the doorbell downstairs rang. Teazle barked and went to the door.

"Shall I go down?" Cam offered. "It must be Nick, mustn't it? No one in their senses would come farther than from next door in this weather."

"One of our detectives will get it," Eleanor said, glancing back at the sitting-room window. Rain battered the glass. She needn't have looked, she could hear it. Yet only occasional flurries hit the kitchen window, because of the lie of the land and the force and direction of the gale. The wind whistled down the street between the buildings, though, and down the chimney in spite of the closed damper. Thank heaven they had got home from Launceston before it really picked up.

She turned back to the potatoes. Fortunately she had bought

several pounds on Friday with the intention of making leek and potato soup. She had also bought a roasting chicken and invited Nick to Sunday lunch. The leftovers would have lasted her through the week, but with Cam and two large policemen to feed as well, she could only be glad she had enough for all. She hoped. Cam was delighted to help with the preparation. She loved cooking and hadn't had a chance to do much for a long time.

Though Eleanor had been careful not to ask questions, Cam had told her quite a lot this morning. Her life had been difficult since she ran away from home, but she had chosen it and she didn't complain. Two things were obvious: that she was eager to see her parents and that she thought Megan was wonderful.

"Why isn't he coming up?" she said now anxiously, stopping with her potato peeler in one hand and a half-peeled spud in the other. "Maybe it isn't Nick?"

"I expect he's talking to our tame policeman, whichever isn't asleep in the stockroom."

Camilla looked dismayed. "You mean, he's being questioned?"

"I mean they're chatting. Probably about the weather."

"Oh, yes, I suppose so. Somehow I can't imagine chatting with a policeman."

"They're just people, Cam, like Megan. They're coming to lunch, remember. I hope you won't refuse to speak to them."

"Oh no, I promise." Camilla went on thoughtfully, "Just people. Maybe I'll go into the police instead of being a vet."

"Concentrate on getting your A levels first, dear. There's Nick knocking now. Come in!"

Nick's slacks were paint-stained but he had put on an old tweed jacket over his shirt, probably to hide the paint on that. His hair was plastered to his head and his ponytail dripped behind. "Something smells good," he said, sniffing. "Chicken!"

"Not in a basket. Roast, with roast potatoes. If your jacket's as wet as your hair, Nick, you'd better take it off."

"It's not. I left my anorak downstairs in the custody of the police. The hood kept blowing off. I walked down to look at the harbour, Eleanor. The brook's up over the bridge, but only by a few inches. The car park's flooded too, of course. Lucky you thought of parking it up top."

"Yes. I need it tomorrow to take Cam to Taunton."

"Do you think the weather will be okay?" Cam asked.

"I hope so! What do you think, Nick?"

"The harder it blows, the sooner it goes. If that isn't an olde Cornish proverb, it ought to be."

Whether it was an old Cornish proverb or not, Nick's saying proved accurate. At about four, the wind suddenly dropped completely. The squalls turned to a fine mizzle that was not enough to deter Eleanor.

"I'm going for a walk, Cam."

Teazle jumped up, tail wagging madly.

"She knows that word all right!"

"Do you want to come?"

"Would you like me to?"

"I'd be happy to have your company, or happy on my own. It's your choice."

"I haven't got a coat."

Eleanor found a jacket and a headscarf for Camilla. By that time the rain had stopped altogether, and Teazle was whining impatiently at the door. They went downstairs. Polmenna and Wilkes jumped to their feet from the cane-bottomed chairs Eleanor had provided from the stockroom. Now she would find out whether the two officers were guarding the premises or the people.

"It's cleared up. We're going for a walk."

"Oh!" They looked at each other. Polmenna said, "Er, would you mind awfully waiting for a few minutes, Mrs Trewynn? Wilkes has just been up to the car and radioed, and our reliefs'll be here very shortly."

"You can send them after us, then. We're only going up the hill and along the cliff path."

"But—"

"I'm sure you can sort it out between you," Eleanor said with a smile. "Come on, Cam, in case the rain starts again. Goodbye, gentlemen."

They went on their way. It wasn't till they reached the top of the hill and gazed down at the stormy sea, beating against the headland in great clouds of spray, that Eleanor realised she not only hadn't locked the flat, she hadn't even brought her keys.

Oh well, she thought, she had two policemen guarding it, or at least one, if the other had followed them. She refused to look back to find out, and Camilla seemed to have forgotten them altogether. The seaside to her meant a summer day trip to Minehead on a crowded coach, with sandwiches on the beach and an icecream for a treat. She was thrilled by the crashing waves, thunderous even here high above the flying spume.

The last clouds dissipated and the sun shone. A herring gull came to tease Teazle, floating in effortless circles above them.

Cam flung her arms wide and cried, "Isn't it wonderful?"

When they turned back, there was no sign of the detectives. But as they approached the village, they saw Polmenna leaning against the fence of the first house, a bed-and-breakfast place.

"Oh no!" Camilla groaned. "Why can't they leave us alone? I don't want them following me home."

"No. I'm not acquainted with your parents but somehow I

don't think the return of the Prodigal Daughter with the police on her tail would go down well. Don't worry, if they're still around tomorrow, we'll evade them."

On Monday, DCs Wilkes and Polmenna were back on guard duty. The weather was still fine, though the early morning air was chilly. Eleanor, tired of being constantly under surveillance, hardened her heart and didn't invite them into the passage.

When the shops opened at nine, she and Camilla and Teazle went out to restock her depleted larder. Wilkes, looking embarrassed, trailed them up the hill to the mini-supermarket, back down to the greengrocer, and lastly to the bakery. Obviously the police were determined to keep an eye on her and Camilla as well as the site of the murder.

To Eleanor's relief, he didn't go so far as to follow them into the shops, instead staying outside with Teazle. She chatted with several people without being asked about the murder— apparently it was a six-day wonder, or else the villagers had resumed their natural polite reticence.

Coming out of the bakery, she saw Jocelyn going into the LonStar shop opposite.

"Oh, good," she said to Camilla, who was carrying the basket. "Let's go and put this stuff away and then we can find you some decent clothes, I hope. I've still got most of the money the police gave me to outfit you. I'll have to give it back if we don't spend it, so let's hope Mrs Stearns can find things you like. She knows exactly where everything is."

Camilla sighed. "It'll be nice to buy some clothes, but I expect I'd better get what Mum and Dad would like me to wear, not what I'd choose for myself, don't you think?"

"That's a very good idea." Sensible was the word that came to mind, but Eleanor wasn't sure Cam would care to be called sensible. "What do they like to see you in?"

"Skirts," she said gloomily. "And not mini-skirts, either."

"Oh." Eleanor looked down at the tweed skirt she wore for shopping at this time of year. "Then I expect I'd better keep this on instead of changing into the tracksuit I usually wear for collecting in the country. You won't mind if we stop here and there on our way, to pick up donations for LonStar."

Jocelyn had just opened the shop. She managed to find several parent-pleasing outfits for Camilla. While the skirts and tops didn't exactly thrill the girl, at least she didn't say she wouldn't be seen dead in them, though that might have been because she seemed to find Jocelyn rather alarming. A pair of shoes in the latest style cheered her up. They were in perfect condition, probably a donation from someone trying to fit into a size smaller than was practicable. Jocelyn also dug up a pair of walking shoes and a bag to pack everything in.

"Thank you, Mrs Stearns," Cam said earnestly. "It's ever so kind of you to go to so much trouble."

"I'm glad we were able to fit you out. Now run along, dear. I have some business to discuss with Mrs Trewynn."

"Put a kettle on, will you, Cam?" said Eleanor. "I'm dying for a cup of coffee. Thanks, Joce," she went on as the girl departed, laden. "I hate shopping for clothes for myself, and shopping for someone else is even worse. I'm exhausted."

"Who is she?" Jocelyn demanded. "All you've told me is that she's a witness."

"She's a child who made a bad mistake. Thanks to Megan, it looks as if we're going to be able to put things right. At bottom, she's a very nice girl, and bright. I really can't tell you any more now, or Mr Scumble would have my blood. Not that I know very much more."

"That man! I take it he's responsible for the policemen keeping the shop under surveillance?"

"Oh dear, they're not very good at being inconspicuous, are they?"

"Since at least three people have asked me this morning what they're up to, I'd have to say no, they're not."

"If it's any comfort, they seem more interested in Cam and me, not the shop. One of them came to the shops with us. Joce, I'm taking Cam home to her parents this afternoon, and I don't want those two following us. How can I get her away?"

"Do you think that's wise? After all, that man *is* investigating a murder, though he doesn't seem to be getting very far."

"I'll be coming straight home after dropping her, and if he can persuade me he really needs to know, of course I'll tell him how to find her."

"You'd better tell me where you're going, just in case. You can write it down, and I won't even look myself, unless that man can persuade *me* he really needs to know."

"And you're much less persuadable than I am," Eleanor said, laughing. "All right. But I'm going to do some collecting along the way, so I'll have to work out exactly which way we'll go. I'll drop off our itinerary before we leave. If you can suggest how to elude our watchdogs."

"I've got an idea." She explained.

"Good heavens, Joce, I'd never have expected such deviousness from you!"

"Only because you're escaping from that man."

"Never mind your justification. It's positively sneaky. We'll try it."

TWENTY-SEVEN

Eleanor went up to the flat and explained Jocelyn's plan to Camilla, whom she found looking very respectable in a green woollen skirt and pale yellow blouse.

"Gosh, I can't believe Mrs Stearns came up with anything so . . . so . . ."

"Devious? Nor could I. I'll go and tell Nick."

"Is it all right if I come too? I'd love to see his pictures. I've never met a real artist before."

They went out the back way, taking Teazle. Tail wagging, the dog headed straight to the semi-concealed DC Polmenna. He stooped to pet her and muttered a sheepish, "Good morning," to Eleanor and Camilla.

They returned the greeting and proceeded a few yards down the path. Eleanor knocked on Nick's window. As he came to open his back door, she had a dismaying thought.

"Nick, the flood! Will I be able to get the Incorruptible out?"

"I haven't been down there today, but when I went to the pub last night the water was going down fast, already off the bridge. Do you need it now? Shall I go and check? Fend off the ravening hordes of customers for me and I'll be back in half a tick." He headed for the shop.

"Wait! Let me explain. Cam, why don't you go into the shop and look around while I tell Nick our plan."

"But what about the customers?"

Nick laughed. "They're a myth. Don't worry, if anyone comes in I'll hear the bell and come rushing to the rescue. What's up, Eleanor?"

"We want to get away from our watchers. Jocelyn suggested you should take the car up the other side, past the Wreckers, and leave it in the car park at the top there. Then Cam and I will walk up to the hairdresser—I can't remember what Miss Hatchell calls it—"

"Delilah's."

"That's it. Definitely a mistake. The chapel people won't go there. We'll get Cam a quick trim. Lord knows she could do with it! I'm sure Miss Hatchell will fit her in at noon prompt as a favour, if I ring her now. She's only really busy in the summer. Then we'll go out the back way—"

"Brilliant! This is Mrs Stearns's plot? What devious minds the Anglicans have. If there's any shop the 'tecs won't follow you into, it's the ladies' hairdresser. I'll go right away and move the car. Then I'll bring you back the keys. I'll go up the street and come back the back way, so Wilkes will see me go but won't see me return."

"What devious minds artists have! Here are the keys. Thanks, Nick. Anytime—"

"May the time I need help evading the police never come!"

"You never know. Cam! Let's go."

Camilla came through from the shop. "Thank you for letting me look," she said to Nick. "I really like the scenery ones, but the others, the ones I don't really understand properly, they're super-special, aren't they? They make you think."

Nick looked startled and pleased. "You've got an eye for the real thing, Cam. A better eye than Eleanor, for one."

"Oh dear," said Eleanor, "I hope you aren't going to decide to be an artist, Cam."

"Don't worry, I can't draw for toffee. I'm not going to keep changing my mind now. I really and truly want to be a vet. Is everything arranged for our escape?"

"We're all set. Now I have to go and put my mind to which route we're going to take."

They went back to the flat. Eleanor made a list of villages, some no more than hamlets, that she expected to pass through, along with a few isolated farms and summer bungalows where she might stop along the way. She pictured the route as if she were driving it and had no difficulty recalling the places and the people who lived there. The quirks of memory were inexplicable, she decided—of her memory, at least.

Shortly before half past noon, Eleanor, a newly shorn Camilla, and Teazle stepped out of Miss Hatchell's back door onto a narrow asphalt path. On the other side was a drystone wall with a white-painted gate, enclosing a tiny patch of garden ablaze with scarlet tulips. An elderly woman looked up from her weeding and waved to them.

"A magnificent show, Mrs Pertwee," said Eleanor, but didn't stop to chat.

They turned right up the hill. The front door of the next cottage opened directly onto the path. Just beyond, the path turned into steps. At the top of the flight, they turned left on a cross-path, and so made their way upward by twists and turns and slopes and steps, past houses and pocket-handkerchief gardens, till they came out onto the road just opposite the car park. There the Incorruptible awaited them.

The car was a bit muddy around the skirts, but started imme-diately, "Which is the important thing," said Eleanor.

She drove on up the hill a few yards then turned into a lane not much wider than the car, with hedge-banks on each side where primroses and violets were still in bloom, joined already by ragged robin, stitchwort, and great umbels of cow parsley. They went without stopping, as directly as the wandering lanes allowed, until they had crossed the B road. Then they started col-lecting, calling at Trewennan, Trekee, Treburgell, and Pengenna, picking up odds and ends which nearly filled the boot. A farmer's wife gave them the inevitable pasties for lunch, then they went on: Trewane, Trelill, Pennytinney, Trequite. Donations crowded Teazle on the backseat.

"I'll do St Kew on a separate trip," Eleanor decided. "The vil-lage is big enough to fill the car on its own. We'll go round by Brighter, then straight on to Bodmin."

"Is Bodmin on the way to Taunton?"

"Bodmin, Plymouth, Exeter, Taunton. We've quite a drive ahead of us still. Perhaps I should skip Brighter. There's not a proper road up to the farm and the track is probably knee-deep in mud after that rain."

Between Trequite and the A39, the lane crossed over a small stream. Just on the far side of the bridge, an isolated cot-tage stood on the bank, facing the stream, half hidden by golden-green willows. Once derelict, it had been nicely restored and enlarged by a Londoner, who couldn't be called either a summer visitor or a weekender, as Eleanor had found him there at odd times on weekdays and weekends, spring, summer, and autumn. When the owner was there, he usually gave her some-thing.

There was his sleek maroon Jaguar (she could tell the make

from the emblem on the bonnet) parked on a patch of asphalt to one side.

Eleanor drove past and pulled the Morris Minor as far over to the side of the lane as she could. "I'm afraid I may be blocking the way," she said to Cam. "If someone honks to get by, come and fetch me, will you, dear? I'll just pop in and see if Mr Donaldson has anything for us."

"We hardly have any room left. Never mind, Teazle can sit on my lap."

"She'll love that. Stay, Teazle. I shan't be a minute."

As she opened the gate with the name of the cottage, Withy's End, painted on it, Eleanor cast her mind back to the owner's previous donations. He had several times donated jewelry, she recalled, nothing terribly valuable, mostly silver set with semi-precious stones, turquoise, cairngorm, onyx, jade. He was a jeweller, and he had told her he brought items that weren't selling to Cornwall specially to give to her for LonStar. Unlike ordinary household donations, they required special paperwork. She had seen his full name, and it was Wilfred A. Donaldson.

She started putting two and two together.

D A W, she thought—or *W A D*. Surely he must be the jeweller who had been robbed. What an odd coincidence that his jewelry had been recovered so near his holiday cottage.

A very odd coincidence indeed. Eleanor's thoughts raced. It was not the only local connection—DI Scumble seemed convinced that her sometime helper Trevor was mixed up in the business.

Was Donaldson the uncle Trevor had told her about?

Trevor had always seemed such a nice boy, though a hopeless layabout. She found it hard to believe, but he and his friend must have held up, and beaten up, his uncle. What a horrible shock to the poor man.

But could it have been Trevor? According to the newspapers, the police were looking for a couple of tall, burly, well-dressed men. That description in no way fitted either Trevor or the dead youth. Had Mr Donaldson lied to the police, to protect his nephew?

What was it Trevor had said about him? He had promised Trevor's mother, his sister, to take care of him. Even in these appalling circumstances, he was trying to keep his promise. Presumably he had come down to Cornwall to escape persistent questioning by the police, for fear of revealing something that would lead them to Trevor.

Which was exceptionally kind and generous of him, yet it didn't explain why Trevor should have brought the loot to this part of the country. Wouldn't the jewelry be much easier to sell in a big city? In fact, rural North Cornwall seemed about the most unlikely place in the world.

The only reason Eleanor could think of for Trevor to come here was to see his uncle. Suppose he had repented and decided to return the proceeds of the robbery, and his friend had refused to go along, leading to a quarrel, a fight, a death.

No, that didn't work. Trevor must have been in Cornwall on Tuesday, when Mr Donaldson had still been in hospital in London. How could the boy have guessed his uncle would come down here? Surely it was much more likely that the jeweller would stay in town to monitor the police hunt for his valuables. Unless—

Unless the whole business had been engineered by Donaldson, for some fraudulent purpose Eleanor couldn't even begin to decipher, ignorant as she was of the business world.

While thinking, she had unconsciously continued slowly

along the path to the front door, and even raised her hand to knock. Now she thought better of it. She ought to find a telephone box and report her theory to Megan. Or even Scumble, though he would certainly castigate her for wasting his time with her guesswork.

She had started to turn away when the door was flung open. Donaldson stood on the threshold, a short, tubby, balding man, who always wore a jacket and tie even in the depths of the country in the summer. Eleanor had always considered his round pink face almost cherubic when he handed over his generous gifts to LonStar. Now, however, blotched with yellowish green fading bruises, it wore a ferocious scowl.

"You! You're the woman from that charity shop. It's all your fault everything's gone wrong!"

"My fault? I had no idea—"

"You can't really imagine the police haven't worked it out by now," he raved. "I'm not sticking around to be arrested as an accessory to murder because my idiot of a nephew killed the creep who beat me up! I've got to get away." He grabbed her wrist and pulled her into the hall. "I'm going to tie you up and hide you where you won't be found till after I've left the country."

Eleanor had no intention of letting that happen. What if she wasn't found in time? Her reflexes were slower than they used to be, or she would have reacted the instant he reached for her, but though he was younger, a few inches taller, and heavier, those apparent advantages could be used against him, especially as he was obviously out of shape. Better still, the way he stood and moved told her he had no training in the martial arts.

It was a pity she was wearing a skirt, but it couldn't be helped. She'd just have to make allowances, to adjust her moves. As all this flashed through her mind, she was already stepping back into *hanmi* stance, knees bending to drop her centre of gravity—

"Uncle Wilfred!"

Still gripping her wrist, he swung round. "Trevor!"

Two to contend with, one of them young and capable of murder, though he looked more like a scarecrow than ever. Reassessing her tactics—and her chances—Eleanor broke Donaldson's hold.

"Trevor! I'm so glad you're here!" Camilla was behind her, blocking the doorway and the only way of escape.

TWENTY-EIGHT

The phone on Megan's desk rang a couple of minutes after Scumble had sloped out without explanation but with that shifty look that meant he was going to the loo. He still couldn't bring himself to tell her he was going to the bog, or whatever male euphemism he preferred.

"Everett here."

"Hello, Inspector. How are your floods?"

"Going down nicely, thank you, though there's a lot of people won't be able to go back home for a while. Including the bunch you're interested in. You mentioned a laddie by the name of Jake—that helped sort them out."

"Wonderful. Are they talking?"

"Singing like dicky-birds, they're that grateful for being rescued from the rooftop."

"Do you want to talk to DI Scumble?"

"No, you're the one that was there, Miss Pencarrow. I won't have to do so much explaining."

Megan took down his report verbatim, easier than trying to reconstruct it from notes. Scumble came back halfway through.

He looked over her shoulder, but seeing she was writing short-hand, he sat down at his own desk. He sat there looking ostentatiously patient until she had thanked Inspector Everett for his help and hung up.

"Well?"

"Bristol, sir. Camilla's friends had to be rescued from the roof of their squat."

"So they decided the fuzz aren't so bad after all?" He rubbed his hands together in satisfaction. "What've you got?"

Megan quickly scanned her notebook. She never managed to absorb the information properly while she was taking it down in shorthand. It went straight from her ear to her fingers without, apparently, passing through her consciousness.

"Well?"

"Uhhh . . ."

"Can't read your own shorthand? Need a refresher course, do you?"

"No, sir! They confirm that the victim was known to them as Norman Wilmot."

"Known to them? Cautious buggers!"

"None of them knew him before he turned up and joined their squat. But I gather that's nothing out of the ordinary. People come and go."

Scumble grunted his incomprehension of young people today.

"None of them liked him particularly, but it's against their principles to turn anyone away."

"Spare me the sermon!"

"If he was friendly with anyone, it was Trevor—Trevor Brand, one of them thinks. They all recognised the composite picture as Trevor."

"Aha! Now we're getting somewhere."

"Trevor, unlike Norman, was generally considered a 'good

bloke.' He has an uncle he visits now and then—could be once a month, but they're all very vague about time."

"Dopers! They're going to make lousy witnesses."

"At any rate, the uncle apparently gives him an allowance. Not generous, but he always came back to Bristol with money in his pocket."

"What about their recent comings and goings?" Scumble demanded impatiently.

"There was a good deal of disagreement but one, who has a part-time job and has to keep track of the days of the week, is pretty sure—"

" 'Pretty sure' convinces no juries!"

"No sir, but as you said, they'll make lousy witnesses anyway. To the best of his recollection, Trevor and Norman left together the day before the robbery. They returned very early Saturday morning and left again on Monday. I'll have to check the report, but I think Camilla said she didn't see Trevor again—"

"That's right."

"A couple of the others claim he came back after they'd seen the photo of Norman in the chip paper. They told him to bugger off. They wouldn't turn him in but he wasn't welcome any longer."

"Good to know there's something they draw the line at!"

"Norman had had a warning. He blacked someone's eye, and—" Her phone rang.

Scumble nodded to her to take the call. As she lifted the receiver, his phone followed suit. Before she became involved in her own call, she heard him say in a tone of horror, "Reverse the charges? Who—?"

"Megan?"

"Ken! You have something solid for us?"

"As solid as a neighbour's memory of a chance remark a couple of years ago."

"Oh. Well, better than nothing. We'll take what we can get."

"It's the neighbours who were in Majorca. They came home late last night. The wife, Rosalyn McLoughlan . . ." Ken spelt it and added the address and telephone number. "She found out this morning about the robbery and Donaldson's disappearance, and she rang us. At a guess, she's the sort who buttonholes people whether they want to chat or not and winkles their life histories out of them willy-nilly. We know Donaldson isn't the sociable sort. Why should he tell her he has a cottage in Cornwall—"

"In Cornwall!"

"I thought you'd be interested," he said smugly. "Near one of your odd saints that no one's ever heard of. She remembers the name because she'd recently visited Kew Gardens."

"Not St Kew?"

"St Kew. I looked it up, and it's not far at all from Port Mabyn. Believe it or not, she even got the name of the cottage out of him."

"Don't tell me she remembers that!"

" 'Such an odd name, Sergeant,' " he said falsetto. " 'And I do love willows, don't you? They always remind me of Henley.' "

"Willow Cottage?"

"Withy's End. Apostrophe *s*."

"Withy's End, near St Kew. We'll find it."

"You have a photo of him?"

"I stuck one from a newspaper into the file."

"That's all we've got. Lord knows where they dug it up. We're trying to get the original from them, but you know the press. Oh, and his car's a maroon Jag." He gave her the registration number. "If you don't find him we'll put out a call for that. Don't forget we have an interest in the man, too."

"We'll keep you informed. Thanks, Ken. We're getting some-where at last."

"Assuming he's there, they'll probably send me down again to talk to him. Start thinking of a good place, a really nice place, I can take you for dinner."

"Ken, I—" But he had hung up.

Scumble was staring at her with his eyebrows raised questioningly. His ear was still glued to the receiver and he made occasional inarticulate responses. She guessed he had someone on the line whom it would be impolitic to cut off, though he wasn't learning much of use. Someone who stood on his rights: If he rang the police to offer assistance, he felt they should pay for the call; if they were rude, he'd complain.

But the inspector wanted to know at once what Megan had been told.

"Sir, that was the Yard. They—" Her phone rang yet again.

Scumble rolled his eyes in exasperation but waved to her to pick it up.

"Sergeant, DC Polmenna just radioed in. Wilkes and him, they've lost Mrs Trewynn and the girl."

"They *what*? How the hell—No, don't tell me. How long ago?"

"Last sighted going into a hairdresser's at noon."

"Noon!" Once they realised the pair was missing—which might have been quite a while considering how long some women spent at the hairdresser's—they'd have made frantic efforts to find them before reporting the fiasco.

"They want to know if they should stay in Port Mabyn."

"Yes! No, wait, I'll have to ask Mr Scumble. Hold on. Sir, Wilkes and Polmenna have lost Aunt Nell and Cam. Mrs Trewynn and—"

"*What?* Ye gods, I'll—No, sir, I beg your pardon, I was not speaking to you. I'm afraid a bit of an emergency has come up. I'm going to have to ring off. Thank you for your assistance, sir . . . Yes, yes, of course I'll ring you back." He hung up. "When hell freezes over," he said to the phone, then addressed Megan as he shrugged into his coat. "The bloody schoolmaster. They lost your aunt, or your aunt lost them?"

"I didn't get the details, sir. They want to know if they should stay in Port Mabyn."

"Of course they should bloody stay in Port Mabyn! And go on searching. And if they haven't found them by the time I arrive, then God help them! Let's go!"

As Megan drove out of Launceston, she told Scumble about Donaldson's country cottage. "So do you want to go there first, rather than to Port Mabyn?" she asked.

"Do you know how to find the place?"

"I know roughly where St Kew is, sir. There's a signpost off the A39. But the cottage, no. Aunt Nell's bound to know. If we can find her."

"Port Mabyn first. We may want to take those bloody useless idiots with us when we call on Mr Donaldson."

Surprised, Megan was going to ask why they needed back-up when going to talk to a crime victim. She didn't get a chance. Scumble started talking on the car radio, giving instructions to contact the GPO, PC Leacock, or as a last resort the local milkman to get directions to Withy's End. She was quite glad he was distracted from her driving. Worried about Aunt Nell, she zipped along as fast as the traffic allowed. The trunk road was quite busy for Cornwall, but still quicker than the twisting, turning back lanes, however empty.

She was very much afraid Camilla must have something to do with Aunt Nell's disappearance. Why had she ever thought it was good idea to dump the girl on her aunt?

What worried her most was that DI Scumble was worried. He

was trying now to raise Wilkes and Polmenna's car, without success. They must be combing the village. He switched back to the Launceston nick. Megan concentrated on overtaking a pair of lorries dawdling up the hill onto the moor.

"Leacock's out and his radio's malfunctioning again," Scumble said savagely. "The postman is out on his rounds. The milkman's gone home to some obscure village and he's not on the telephone."

"My aunt's bound to know where Donaldson's cottage is. She knows all the lanes like the back of her hand. With any luck, she'll have turned up by the time we get to Port Mabyn."

Scumble closed his eyes as she took advantage of a gap in oncoming traffic to pass a tour bus. He remained silent until they turned off the A39 at St Teath.

Then he said, "We'll go to the shop first, the LonStar shop. That woman, the vicar's wife—"

"Mrs Stearns."

"—probably knows where your aunt's gone. D'you know what it smells like to me?"

"Cows?" said Megan, jamming her foot on the brake as a lowing herd of Guernseys strolled down the lane in front of her towards their milking shed, a black-and-white dog at their heels.

"Insurance fraud."

"But that would mean . . ." She turned her head to stare at him. "Donaldson's a crook?"

"Keep your eyes on the road!"

Not another word would he utter until they were safely parked. Megan spotted Wilkes and Polmenna's panda car in the car park at the top of the hill and pulled in beside it.

As they hurried down the hill, he said, "Find out whether your aunt's taken her car. Meet me at the shop. And if you come across that pair of nitwits, bring them with you."

"Yes, sir." If the nitwits had read the reports, they'd have known Aunt Nell kept her car in the shed in the car park by the stream. They would have checked. But they'd been sent up to Launceston from county headquarters in Bodmin and then rushed off to Port Mabyn. Maybe they hadn't had a chance to catch up on all the details.

Megan hurried down, picked her way across the soggy field, and opened one of the shed's double doors. No Incorruptible.

Or maybe they really were nitwits. They were the same two who had followed the car from Launceston the night of the gale. Surely they had seen Aunt Nell leave it in her shed. If they had been watching, they could hardly have missed the departure of a pea-green Morris Minor.

Except, Megan remembered as she squelched back across the grass, Nick Gresham had been driving when they were following. Had they been told it was Aunt Nell's, not his? Nick would have parked it for her that night. Could he have taken it out for her today, because the field was boggy? In fact, the layer of mud presently wrecking her shoes suggested it had been flooded, so perhaps he'd parked up one hill or t'other? But that was beside the point. Wherever the car had been, might he have moved it to help Aunt Nell elude Wilkes and Polmenna? They hadn't been told to keep an eye on him, only on Aunt Nell and Camilla.

Instead of hurrying to join Scumble at the LonStar shop, Megan pushed open the door of Gresham's gallery. He was sitting on a high stool behind his counter, wrapping a parcel. He looked up when the bell jangled.

"Hello," he said cheerfully. "I thought we might be seeing you."

"Did you help Aunt Nell evade the constables watching her?"

"Yes. She's not a suspect. Why not?"

"Why? Why was she so keen to get away unseen?"

"She was fed up with having her every step watched. But actually, I think it was mostly Camilla's idea. She didn't want the cops following her—"

"I knew it!" Megan's thoughts whirled. Camilla was a friend of Trevor's, and Trevor was Donaldson's nephew, and Donaldson was a crook. "Where did they go?"

"Eleanor intended to take Camilla home. To her parents."

"We must find them. Come on."

He tapped the parcel. "I've got to get this to the post."

"Don't be so bloody bolshie! She may be in danger. Come *on!*"

"In danger?" Gresham said incredulously, but he followed her, locking the gallery behind him. "Eleanor? From that child? What the hell are you talking about?"

In the LonStar shop, they found Mrs Stearns at bay.

"I've *told* these officers," she said, speaking to Scumble and gesturing at DCs Polmenna and Wilkes. "I won't lie and claim Eleanor didn't say where she was going, but I promised I wouldn't tell."

"Madam," said Scumble sternly, "you are obstructing—"

"Mrs Stearns," Megan interrupted, "Aunt Nell may be in danger. We *must* find out where she's gone."

"In danger? Are you sure?"

"No, we're not. Do you want us to wait until we're sure? Too late?"

"Oh dear! Nick . . . ?"

"Better safe than sorry. Tell them."

"She's taking Camilla to Taunton." Mrs Stearns took a folded paper from her pocket and handed it to Scumble. "Going by the back roads to start with, and picking up donations on the way. This is her route."

Megan wasn't tall enough to read over the inspector's shoulder, but she peered round his bulk and her finger shot out at the same moment his pointed at a name on the list. In unison, they pronounced, "St Kew!"

"It's one of my husband's parishes," said the vicar's wife. "I know it well. Eleanor can hardly come to any harm there."

Scumble gave her a hard look. "Do you know a house called Withy's End?"

"It sounds familiar. It's not one of our flock . . . Oh, I know where I've seen the name. We've had paperwork. One of our donors, LonStar, not the church, lives there, so Eleanor might well call in."

"Can you tell us how to find the place?"

"I'm sure I've driven past it. I couldn't give directions but I can picture it—"

"I know where it is," Gresham interrupted. "I've biked past it. I can show you the way."

"So can I," Mrs Stearns put in.

"Let's go!" said Scumble.

Megan, Gresham, and DC Polmenna reached the car park ahead of the other three, older and slower. Megan unlocked the unmarked car, but when she looked round, Polmenna was already behind the wheel of the panda car, starting the engine, and Gresham was about to get in.

"Wait, I'll come with you!" They should have someone with them who had at least some idea of what was going on.

She dropped the keys on the driving seat. Gresham stood back to let her climb into the back, then folded himself into the front passenger seat and slammed the door as Polmenna put his foot down.

"Left, through the village," said Gresham.

They roared down the hill, over the bridge, and up the other side. Fortunately the street was not very busy at this time of the afternoon. By the time they were out of the village, Scumble and Mrs Stearns were on their tail, with Wilkes at the wheel. When they reached the main road, Gresham told Polmenna to turn right.

"And then the second left."

The others followed them until they came to a crossroads.

"Right," Gresham directed, and they turned into a narrower lane. Looking back, Megan saw the plainclothes car go straight past.

"They're not coming this way!"

"Oh damn! No, go on," he said as Polmenna braked. "This may be a bit slower but by the time you stopped and turned . . . We'll go through Trequite, so assuming they'll go on as far as the A39 junction and turn back, we'll come upon the cottage from both directions and box him in. Besides, if one of us is slowed by a tractor or—"

"Cows," Megan suggested.

"—or cows, the other will get through."

Polmenna drove on, taking the curves and turns at a reckless speed. Megan clutched the strap, once more sympathising with Scumble's feelings when she drove him. She had to trust that Polmenna was in control, but to a passenger it was scary.

On the way, Megan had told them they were after Donaldson. She couldn't say much more in Gresham's hearing, and she wouldn't in any case have told Polmenna about Scumble's new theory, based, as far as she could see, solely on the "smell" of the case. The remote possibility that the jeweller might be a danger to Aunt Nell was enough to arouse blood-lust in both her companions.

A left turn at the crossroads in Trequite, into a lane barely wider than the car, hedges brushing the windows. It forked.

"Keep right, keep right!" Gresham cried.

A moment later, Polmenna jammed on the brakes as they came nose to nose with a maroon Jaguar.

The driver stared at the panda car in horror, mouth open, eyes popping in his round, oddly blotchy face. Then he flung open the door, jumped out, and set off back down the lane at an awkward trot.

Bruises and a maroon Jag—"It's Donaldson!" Megan shouted.

Polmenna and Gresham sprang out and took off after him. Megan disentangled herself from the seat in front of her and followed.

Donaldson veered towards the hedge. There was a gap, a five-barred gate. He scrambled clumsily over it and set off up a slope of close-cropped grass dotted with sheep and lambs. Gresham and Polmenna vaulted over. Cursing her skirt—surely it was about time women officers were allowed to wear trousers!—Megan opened the gate just enough to slip through. Being country-bred, she banged it shut behind her though it delayed her further.

The two men were already closing in on Donaldson.

"Stop! Police!" Polmenna shouted.

Donaldson stopped. For a second Megan thought he'd seen sense. But what he'd seen was a barbed-wire fence. Whirling round, he pulled a pistol from his pocket. His aim wavered wildly between his pursuers.

Nick Gresham was closest. A report rang out and he stumbled, clapping his hand to his side.

Polmenna dived for Donaldson's legs and brought him down. He struggled feebly for a moment, but the detective was half his age and twice his size. He went limp.

Megan reached Gresham. He was on his knees, very pale, an ominous red stain seeping through his shirt.

"That was fun," he said feebly. "I should have joined the police." And then he passed out.

TWENTY-NINE

"I do wonder if I shouldn't have gone after him," said Eleanor, "if only to see which direction he went in."

"His car's a *Jag*, Mrs Trewynn," Trevor repeated patiently the argument he had used to stop her pursuing his uncle in the first place. "Yours is a Moggie. You wouldn't have seen him for dust."

"Your car is blocking the lane," Camilla pointed out, fondling Teazle's ears. The dog had followed her from the Incorruptible. "Trev's uncle didn't have any choice about which way to go."

At that moment the sound of an impatient car horn drifted through the windows of the kitchen, where they sat.

"There," said Eleanor, "someone's trying to get past now. I'll go and move it."

Camilla looked frightened. "D'you think he's come back?"

"No, dear, not after the way he raced off."

"I'll move it," said Trevor, hand out for the keys.

Eleanor hesitated. "Better not, dear. It would be a terrible temptation just to keep on driving. You're going to have to stop running away and talk to the police sometime. The sooner you get it over with, the better."

"But I—"

"*Police!*" Scumble's instantly recognisable bellow from the front door was followed at once by DC Wilkes bursting into the kitchen through the back door. He stopped and stared.

"Cam, you'd better put more water in the kettle, please," said Eleanor. "It looks as if we have company."

Wilkes cast a swift, astonished glance at the assembled company, then grinned at her. "Everything under control, Mrs Trewynn?"

"Yes, thank you, Mr Wilkes." She was relieved to see he still felt enough gratitude for the shelter she had provided to offset any resentment at her having tricked him and his partner. "We were just discussing what to do next. It looks as if that's out of our hands now."

"Donaldson's here?"

"He drove off just a minute ago, in rather a hurry. As he was waving a gun around, it seemed unwise to try to stop him."

Wilkes strode past them into the front hall. Eleanor heard him say, "Donaldson's done a bunk, with a gun."

Scumble growled something she couldn't make out. Heavy footsteps approached. He came into the kitchen, leant with both fists on the table, and glared at Trevor. "Trevor Brand, you're under arrest. I can't spare the time now to deal with you, but if you try to hop it, you'll be in even more trouble than you're in already when we catch you. And we will. Mrs Trewynn, your car keys, please."

Eleanor felt in her pockets, then searched her handbag. "I'm sorry, Inspector, I must have left them in the car."

"You did," said Camilla, turning from the stove with a look at Scumble as hostile as the one he had just sent Eleanor's way. "I brought them." She held them out towards Eleanor, dangling by the keyring from her forefinger. Scumble snatched them and left without another word.

In the hall, he yelled at someone unseen, "For pity's sake, keep them all here till I get back!"

Jocelyn stalked into the kitchen. "That man!" she said indignantly. "He seems to think we're in the Wild West and he can deputise me—if that's the word—without so much as a by-your-leave! Eleanor, my dear, I'm so glad to see you safe and sound. What on earth is going on here?"

"I'd like to know what on earth *you're* doing here, Joce!" Eleanor retorted.

"Showing that man how to get here. Nick's in the other car with Megan. They seemed to think you were in trouble."

"Sit down and have a cup of tea. Trevor was just about to tell us his story."

"Yes, go on, Trev," Camilla urged. "If the fuzz come back, they won't let us hear it."

"I need something to eat first." Wan and exhausted, Trevor was even dirtier and more dishevelled than his usual state. "I haven't had any food for two days. I dumped the car and took the train to the Smoke, but Uncle Wilfred wasn't there. I ran out of money, so I've been hitchhiking and sleeping rough."

"I'll see what I can scrounge," said Camilla, heading for the larder. "He's bound to have eggs, and cheese probably, and bread for toast. There's gas so it won't take a minute. But talk while I cook, in case they catch your uncle quickly."

"I think it would be a good idea, Trevor," Eleanor said gently. "You'll get it all straight in your mind before you have to tell Inspector Scumble. He can be a bit . . . disconcerting. I made an awful muddle of telling him things."

"You certainly did," Jocelyn agreed grimly. "Go ahead, Trevor."

The boy sank his head in his hands, staring down at the table. "It was all Uncle Wilfred's idea. He's been giving me an allowance since I left school, and he said he was having business troubles and couldn't afford to keep it up unless I helped him."

"Helped him do what?" Jocelyn asked impatiently.

"Let him tell it his own way, Joce."

"He wanted me to take some jewelry off him. He was going to tell the fuzz he'd been robbed by a couple of big, burly toughs with short hair so they wouldn't come after me. Then he'd get money from the insurance and sell the stuff abroad, and he'd be able to keep on with my allowance."

"What made him think you wouldn't take the jewels and run?" Jocelyn enquired. "He couldn't very well change his mind about the robbers' appearance and set the police onto you."

Trevor raised his head to give her wounded look. "I wouldn't do a thing like that, even if I knew where to sell them. He's all the family I've got left, my mum's brother. So when he said I had to hit him—"

"What?" Camilla whirled, wooden spoon in hand. "Trev, you didn't!"

"Course not. I swore peace and love and that like you did, didn't I. After what my dad used to do to me before I ran away . . . But Uncle Wilfred said it had to look like he'd tried to fight off the robbers. That's why I got my mate Norm in on it. He said he'd sock Uncle Wilfred in the nose and it'd bleed buckets and look spectacular. But he went sort of mad. He kept hitting him and hitting him. He had knuckledusters on. I never knew he even had any, I swear it. I thought I'd never get him to stop."

"Oh, Trev!" The girl put a bowl of steaming tomato soup, toasted cheese, and a glass of milk in front of him and patted his shoulder. "How awful!"

"It was. Ta, Cam, this smells like heaven."

Teazle agreed. She sat hopefully beside his chair, her nose quivering.

"The soup's tinned—sorry. Wash your hands," Camilla said, and he obeyed.

The rest of his story emerged between mouthfuls. "After I pulled Norm off Uncle Wilfred, I wanted to phone for an ambulance, but he said he'd be all right and we'd better just tie him up and go. His face was all swollen so he could hardly talk." Trevor shuddered. "He'd given us money earlier to buy an old car. We got a mate to do that, so the dealer didn't see us. We were supposed to drive down to meet him here that Monday. I don't know what day it is today."

"Monday again," Jocelyn told him.

"Only a week! It feels more like a month. We got here and he wasn't here. He never gave me a key. Norm wanted to break in, but I wouldn't let him. We didn't want to hang about in case someone saw us, so we just drove around for a bit. We slept in a barn and came back next day but he still wasn't here. We didn't know what to do except it seemed safe to keep moving. That was when we saw the police car, Mr Leacock's panda? Norm said he was staring at us. He got the wind up—well, I did too, rather, because of him knowing me."

"And the next thing you saw was my car," said Eleanor, "and me and Teazle going off for our walk, so you decided to hide the case of jewels in it."

"I'm sorry, Mrs Trewynn," Trevor said earnestly. "I really am. I shouldn't've told him about the shop and how you hardly ever remember to lock up."

"Eleanor," Jocelyn said severely, "none of this would have—"

"Oh no, Mrs Stearns, it didn't matter if it was locked because Norm had a jemmy. It's not your fault at all, Mrs Trewynn. It's all my fault. We put the case under some stuff so you wouldn't find it before you got home. Then we came back here to see if Uncle Wilfred had arrived yet."

"Which he hadn't," Camilla put in. "He was in hospital, wasn't he? That's what it said in the chip paper." She was listening with obvious disapproval, Eleanor was glad to note.

Trevor looked as baffled by the chip paper as Eleanor was, but he continued his story. "We waited till dark, and went to Port Mabyn. We went round the back way, down that little path. The back door wasn't locked and the light was on over the stairs. We saw the case right away, standing against the wall at the bottom of the stairs."

"I put it down out of the way when I went to organise the children unloading the car. I meant to take it to the stockroom later, but what with one thing and another . . ."

"Norm was livid when it was empty. I said the stuff would be in the stockroom. We searched everywhere. We wore gloves because of fingerprints, and we tried to leave everything the way it was—"

"Good of you," said Jocelyn acidly.

"—so no one would guess we'd been there. We couldn't find the jewelry anywhere. Norm said it must be in the shop but I remembered you said once you didn't have the key to the shop. It would've been closed by the time you got home, considering when we'd seen you. He said he was going to go up to your flat and make you tell him what you did with it."

"But—" Jocelyn started, then pursed her lips as Eleanor shook her head at her.

"I told him he mustn't. He just laughed. He had a scarf he found in the stockroom and he started tying it round his face like a bandit in a Western. He was going towards the door. I couldn't let him go up, not after what he did to Uncle Wilfred, could I?"

"No!" said Camilla.

"I got between him and the door and grabbed his arms and

shook him. I think I was shouting at him, I can't remember. Then I let go and gave him a shove away from the door." Trevor started crying. "He lost his balance and sort of stumbled backwards and then he fell and hit his head on that table thing. I could see he was dead. His neck was crooked and his eyes went blank. I *must* have been shouting, because I remember I couldn't understand why no one came. Teazle wasn't even barking."

"Eleanor—Mrs Trewynn—was out," said Jocelyn.

Trevor, tear-stained, stared at her in horror. "You mean I could've let Norm go up? She wasn't there, so he couldn't have hurt her?"

"She wasn't there," Jocelyn confirmed. "The jewels were shut up in the safe. He'd never have got hold of them if he had gone upstairs. It was all for nothing."

Eleanor was furious with her. The boy had enough to face without that.

But Camilla said stringently, "That's rubbish. You can't tell me that when Norm didn't find the jewels, he wouldn't have waited till Mrs Trewynn came back. It was awful for you, Trev, but you had to stop him. You didn't mean to kill him."

"I didn't. I swear I didn't! I came back next night to explain to you, Mrs Trewynn. And I sort of hoped if I saw the shop again, the stockroom, I'd be able to stop thinking about . . . But there was a cop lying in wait and I ran."

Eleanor reached out and took his hand. "All I can say is thank you, Trevor."

He clung to her hand. "Will I have to go to prison?"

"I don't know, my dear, but you can be sure I'll do my best to prevent it. You've saved me twice."

"Twice?" asked Jocelyn.

"When I arrived here this afternoon, Mr Donaldson jumped to the conclusion I knew all about his . . . er . . . misdeeds. He was going to tie me up and hide me away somewhere while he made his get-away abroad. Trevor arrived just in time to rescue me."

"And I came in, too," said Camilla. "I saw Trev going round the back, so I thought I'd better follow Mrs Trewynn."

"Between the two of you," Eleanor agreed, "he had no choice but to flee." And neither of the children, nor Jocelyn, would ever know that she had been pretty confident of extricating herself from Donaldson's toils. "I wonder if Mr Scumble's caught up with him."

All at once, their attention no longer absorbed by Trevor's narration, they heard the sound of cars outside. They trooped out.

The Incorruptible had been moved to Donaldson's parking spot. Down the lane and over the stream came a plainclothes Mini, driven in reverse by DC Wilkes. It stopped several yards beyond the cottage. He jumped out and set up a POLICE barricade behind the car. After the Mini came the maroon Jaguar, also in reverse, driven by Megan. Last in the procession, right way round, came a panda car, its roof light flashing, driven by Polmenna. He stopped with its front bumper a foot from the Jaguar's.

Approaching the Jaguar, Eleanor saw Megan twist to look anxiously over her shoulder at the backseat. "Aunt Nell," she called, "Nick's hurt!"

Jocelyn hurried forward. "I was a nurse during the war. What happened?"

"Donaldson shot him. I don't think it's terribly serious—" A heartrending moan from the backseat belied her words. "Unless he's got a cracked a rib or something. But it keeps bleeding. We only had Polmenna's shirt as a bandage. Luckily he wears cotton. My slip's nylon, of course."

"We've radioed for an ambulance," said Scumble, hurrying from the panda. He looked thunderous, but that was nothing out of the ordinary.

"Trevor, go and see if your uncle has bandages and gauze," Jocelyn ordered as she opened the back door and dived headfirst into the Jaguar. Muffled questions and responses emerged. Megan was kneeling on the driver's seat now, joining in.

Trevor and Camilla disappeared into the house.

"Did you catch Mr Donaldson?" Eleanor asked Scumble.

"The others did. Pencarrow and Polmenna, and the artist." He gestured at the panda.

Eleanor saw the jeweller slumped on the backseat. Polmenna sat stolidly in the driver's seat, shirtless, his unbuttoned jacket showing a glimpse of a string vest.

"Is he hurt too? Donaldson?"

"Not so's you'd notice, unfortunately. When he started shooting, that fool Polmenna tackled him, but the ground was soft after the rains. He was handcuffed to a barbed wire fence for a bit, while they saw to the artist, but he managed to stand still enough not to scratch himself. Don't need a warrant for *him*, not after he shot someone in the presence of police officers."

"But you do for Trevor?"

He looked surprised, as if she had displayed unexpected deductive powers. "Well, yes, strictly speaking."

"You told him he was under arrest."

"Yes, well, I was in a hurry, wasn't I. We've got more than enough to take him in for questioning."

Eleanor sighed. "Yes, I expect so. But it wasn't murder, you know. Norman's death was an accident. Trevor was protecting me. Or thought he was."

"Been telling you a sob-story, has he?" Scumble said nastily.

"I believe him." His sceptical look made her add, "What's more, so does Mrs Stearns," though she wasn't absolutely certain of Jocelyn's opinion. At least it gave him pause. "His uncle will tell you it was Norman who beat him up, not Trevor."

"Hmph."

Camilla and Trevor came out with a roll of two-inch bandage, some cottonwool, and a bottle of TCP. By this time Nick was inching his way out of the Jaguar, feet first, with Jocelyn urging him on and Megan telling him to take care.

"This is all we could find," said Camilla, Trevor lurking nervously behind her.

Examining their finds, Jocelyn snorted and said, "Clean teatowels?"

Nick stood, bent slightly at the waist, supported by Megan. The torn shirt wrapped round his chest was soaked with blood on one side. He was pale and obviously in some pain, but he gave Eleanor a crooked grin and croaked, "'See the conquering hero come.'" She thought he looked dreadful, but obviously Jocelyn didn't consider him to be at death's door, and Jocelyn was usually right. Wilkes hurried to help Megan support him into the house.

Jocelyn took charge of the operation. "Bring him in here," she said, leading the way into a sort of study. "We don't want to tackle the stairs, and this appears to be the only room in the house with a sofa."

How she knew, Eleanor couldn't guess. They had all stayed in the kitchen before, but Jocelyn was omniscient. The study had a wide window looking out over a patch of rough grass to the row of willows and the stream. In spite of the pleasant view, it seemed to Eleanor an uninviting cross between an office and a sitting room. The large desk, four-drawer file cabinet, and bookshelves were functional modern metal. The seats were a particularly hideous maroon leather, a colour Donaldson seemed fond of, though comfortable enough to judge by the sigh of relief with which Nick subsided on the sofa. There were no pictures on the walls. The only homely touch was a Dutch tile stove in one corner.

Scumble made straight for the stove and opened the stoking

door in the front. "Safe," he said, jingling keys in his pocket. "Ah well, it can wait for a search warrant. Your statement can wait, too, Mr Gresham, as I have two official witnesses. Pencarrow, you stay in here and take statements from Mrs Trewynn and Miss . . . Camilla. Wilkes, you and I will have a word with this young feller-me-lad in the kitchen." He gestured at Trevor and jerked his thumb towards the door.

Jocelyn straightened abruptly from leaning over her patient. "Oh no, Inspector! Trevor isn't going to talk to you until he has a solicitor to advise him."

Scumble glared at her. "All I want just now is a preliminary statement."

Trevor stammered, "I d-don't mind—"

"How old are you, Trevor?" Eleanor asked.

"Seventeen. Nearly eighteen."

"A juvenile!" Scumble was disgusted.

"I don't care how old he is, he's not answering questions without a lawyer," Jocelyn said adamantly. "I shall telephone Freeth and Bulwer as soon as I've seen to Nicholas. Come to think of it, Timothy must be wondering where on earth I've got to. Eleanor, would you mind ringing him for me? Just tell him I've been a little delayed. Mr Wilkes, bring a basin of water, if you please."

Dear Jocelyn, Eleanor thought as she went to the desk and dialled the Stearns's number. At times her bossy nature might be irritating, but in times of crisis she came through with flying colours.

"Hello, Vicar, this is Eleanor. Yes, Eleanor Trewynn. I'm just ringing to say Jocelyn's been delayed . . . No, nothing serious . . . No, of course not another murder . . ." Not quite.

Megan was about to ask Camilla to describe events at Withy's End when Scumble, his intent to interrogate Trevor foiled, decided to take her and Aunt Nell's statements himself. He sent Trevor to the kitchen with Wilkes so that he wouldn't hear the evidence. By the time he was finished with Aunt Nell, Nick was feeling well enough to give his statement.

"You'd better ring the Yard, Pencarrow," the inspector said. "The boy wonder'll be wondering what's going on."

Waiting to be connected, Megan listened with amusement to Nick's highly coloured account of the encounter with Donaldson. She didn't really expect Ken to be at work so late—it was half six by now—but the switchboard put her through. In rather more temperate terms than the artist's she told him what had happened.

"Strewth, Megan, you have all the fun down there! I should have gone back with you. So Donaldson's going to be facing a charge of attempted murder?"

"Yes, I haven't had time to think about it but that's what it amounts to."

"Silly git. Without that, the worst he could have been nailed for is accessory before, and if you ask me it'd be practically impossible to get a jury to convict. Besides, assuming your aunt's account is correct, the boy's death was manslaughter, not murder."

"But there's the faked robbery. Donaldson didn't want to go to prison for making a fraudulent claim—"

"That's why I said he's a fool. You can't charge someone with insurance fraud unless they make a claim. And he hasn't. On the other hand, perhaps he's just anticipating trouble. Our Fraud laddies are finding some interesting bits and pieces among his papers. They think he may have kept some of his records elsewhere."

"Here, I'm sure. This place is more like a cross between an office and a hideout than a holiday home. There's a hidden safe, too."

"Is there now! Be so kind as to ask your lord and master not to muck about with anything till we can send someone down. Beg him, plead with him on bended knee."

"Don't hold your breath. I'll pass on your request. The Fraud Squad didn't start looking till Donaldson staged the robbery, did they?"

"No. If he'd been patient, he might well have got away with whatever it is he's been doing."

"The gaupus!"

"I beg your pardon?"

"A Cornish silly git," Megan explained. "I'd better ring off. This is going on the gaupus's phone bill."

Ken laughed. "Just one more point. As the insurance company hasn't forked out, I imagine they may not feel obliged to pay the usual percentage for recovery of the jewels. But there's a good chance your aunt will get some sort of reward."

"Are you serious?"

"Certainly. I've no idea how much it might be."

"Never mind. It'll all go straight to LonStar, I expect."

"Don't tell her yet, in case it doesn't materialise. Have you thought of a good place for me to take you to dinner when I come to interview Donaldson?"

"I haven't had a chance! 'Bye, Ken."

The phone rang the moment she put down the receiver. It was the solicitor in Port Mabyn. To Scumble's irritation, in accordance with Mrs Stearns's request, he had already arranged for a Bodmin solicitor to meet Trevor as soon as he arrived at the Bodmin nick.

DI Scumble was not a happy man, and for once Megan could sympathise. His murder case was dissipating before his eyes, turning into manslaughter—or even an act of heroism—by a juvenile, and he had a wounded civilian to account for, never popular with the top brass. If any laurels were proffered, they would no doubt have to be shared with Scotland Yard, in the person of Kenneth Faraday. Certainly none would reach Megan, who might conceivably be blamed for letting Nick Gresham put himself in danger.

As if she could have stopped him! She hadn't even known Donaldson was armed. But in spite of the casualty, she couldn't help feeling a sense of triumph: Ken was hunting for the jeweller, but she had found their quarry first.

When the ambulance arrived, Nick refused to let himself be carted off to the county hospital in Bodmin. Properly bandaged by the ambulance men, he promised them he would see his own doctor next day.

"He shouldn't come to no harm in the backseat of that Jag," said one. "Mind, if you was thinking of cramming him into one of them Minis, let alone the Moggie, you'd be asking for trouble."

They watched with interest as Scumble turned an unlovely shade of puce, not very different from Donaldson's sofa.

"Want to watch your blood pressure there, mate," said the second man. "I'll just check it for you, shall I?"

"It'll go down as soon as you get out of my sight!" Scumble bellowed.

They scarpered, leaving him with no alternative but to make use of Donaldson's Jaguar. Neither Aunt Nell nor Mrs Stearns was willing to drive so high-powered a car, so he told Megan she would have to take Nick Gresham home to Port Mabyn.

"Then bring the car to Bodmin. It'll have to be searched."

"Before anyone goes anywhere," Mrs Stearns pointed out, "you're going to have to move cars out of each other's way."

Scumble gave her a look, but sent Megan and Wilkes out to sort out the vehicles. When they returned, Camilla was saying goodbye to Trevor, with Scumble eavesdropping. Mrs Stearns and Aunt Nell were fussing around Nick with a pillow and blanket presumably purloined from Donaldson's bedroom. Joining them, Megan noticed that her aunt looked tired and worried.

"What's wrong, Aunt Nell?"

"Shhh. I don't want Mr Scumble to hear. I've just remembered I have to leave for the Scillies tomorrow morning—I don't know whether he'd try to stop me. But the real problem is that I can't take poor Camilla home to Taunton."

"I'll take her," Mrs Stearns volunteered, her voice lowered. "That man can't stop me. In fact, she'd better spend the night at the vicarage. Eleanor, why don't you go with Megan and Nicholas in the big car and I'll drive Camilla home in yours. It will be as easy for you to fetch the Incorruptible from the vicarage as from the car park in the morning."

"It's full of stuff for the shop."

"We'll unload it tonight."

"It does sound very tempting. I *am* a little tired. If I hold Teazle on my lap, she won't scratch the car seat."

"I wouldn't worry about that," said Mrs Stearns ruthlessly. "Its owner is a criminal."

Resisting temptation, Megan drove the Jag at a decorous pace. By the time she had helped Nick up the stairs to his bedsitter above the gallery, the Incorruptible was pulling up next door.

"I'd better help them unload," she said as Aunt Nell tucked a cushion behind Nick's head and spread a rug over him. "Then I'll come back with fish and chips for three."

"Just for two, dear," said Aunt Nell. "I'm not very hungry, but Teazle's dying for her dinner, and chips aren't at all good for her." Teazle yipped a protest. She liked chips, not to mention battered fish. "Besides, I really am quite tired, and I have to pack. I want to leave early to be sure to catch the helicopter. You know what traffic can be like on the road to Penzance. You two have a cosy supper together, and I'll see you when I get back from the Scillies."

Megan wasn't at all sure she wanted a cosy supper with Nick Gresham. However, tackling the stairs had taken it out of him and he was in no state to get himself something to eat. She could hardly back out now.

He caught her studying him. "Am I looking pale and interesting?" he enquired.

"Pale, anyway. Perhaps I'd better ask Mrs Stearns to come and look you over."

"Heaven forbid! All I need is a nice piece of cod and lots of chips."

She went down with Aunt Nell and made sure she went straight upstairs to her flat. Then she had to dissuade Mrs Stearns from going to inspect Nick, and to suggest it would be a good idea to make sure he actually saw his doctor tomorrow.

Half an hour later, after haggling over who was paying for the fish and chips, Nick said casually, "By the way, I've been wondering, who's the 'boy wonder'?"

"Oh, it's what Scumble calls an old acquaintance of mine from my days with the Met."

Nick looked startled. "The . . . ? Oh, the Metropolitan Police, I take it, not the New York opera company."

"Of course. He's been handling the Scotland Yard end of the enquiry."

"I'm afraid Scumble isn't very happy with the outcome. 'A policeman's lot is not a happy one.' I like G&S but I'm not a great fan of opera in general. Too obvious. Why don't you put on a record and relax? The Brahms Second Serenade—I think it's on top."

Megan held up greasy fingers. "You don't want me touching your LPs like this. And when I've finished eating, far from relaxing, I've got to deliver the Jag to Bodmin. I only hope Scumble isn't waiting and wondering why the hell I'm not there yet."

Finishing before he did—chewing was all right but swallowing, he said, was painful—she washed her hands and put on the record. She listened while she made tea. She had always vaguely thought of Brahms as 'difficult' music, but the serenade was pleasant enough.

When she took him a cloth to wipe his hands and a cup of tea, he thanked her, but his mind was obviously elsewhere. "A dark palette," he muttered, "but not sombre."

With a sudden flash of insight, she realised that some of those paintings downstairs that she hadn't understood were visual depictions of music. She could practically see shapes and colours burgeoning in his mind. Perhaps if she listened to the right sort of music, she'd have some chance of working out what the paintings were about.

The question was, did she want to put that much effort into understanding his art?

"I've got to go. Will you be able to get yourself to bed?"

He looked at her vaguely. "I should think so. Could you pass me my sketch pad? And put the transistor over here where I can reach it."

She set the wireless on the floor beside him and found a large pad of paper and several pencils on a shelf. "Here you go."

"Ta muchly."

"Take care, won't you. If you have any trouble, just ring Mrs Stearns. I'm sure she'll be down in a flash."

At that he grinned. "Not on your life. I'll be fine. Thanks, Megan. Drive carefully."

"And you move carefully. Good night."

Walking down to the car park, she found a bit of Brahms circulating in her head. It didn't conjure up any pictures, but the idea that it could was intriguing. When she got into the Jaguar, equipped of course with a car radio of the non-police variety, she tuned it to a concert on the BBC Third Programme.

Eleanor got out a packet of soup, looked at it, thought about washing up the pan, and put it away again. She dined on Weetabix and an orange, then packed her suitcase.

She took Teazle down for her last outing. No policemen lurked in the gorse bushes, thank heaven, and if she forgot to lock up when she went upstairs, no one would scold her.

In the aftermath of the gale, breakers boomed as they crashed against the rocky cliffs of the inlet and the jetty sheltering the harbour. From Nick's open window came the voice of an announcer, followed by music—Mozart, she thought. The intermittent flash of the Crookmoyle light reflected off a layer of low cloud. A breeze brought the salty smell of seaweed to mingle with the scents of gorse and blackthorn. Eleanor breathed deeply.

On such a peaceful evening, it was difficult to believe the events of the past week had really happened.

"Come on, Teazle. Time for bed, girl."

At last she snuggled down under the covers, with Teazle keeping her feet warm. Tomorrow she'd have to turn her mind to the dire situation in Nigeria. Before she left, she must make sure Jocelyn would keep an eye on Nick's injury, little though he'd appreciate her interference. When she returned from the Scillies, she'd have to see what she could do to help Camilla and poor misguided Trevor. Then she ought to go up to London for some work with her *Sensei*—practising Aikido on her own was all very well, and she'd considered it sufficient in peaceful old England, but obviously she badly needed to hone her reflexes.

So much for the future. Tonight she drifted into sleep already dreaming of Nick and Megan living happily ever after.